About the Author

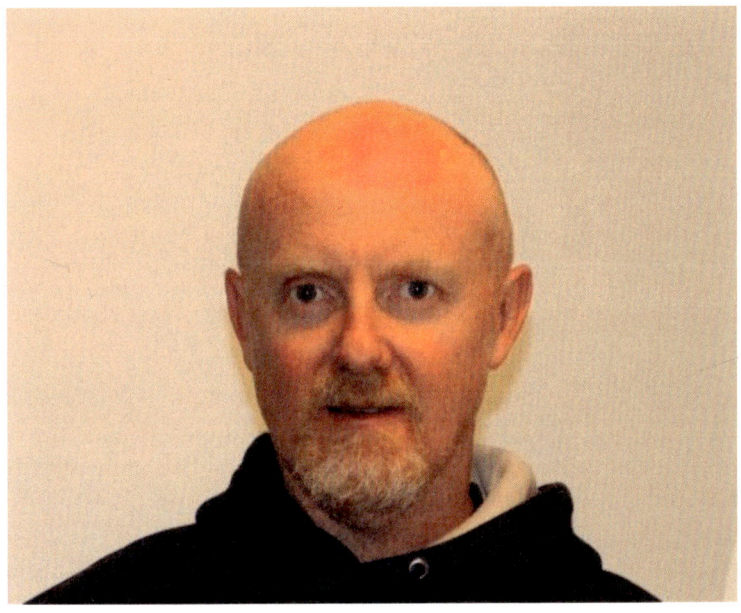

I started writing in 2017 when I started thinking about my mortality. A big part of who I am as a person is in my daydreams and imagination. We do not know what the future will bring, and I wanted to make sure I have a record of the stories I have been playing in my head. That was the start of the passion I now have for writing.

I am a new writer who has found his artistic self in his writing.

I am the father of four young adults and teenagers. I see my writing appealing to this age bracket or older.

My hobbies include writing, gardening, looking through abandoned houses, running and camping.

Writing is a hobby as I have a full-time job as a mining engineer and a family which keeps me occupied. I am grateful for the opportunity I have been given to publish this story.

The First King of England

The Worchester Chronicles
Book II

Dennis Hunt

The First King of England

The Worchester Chronicles
Book II

Vanguard Press

VANGUARD PAPERBACK

© Copyright 2024
Dennis Hunt

The right of Dennis Hunt to be identified as author of
this work has been asserted by him in accordance with the
Copyright, Designs and Patents Act 1988.

All Rights Reserved

No reproduction, copy or transmission of this publication
may be made without written permission.
No paragraph of this publication may be reproduced,
copied or transmitted save with the written permission of the publisher, or in accordance
with the provisions
of the Copyright Act 1956 (as amended).

Any person who commits any unauthorised act in relation to
this publication may be liable to criminal
prosecution and civil claims for damages.

A CIP catalogue record for this title is
available from the British Library.

ISBN 978-1-80016-458-1

This is a work of fiction. Names, characters, businesses, places, events and incidents are either the
product of the author's imagination or used in a fictitious manner. Any resemblance to actual persons,
living or dead, or actual events is purely coincidental.

Vanguard Press is an imprint of
Pegasus Elliot Mackenzie Publishers Ltd.
www.pegasuspublishers.com

First Published in 2024

Vanguard Press
Sheraton House Castle Park
Cambridge England

Printed & Bound in Great Britain

Chapter 1

Irony

Swindhun was riding back at pace which did not bode well. I never liked seeing a message being carried with such haste as it has always been bad news. We are in the south Yorkshire Dales on a cold Autumn's day. The rolling hills are mostly grazing lands at best as they are rocky and barren. They are as free of trees as Hereweald's head is lacking hair.

Swindhun is Hereweald's eldest son and on his first campaign with the English Guard. Hereweald is captain of the newly appointed English Guard. It is an amalgamation of the old Wessex and Worcester guards. Immediately after uniting as a country the new guard was established. The Worcester guard had been the backbone of the movement which had united the countries of Britannia to destroy the Viking armies. It was important that a new army be formed to carry the hopes of this new country by name of England.

Hereweald is back in Wessex continuing the work of establishing law and order in the newly acquired lands of the realm. Swindhun is an experienced swordsman well and truly in the make of his father.

We are a unit of a thousand men travelling to Bamborough to support Dunstan in negotiations with the Picts. Bamborough was the last stronghold of the Vikings in Britannia and was taken by Dunstan and the English guard around the time of my coronation as the first King of England. I had left Dunstan and the guard at Torksey as I had word that King Alfred of Wessex had died. Dunstan continued as commander of the campaign to free our lands of Vikings while I headed back to Wessex for the royal funeral and my coronation. I do not know if the trouble is with the Picts from Strath Clyde or Pictland however, I hoped for the later as I have no history with them.

My brother Tata is also on his first campaign and apart from hunting trips it is the first time we have ridden together to a potential conflict. Tata has not seen much of the land as he has always been stuck at home with the responsibility of looking after the forges. Being a blacksmith in a time of war and expansion has been hectic and a critical role. I have known of his desire to go into battle with me and at the same time see a little of the world however the time was never right. Tata is a member of the Worchester guard and a skilled archer but there is still the fact that he is my only brother and I feel very protective of him. Tata is now twenty and able to make his own decisions, as dictated to me by my sister Hilda and wife Aethelswith. Bowing to their wisdom Tata and I are riding for Bamborough and the negotiations.

Swindhun finally caught up with us and was surprisingly out of breath. Before I could say anything, he blurted out that we are surrounded. Deorwine snapped back, 'What do you mean surrounded'? I did not have a good feeling about this as I began looking around us. I could see we were in the lowest point between three of the rolling hills which could look like a bowl if viewed from above. Sitting in the bottom of the bowl I could now see heads starting to get nearer as they lined the ridges which surround us. There were still at least five hundred yards between us and the ridge however the desperation in Swindhun's voice gave me great cause for concern.

Before I could ask, Swindhun told me there were maybe eight thousand Picts surrounding us. He quickly chimed in that there was nowhere to run, they are all around us. Looking back up I could see the ridges were all lined with heads silhouetted against the sky. They had started moving down the slopes towards our position. They seemed to be evenly dispersed around us which reduced our options for escape. We are all on horseback so a possible counterattack into one point of the enemy line was my first thought. I could see that this would be a futile attack, with our chances getting less as the moments passed. There were just too many Picts. There were flags however I did not recognize their origin. This meant they were probably from the true north and Pictland.

Tata and Deowine were nearby, and I found myself looking at them and wondering about how fleeting life can be. Tata had wanted to go on campaign with me for at least two years. I had always managed to keep him safe by finding other critical work for him. The lands of England are meant to be safe now that the Vikings are defeated. It is ironic as peace and security is what all the fighting was for. In times that have never been safer I have now led Tata to his possible death. This is the irony of our situation.

I snapped out of my reflections with Tata and Swindhun yelling at me for instructions. 'What do we do and what is the plan?' I realized I had probably been staring at them for longer than was comfortable. It did not matter now for we needed to act and decisively.

Scanning the ground around us I could see that most of the horses were not needed. I have this ability to picture a battle before it is fought. Experience and my knowledge of many of the great historical battles have helped me to enhance this ability. I could see our best hope of success being a truce with this attacking force. There was no delegation or rider with a parley flag, so I guessed they knew their advantage and intended to make the most of it. We would have to do them damage with significant losses to draw them to a settlement.

I ordered that all bar one hundred senior archers are to release their horses and form a spherical shield wall. This was nine hundred horses which we were releasing to our attackers. The intent is to use the dense shield wall to protect the archers who will be on horseback in the middle. The archers will have extra quivers from those archers who are in the shield wall. This will give us a massive supply of arrows. The longer the wall can hold the more damage we can continue to inflict. The plan was relayed to the commanders around me, and everyone was told to take their positions. The problem with this plan was that the archers will be sitting ducks to archer attacks however I could not see a way to remove this risk and we did not have a better plan.

The men needed confidence so I quickly rode the line to remind them that they are men of the guard and that we have been in sticky situations before. 'We can only control what we can control so clear your mind of worry and fear. God rides with us and if it is our time then God will welcome us into his kingdom. If it is not our time, then God will give us this day. Hold your positions and do not let your neighbors or friends down. Fight with all God gave you and fight until the end.' I gave the speech several times as I rode around the infantry. Speaking to the warriors gave me hope and steeled my spirit as prior I had been a little resigned.

Coming at us from every direction the Pict came at us hard, charging the last twenty meters. Our shields clashed with a loud crack which reverberated along our lines. Our archers had started firing long before the charge. Most of our arrows were deflected by shields however the odd arrow made it through as we saw Picts drop as they came forward. Along the front there was one continuous line of skirmishes. It is critical that the outer shield wall holds. If one of our men is hurt and needs to pull back a replacement quickly takes their place. This is exhausting work, and I knew it would test the men and force them to draw on all their strength.

    A cacophony of sound rang out across the battlefield. Our men fought and died defending our archers for what seemed like hours. The Picts did not use their archers until late in the battle. At this time, our men were getting exhausted, and our numbers had been cut by half. Our shield wall had consequently halved when the arrows came. Most of the men were too exhausted to protect themselves and I saw many of them take direct hits. Consequently, this put holes in our shield wall which became more and more difficult to close. At this time many of our archers were also hit and even more horses. The fear of the horses caused more damage to our defense as the horses started to kick and panic. Those of us who were not hit kept firing and killing as quickly as we could. Looking out I could see that this was a lost cause as we were still surrounded by a wall one hundred thick in every direction.

    My horse was hit and as it panicked and went to throw me off his back I was hit in the shoulder by an arrow. Hitting the ground, I was lucky as the angle and impact snapped the shaft of the arrow leaving the head of the arrow in my shoulder. Although agonizingly painful I still had the use of both arms, as I drew my swords, which I thought was fortunate. Looking around I could see that most of the horses had fled or were dying, kicking themselves silly on the ground in pain.

    Noticing that Tata was being pressed I pushed over to give him some support. I was almost by his side when I saw him get a cut across the front which doubled him over. Up until this point I had been fighting as in a dream however seeing my brother take a hit was like having a bucket of water tipped over my head. Every one of my senses came to life and I snapped into the zone. Around me I was seeing everything in slow motion as I took advantage and began cutting a safe zone around Tata. Everything became too easy for me as I danced from one enemy warrior to another. I continued like this for what would have been minutes. After clearing a significant zone, I had a quick breather and looked around me. There were no horses left and our numbers looked to be less than a hundred. Looking more closely I could see that Deorwine was dead with his head half hanging off. Swindhun was battling on and I could see Tata scrambling to his feet. I could not see the point of it all, we were going to die.

For the first time in my life, I searched for something white. Ripping off a strip from my tunic, I wrapped it around my sword and lifted it high into the sky. I was trying to surrender. Perhaps it would give my baby brother and Hereweald's son a chance of living. We cannot fight another day if we are dead, so I hoped this was our way out, even if it was through slavery.

The battle continued around me until at last I heard a horn and the Picts stepped back from their engagement. I called for our men to come together and standdown. Our numbers were worse than I thought, maybe fifty men if lucky. It was hard to see who had lost the most as the piles of bodies around us were immense and sickening.

It was then that a group of men came forward and I guessed that they were the Pict leaders. I stood my ground with my weapons lowered and then I dropped them to the ground. What good were they to me now. I had put my life and the lives of my remaining men into the hands of this unknown army and these unknown men.

One of the men came directly to me with his sword raised. 'You are Godric of house Amity?' Answering yes, I soon found out it was probably not my wisest move. The man in front of me ran is sword straight through my guts, at the same time telling me, 'That was for what you did to Kenner.' Doubled over I saw a whack from the butt of a sword coming my way. The whack was aimed directly at my head, but I could do little to stop it. That was the last thing I remembered from that day.

Chapter 2

Imprisonment

I knew I was in a dungeon the moment my consciousness returned. Having spent weeks in the Wessex dungeons I knew the smells, sounds and the cold hard stone. I felt a sense of relief which was far from being disappointed. Given the situation on the battlefield I did not expect to wake in this world. I expected to find myself at the gates of heaven as I had been taught happened to believers when they died. The dungeon was dark and cold with only a slither of candlelight coming through around the edges of the door.

My feelings of relief did not last long as I began noticing my pain. Any movement was excruciatingly painful all over. I had a concentrated sharp pain in my shoulder and through my stomach. I remembered I had taken an arrow in my shoulder and that the Pict leader had put a sword through my stomach. I moved my hands to my wounds as carefully as I could. The pain from the movement was acute but necessary. I found that the head of the arrow was still in my shoulder and the stab wound to my stomach had not been stitched or cleaned. As best as I could I inspected my hands and could see that there was no fresh blood. This was good as it meant that the wounds had started to heal. The arrowhead would need to be removed however it was secure where it was and could wait until I was in a better situation. If I was going to die it would not matter anyway.

Looking around the room I could see that it was not much bigger than the space I occupied and that I was alone. With no other option open to me and still infused with exhaustion I closed my eyes and let sleep take me again.

I woke to the pain of a boot in the side. 'Oh, you're still alive. Get up and have some grub.' Looking around I was still in the same cell, and I could see a bowl of something steaming sitting on a tray close to the door. My guard gave me a shove with his boot and told me to hurry up. His words were far from clear but having grown up on the Welsh border I could follow his Celtic language. Thinking it best to be polite I thanked him for the food using the same language. Although dark this use of his language seemed to surprise him. Pressing the advantage, I asked him where I was however this was received with a grunt and a kick. 'You are in the dungeon,' he shouted back at me before leaving the cell and slamming the door. He was chuckling to himself as he left.

Still in immense pain I eased my way over to my food. It smelt odd and unpleasant however I knew I needed to eat it if I was going to regain my strength. Fortunately, it tasted much better than it smelt and before long I had finished. Being my first food in god knows how long I now felt desperately hungry and in need of more. Sitting back against a wall gave me an opportunity to test out the rest of my body. My head also ached from where I received the blow which knocked me out. Apart from this the rest of me seemed intact. I decided to try and get to my feet to test out my legs. The movement alone was extremely painful and despite my weakness I was able to pull myself to my feet. Although stiff and sore it felt good to be on my legs again. Feeling my stomach and again checking for blood I found layers of dried blood over my stomach and on my underclothes but no fresh blood. I knew about my shoulder so my overall assessment was much better than I could hope.

A trap door was opened at the bottom of the door and a boy's voice requested that my bowl be put on the tray at the base of the door. The voice was gentle and scared, so I did what was requested and did not give him a hard time. Hearing the boys voice reminded me of the lost battle and of my brother Tata. I had been self-absorbed and failed to consider those who were captured with me. That I had been kept alive meant there was a good chance that Tata and Swindhun may also be alive. I had to hope, and I had to stay alive to find out where the remaining English souls were being kept.

My strength was returning to me slowly even though I was only receiving one bowl of food each day. I guessed it was daily although without natural light it was difficult to be certain. It was the same boy who brought my food and took away my empty bowl but still he would not converse with me. As he sounded timid, I had held off from asking him anything for the first six bowls. From then I had been saying hello and asking him for his name. Failing to receive a name I tried finding out where

I was however this was also met with silence. The guard had not returned, and it seemed as though I was being left down here to rot.

Life went on like this for months with no variation. I would fail to put my bowl back at the door just to confirm that I still had the same helper. He would ask in the familiar voice for me to put my bowl on the tray. I would thank him and ask him how the weather was and get back the same dead reply.

The seasons had changed as I could feel my cell getting colder and colder. It was already cold hard stone which I was sleeping on only now the cold was really damaging my health and spirit. The head of the arrow had become a constant throb and companion notifying me that I was still alive. It was the metal which was cooling as if it was stone.

I started asking my boy for a blanket or jacket but again was given no response. Weeks later a thick blanket was pushed through the service hole. I greedily grabbed the blanket and wrapped in around my body. It felt like the greatest gift I had ever received, and I thanked the boy although the service hatch was closed so I suspected he could not hear me.

I was still optimistic of some sort of escape now that I had the blanket and my recovered health. Maybe a rescue was a day away and I was to be surprised or maybe the king of wherever I was would ask to see me. There was now every reason to be optimistic.

Chapter 3

Queen of England

I was still in tears having received the news only minutes earlier. Godric had set off for Bamborough on a report his army were having trouble with the Picts. They had left ten weeks ago, and we had not heard anything since they departed. A delegation from Bamborough had arrived to tell us that the guard from England had been slaughtered on the road between York and Bamborough. The battle had been inland from the small seaside town of Jarrow on the northern English coast. The battle of Jarrow had been a one-sided affair and it sounds like Godric and the men had very little chance of survival. I cannot believe that Godric is dead after all that we have been through. Better times were promised and our dream of uniting the land had become a reality. I have more tears as I contemplate the meaning of the message.

The room has been cleared from all but the messenger, Hereweald, Andras and Ebba. Ebba, my personal maid, was comforting me with her arm around my shoulder. Hereweald was talking to the messenger to get as much information as he could. In between my tears I was listening to the exchange.

He told Hereweald that there were no survivors which could be identified. The bodies had been piled up and burned. The land north of York was swarming with packs of Picts attacking villages, travelers, and farmers. This is the third delegation which was sent to Winchester, and it was only when they did not get confirmation that the delegation had arrived safely that they sent the second and third delegations.

Hereweald's eldest son was travelling with the guard along with many men who are close to us. Tata was on his first campaign with his brother and the ever-popular Deorwine. Godric is much loved by the people and is seen as the inspiration which had brought peace to our land. What would happen now that he was dead? Will we be open to attack from foreign powers once they get the news about Godric?

Hereweald thanked the messenger and dismissed him. He told him and his men to have a break until called upon again. Hereweald seemed to be taking control of the crisis even though he must be hurting inside knowing his son was dead. He asked Andras to fetch Eadwulf who is commander of the Winchester guard and Wulfsige, commander of the London guard.

While we waited, I recovered myself and felt a little self-conscious that I had let my guard down as I had. I am queen of England and should be more stoic and less emotional. My Godric was special though and losing him is as close to being a disaster as it can be. Ebba had comforted me for which I was grateful however I was now feeling myself again. This was to be a war council so Ebba would need to leave. I told her that I was much better and that she could go to attend her other duties. Ebba has proved herself to be the very best of maids, reliable and discrete.

Eadwulf and Wulfsige arrived so the five of us got straight to business. Hereweald filled everyone in on the details of the message. The Picts are harassing English land in the north, and it seems like they want to fill the vacuum left by the departure of the Vikings. We would need a strong response to show them that we are not a small country to be messed with. At my turn to speak I reminded them all that it would be Godric's wish to bring peace and security to the land and its people. Those around the table nodded and without making eye contact with me they all agreed.

The Garrison at both Bamborough and York is two thousand which is necessary for the protection of both castles. We will need to send the entire Winchester guard if we were going to make the impression which we wanted to make. We want to show the Picts that they must stick to their borders or there will be consequences such as our own invasion of their lands.

Wulfsige asked if we knew which Pict tribe it was which we were dealing with. In my misery I had not thought to ask the messenger this question. Of course, there are two large Pict clans, Strath Clyde, and Pictland. We all looked at Wulfsige blankly and confessed that we did not know. Hereweald pointed out that after the war with the Vikings we had discharged half of our guard from both Worchester and Winchester. As it stands, we could send three thousand from Winchester and maybe another three thousand from Worchester, Northampton, and London combined. This would give us six thousand in the field. Wulfsige pointed out that we did not know the size of the force which had attacked Godric. For Godric and the elite men, he rode with to be wiped out the force which attacked them must have been significant. I would suggest anywhere between six and ten thousand men. We must be careful as we know very little of the Pict clans. As an example, who knows if they are working together?

The council meeting went on like this until late into the evening. There was a short break for some supper and mead although this was only a short respite. The decision was made to call up four thousand of the released guard and send ten thousand to Bamborough to engage the Picts. Which clan we would engage we would determine once we got to either York or Bamborough. That intelligence should be available from either one of those strongholds. It will take some time to organize the force so the messengers would be given a message to send back to York. All precaution will be required to ensure the message can get through to Bamborough. It was now too close to the end of the year and deep into winter. The army would leave from Worchester on the first day of spring with ten thousand men. This gives us approximately three months to build provisions and supplies for the campaign.

Hereweald stayed back after the meeting and asked if I would be all right. I was five months pregnant and showing plenty of size in my belly even at this early stage. Telling Hereweald that I would be fine I posed the same question back to him with my sympathies for both he and Cynefri his wife. Cynefri would not have heard the news although we had all been worried for weeks. Being worried is one thing however with Godric leading the mission we did not expect the worst. Oh, how our lives were all going to change now. Hereweald said that the battle of Jarrow will always be a pivotal moment in the history of our nation. 'It is our mission to make sure Jarrow galvanizes us instead of tearing us apart.'

Chapter 4

The Escape

My strength was waning as I continued in the dark cold cell surviving on one meal per day. The only interaction I was getting with another human being was when they switched out my chamber pot and I received my bowl of gruel. I was still grateful to be alive however since being kicked awake I had not seen another human.

Eternal optimism is not enough to sustain someone forever as I was finding out. As my energy and optimism dropped, they were replaced with negative thoughts. Even worse was that I was beginning to embrace the negative thoughts and seek comfort from them. I had no idea of the time however at some point I noticed that it was not getting as cold which meant another change of season.

Self-absorbed by my situation I was wasting away forgotten about in a location I knew nothing about. I could not escape now even if the door were left open and I was told I could go. I was spent and knew I would not last much longer. My highlight was still my bowl of gruel but even the effort to reach across for this was too much on some days. If the boy found my bowl uneaten and or moved, he would leave it there and come back to check the following day. It was in this way that my meals had now reduced to one every second day. Somehow, I kept drinking my water however I am not sure what hand guided me here as I could as easily have given up on this also.

It seemed like a lifetime went by existing in my depressive state. It was lucky I was in the dark as there would be nothing of me and I would be a sight for sore eyes.

Summer must have arrived as one of these days or nights it was humid and almost as unbearable as the extreme cold. It was on one such night that

I finally heard a different sound although I almost missed it. There was a key in the lock and the door was being opened.

There was nothing I could do as I had not stood for months, and any movement was slow and painful. I was more like a slug than a human and I felt just as vulnerable as two men stepped into my cell. One of the men addressed me as Godric in his thick northern celt accent. As I had still been doing my best to thank the boy, I still had use of my voice. I acknowledge the voice that ay I am Godric. 'Get on your feet man, this is a rescue.'

'He cannot stand Ramsay, look at the state of the man.' With that a candle was brought down close to my face. I strained to keep the light out of my eyes as my eyes had not seen any light that bright for as long as I could remember. Whimpering in pain I was picked up and tossed over one of the men's shoulders. The men then left the cell at a trot.

As I was bouncing along on the back of one of the men I started to think about my situation and where I was. As weak and pathetic as I was, I felt shocked out of my depression. What was the significance of Ramsay I questioned myself? It then came to me, Ramsay of Strath Clyde. Ramsay is one of the high-ranking commanders from Strath Clyde. That could mean I was in the dungeon of the Pictland King whoever he is.

I was exhausted from this tiny mental activity and could not stop myself falling asleep. I was lying across the horse in front of one of these men when I awoke. I was probably like a sack of barley to these men as they seemed to carry me with ease. I knew I would not recognize myself if I could see what I looked like. Lying in an awkward position I asked the man for his name. He told me that he was Tadg commander of the Glasgow garrison. He said that he knew me and that I did not look long for this world. I agreed with him and said that I felt dead already. Tadg told me that I had better not die as there was a young lady who was looking forward to seeing me again.

An image of Kenner shot into my mind. It had been years since I had seen and been a part of everything which was Kenner. At that moment I forgot that I was married, a husband or a father and my mind sort the comfort of those beautiful memories. 'I can see that you remember so all will be well.' I asked Tadg how it could all be well as I had abandoned Kenner and disappeared in the night. 'You did what you had to do, and I am sure Kenner was angry however as soon as she heard that you were in the dungeon at Edinburgh the rescue mission was planned. I decided to be silent to process the information I was getting. Tadg finished by telling me that we would get to Glasgow in a couple of hours. Two hours was perfect as it would give my surprisingly alert brain time to think.

Kenner had organized my rescue from Pictland which meant there was no love lost between the two Pict clans. Kenner had been engaged to marry the Prince of Pictland but must have changed her mind after our time together. Maybe this was why I had been left to rot as payback for stealing his fiancé. Maybe he broke it off when he found out about me. I was now going to see Kenner in little more than rags and smelling worse than a sewer. I was emancipated and not much of a man. I asked Tadg when we would be seeing Kenner as I would love to have the chance to wash and have some new cloths. It was hopeless to wish for anything else as this wasted body would take years to recover, if ever it did.

Tadg said that we would be going to Glasgow and Kenner was in Carlisle. He said that I was going to be looked after as I am a king after all. He said this with a cheekiness in his voice which seemed to have some affection with it. I hoped this was the case and from my small understanding of Tadg I am reassured. Tadg opened up a little after that and told me about what had been going on in the land from what he had heard. I listened with some interest but mostly I was waiting on the mention of Kenner and what she had been up to.

It seems that Pictland had marched south with every man and women they could. They attacked Bamborough and finally took it after laying siege to the castle for two months. Apparently, the siege was broken by a massive English army which came against Oengus and his men. The English army was defeated at Darlington in what was being hailed as a historical victory for the north men.

I had to ask who Oengus was as I could not remember hearing of him before. This surprised Tadg as I had been in one of Oengus's dungeons for close to a year. He told me that Oengus is King of Pictland with his castle in Edinburgh.

Oengus had marched south with twelve thousand men and women. Twelve thousand makes it the largest army ever assembled in the north. Oengus is making the most of the vacuum left with the English defeating the Vikings. Everyone would fear an army this large and even Gregor is concerned. Gregor is reassured that he will not be attacked with the knowledge that Oengus has taken all available men and women south and thus is counting on Gregor to maintain their truce and not attack his vulnerable underbelly. With Gregor maintaining the truce he is hopeful the army does not turn its attention west.

This last bit of the story pulled me out of my Kenner brain and had me consider the risks Gregor was taking with my rescue. 'Why did King Gregor risk breaking the truce to rescue me from the dungeons?' Tadg told me that only King Gregor knew the answer to that and maybe it wasn't even his doing as he was not privy to that information.

Tadg continued with the story of Bamborough and how King Oengus and his men were able to defeat the English at Darlington and return to continue the siege. On news of the defeat at Darlington Wulfsige sort parley with King Oengus. Wulfsige was able to negotiate safe passage for his men if they promised to never return north and raise arms against Pictland. Those at the negotiations say that King Oengus coveted Bamborough castle so agreed to such terms. These were considered generous terms as there is a great chance these men would come back that way with a larger army and King Oengus would need to fight them again.

Wulfsige had managed to save his men and could regroup for another push north. I hadn't realized I was smiling until Tadg asked me why I seemed so pleased. I confirmed that I was pleased that Wulfsige had been able to get out of a really difficult situation while saving the lives of his men. Bamborough is just a castle and could be taken again however men are priceless and without them England could not be defended. Tadg nodded and seemed to consider my wise words. I say wise as I have lived by these values in the past. Every attempt is made to protect the lives of all my men.

Tadg reassured me that we were close as he sensed me grimace as his horse stumbled over some rocks. I was still lying across his mount and had been for half a day. I thought we must be getting close and hoped so as the pain in my shoulder was getting worse especially with the hard riding we had started with. I told Tadg that I was sick due to an arrow I still have in my shoulder.

The man riding with us commented that the arrowhead will have to come out. The lead will be slowly poisoning me. Somehow that voice sounded familiar and although groggy I searched my brain for where I had heard it before. It came to me, so I did my best to look around. Shug is that you, you young rascal. I was unable to turn enough to see him however I heard that laugh of his and knew it had to be Shug. Shug was the apprentice blacksmith at the royal estate and would be a trade blacksmith now.

Shug and I had warmed to each other quickly when I was being kept as a slave on the royal estate. Shug was open and friendly and had a cheeky sense of humor. He was quick to work out there was something between Kenner and I and had great amusement teasing me about the affair. My pain and discomfort eased a little knowing that Shug was riding with us. Shug said that he was wondering when I was going to recognize him. He had been in the cell at my rescue however I had not seen past the beard to those blue eyes which would have marked him straight away as eventually his thick accent had.

My exhaustion eased enough for me to continue the conversation with Shug. He told me that he was now the blacksmith at the Glasgow royal estate while Ailpen was still at the Carlisle estate. He has himself two apprentices and Ailpen has another apprentice. Demand for blacksmiths has never been greater with the continued threat of war. Shug told me that Ailpen was furious when I escaped because it made him look bad but also as he had quietly been enjoying my company and skill at the forge. King Gregor had also been angry however for some reason he never pursued me or the others. Tadg jumped in there and said that he would have however he was dissuaded by Kenner. She told him that he had important business in the south and to be patient as he would be back. She convinced him to understand that the south would be important allies. At that stage Shug was the only one who really knew what had been going on between Kenner and me.

Shug went on to say that it wasn't long after we had left that our relationship became common knowledge. 'Months after you left Kenner began to show and nine months later, she gave birth to a son.' If I wasn't already slumped over the horse I would have collapsed from this news. Kenner had a baby, my baby. 'Is he still alive and what is his name?

Shug and Tadg were both amused by how caught off guard I was by this news. 'Godric junior is now seven years and lives at the Carlisle royal estate with his mother. He is a healthy lad being trained in everything required of a future king. Gregor's early disappointment was soon forgotten when he saw the strength and energy of the child. The king's son Munro was not pleased by the entire saga and vowed to one day get his vengeance on you. Munro has also learnt to like and appreciate Godric junior. However, it will be worth staying out of Munro's way until you are fully recovered and can look after yourself. Munro does not know of this rescue, and it is best that it stays this way.'

Exhaustion was taking over me again although I had so many questions. That was when we rode into the estate in north Glasgow.

My next memory was waking on a hard bed with soft pillows. My body seemed to ache all over but nothing like the pain in my shoulder. It seems like they had taken the opportunity to remove the arrow from it while I was passed out from exhaustion. I was now in a room by myself with light coming in through the open window. The wooden shutters on the window were latched back however they were still banging in the breeze. From where I am, I cannot see out the window however I can hear the birds chattering as though they are without a care in the world.

The door opened and in came a maid. She was startled when she saw that I was awake. The maid introduced herself as Anne of house Steward. Anne is a middle-aged woman with long grey hair tied back over her left shoulder. She has pale skin and a stern look on her face. Anne looks like she spends a lot of her day frowning. 'I oversee the household servants and I ask that you come to me if you have any complaints about how you are being treated. I will make sure your visit is comfortable and your recovery is speedy.' Thanking Anne, I went to introduce myself when she put out her hand and told me that she knew who I was. She told me that it was important that I rest as I am in very poor condition and winter is on its way. Anne said that she would be sending for Tadg now that I was awake. Tadg can apparently fill me in on my situation and the operation. With that Anne left the room.

Expecting Tadg I became alert when the door next opened. It was not Tadg but an elderly man who may even be in his sixties. The man is bald on top with long white hair around his monk hair line. There is a jump in this man's step as he apologized for making me jump and introduced himself as the house steward. 'McGregor by name, cheerful by nature. How does your shoulder feel young Godric? The operation was simple enough however there is always risk of infection with an open wound and when the patient is so run down. My assistant will be along shortly with some lamb stew. The food portion will seem small at first however it looks like you haven't eaten for a while, and you will not be able to handle more than we give you. Campbell is my assistant, and he is as chirpy as I try to be so he should have you in good spirits.' Looking at McGregor and thinking of Campbell I could not help but think how they would get on the nerves of a serious woman such as Anne. I am sure they have figured everything out and probably keep out of each other's way.

McGregor came over and removed the dressing from my shoulder. He told me that it seemed to be free from infection which was a great sign. He did nothing but look at it before replacing the dressing covering it and shoulder from the nape of my neck through to my arm. As uncomfortable as it is, I felt what he said to be the truth. I am as weak as I have ever been, and a bad infection could end my life. McGregor told me that I had been sleeping for two days since we had arrived at the Glasgow estate. He told me that Tadg was the estate commander and he and Shug had left with two guards to rescue me from the Edinburgh dungeon. They had known that I had been taken prisoner a year prior however there had not been an opportunity to carry out the rescue. The opportunity had arisen when King Oengus had emptied Pictland for an attack in the south. Tadg did not mess around but set off at once. He was not sure if he was going to recognize you so he took Shug who was sure he would never forget your face. It was fortunate Shug was there as you look little like you did when you were up this way years earlier.

I was surprised that McGregor seemed to know so much about the mission. The surprise was enhanced as I remembered being told that Munro had a dislike for me and that this was to be kept from him. The more people who knew the greater the chance that Munro would find out. I could not face Munro in my current state as I would struggle to protect myself from a maid let alone a hardened warrior. McGregor seemed to have said all he intended to say as he excused himself and left the room.

These small exchanges had made my eyes heavy, so I took the opportunity to close them again. When next they were opened, I could see that the window shutters were latched closed, and it was dark outside. I had no idea what time of night it was as I could not see out and it may have done no good anyway as the first thing I had noticed when being up north was that the sky was forever overcast with clouds. Forever may be an exaggeration however it does seem to be the status quo.

My room was silent, so I closed my eyes again and once again sleep came to me easily.

Tadg woke me up when next I came awake. He had a tray with some more soup in a bowl. He helped me up into a sitting position and placed the tray on my lap. It was good to see Tadg and he had a pleased look on his face. He said that I already looked much better even though it had only been three days since my arrival. The soup was delicious and just what the doctor had ordered as the moment Tadg had woken me I could feel an empty pain in my stomach. He told me that McGregor was pleased with the operation and that my wound was healing well. He said that he was also the local surgeon and had performed the operation.

After eating Tadg took the tray and bowl and told me to get onto my feet. He put the tray onto one of the side tables and picked up a pile of clothes. Putting the clothes next to the bed Tadg said he would give me a few minutes to get dressed and we would head out into the garden. He added that the clothes may not be to my liking however they should fit. Although I was emancipated, I am still a large man with wide shoulders. Tadg may have struggled to find clothes in my size. Thanking Tadg he left the room to allow me to change.

Out in the garden I was reminded of the estate outside at Carlisle. Gregor obviously had a certain taste in gardens and the gardeners intended to please their master. There were large areas of lawn interspersed with flower gardens including poppies, roses and camelias. There are rows of young oak trees providing borders around the open grass areas as they themselves are divided into private groves. I took this opportunity to thank Tadg for the rescue and all he had done for me. I told him that I felt like it was not deserved as I had fled in the night all those years before. Tadg brushed away my comments and said that there was nothing to worry about from the years before. After all I had been taken as a prisoner by a raiding party a long way from Carlisle. Destiny finds a way of working out and we believe that it is this destiny which has returned you to Strath Clyde.

I asked Tadg why I had been rescued however he again changed the subject. He started telling me about the news from south. He told me that

Bamborough has fallen to Pictland and the country between Bamborough and York was now in Pictland hands. He said that the battle at Darlington had gone badly for the English as they were heavily outnumbered and were turned south. Pictland had lost two thousand men however this was nothing compared to the English. King Oengus now has his sights set on York or so the messenger told us. We do not think the English will let King Oengus get away with this victory and that they will be back with a larger army.

'Who led the English army,' was all I could think to ask? Tadg said that Hereweald had led the army and we do not know who lived or died on the battlefield. We are increasing our defenses incase Pictland turns its attentions west. With their large army we would be forced to flee to the highlands should they attack us. King Gregor would not like to lose his estates however better their loss then the loss of our lives.

'Why have you rescued me?' Tadg told me that my rescue had not been his idea and that I could ask Kenner or the King. He told me that he had been asked to conduct the rescue but not told the reasons. He did not care for me either way however he had heard the legend of how I had forged the countries of Britannia into a new country called England. Since the rescue he had grown fond of me and is pleased that he has had the opportunity to get to know me. 'I am heartened to hear your account and I am grateful that you and Shug did come for me. It did not feel like I had long to go living in that dungeon.' Tadg and I did get along well and there was rarely silence as we made our way around the gardens. My legs are very weak and at times I had to reach out to Tadg for support.

Finally, we found a bench opposite to the pond which was filled with lilies and a mother duck and her ducklings. Sitting on this bench with a man easily my match for size we would have made a sight to anyone observing us from across the estate. Tadg would be equivalent to an older brother as he is probably mid-thirties and he seems very similar to Leofric, my close friend who died when I made a poor decision in the battle at Hastings. I still lamented the loss of Leofric and my decision to take a small group of men to fire the Viking boats in Hasting's harbor. We were ambushed and Leofric was killed in the skirmish. Leofric was six years my senior and Tadg reminds me of him and is a similar age to what Leofric would be.

I was getting nowhere with asking for the reason for my rescue, so I changed the direction of the discussion. 'What happened with Kenner and her engagement to the Pictland prince'? Tadg seemed happy with the direction of this discussion and answered my queries. He told me that King Oengus was angered when he found out that Kenner was with child to one of our prisoners. The message was that Kenner was not worthy of being the wife for Prince Causantin. The prince has since married their commander Wen's daughter, Kate of the castle. Kate was said to be a beauty and has since given Causantin three children. This loss of face for Prince Causantin when Kenner lay with me was probably the reason why I was taken prisoner and locked up in the dungeon to rot.

Kenner never married and spends most of her time practicing her archery and riding. King Gregor has attempted to match her with other lords however she has stayed true and has said that Godric will be back. She has doted on her son and has given him all the best teachers for weapons practice and reading. 'Kenner is always telling Godric junior about you and how you can read. When at weapons she if telling him that you are a mighty hero. You must practice like your father she says. She tells him that his father will be so proud of him.' Kenner helps her father manage Strath Clyde and has promoted a building program which includes a library, Cathedral, and schoolhouse. Kenner is a remarkable woman who is envied throughout our country.

The news of Kenner and Godric junior had me fascinated. Could Kenner have really been waiting for me to return all these years. I had never made any promises as I had left without telling her or anyone from Strath Clyde what we were planning. Although I had developed a relationship with many in my short stay, I did not trust any of them to keep my departure quiet. They seem so generous toward me considering what was done back then. I needed to get my strength back if I was to see Kenner as I did not want to see her in this emancipated state. Having this thought made me laugh as I realized the truth of it. I was hoping to maintain favor with Kenner even though I am married to Aethelswith, mother of two of my children by now. Surely god would allow me to have two wives and two families. It was not like I had chosen this to happen but now that it had I thought that it only fair and that God would understand. Once a child was born it was too late to neglect one's responsibilities, or so I thought and hoped.

It sounded like Kenner would understand as I expected she would have heard about my marriage to Aethelswith. The question of whether

Aethelswith would understand may get a different response. Aethelswith is a proud protector and defender of the realm. She will do what it takes to bring security and safety to her people and that would have included an unfavorable marriage. Aethelswith's marriage to me was for love or so I thought it was. I had been a rising star and maybe she had seen that potential and thus directed her love at me. It felt like love when we were together however I was now doubting myself as Aethelswith was also a beautiful woman who had many charms. I had loved Sunngifu, and I am certain that she had loved me. We had grown up playing as children and there were no secrets between us. We had been soul mates before she had been killed.

    Tadg had been sitting quietly with me while all these thoughts had been running through my head. Looking across at him I said that it was probably time for me to go back and rest. Tadg agreed that it was important that I get back my strength. I promised Tadg that I would go easy on my eating and daily walks until I started to feel stronger. Winter was coming around again and Tadg reminded me that should I get lost or collapse in the grounds that I could be dead before someone found me. He reminded me that Winter comes in quickly this far north and that the bite of the cold is far worse than what I would be used to. With that we returned to the house and Tadg left me at my room.

Chapter 5

Collapse

The army arrived back in Winchester bruised and battered. We had sent ten thousand men north and only half had returned. Both Eadwulf and Hereweald were uninjured however many others were not so lucky. By all accounts the campaign north had been a disaster as the Picts were a much larger force then was thought possible and the terrain favored the north men due to its steepness, rocky outcrops, and confined valley's. Godric would never have put the army in a position like that although I am sure the commanders did their best and it will not help thinking of Godric at this time.

It appears my mind has been foggy for the last six months. This is ever since the news that Godric and his men were slaughtered by the Picts. Ebba tells me that it is to be expected with the loss I experienced and with being pregnant and giving birth. Praise god that everything went well with the birth of baby Albert. At least Godric junior has a baby brother. Albert takes after his father which I know would have quietly pleased him. He does not portray a proud man however I know that he was fiercely proud of his family. His older child Egbert is being raised by Hilda back in Worchester. Hilda is Godric's older sister who has four children of her own. They all live with extended family on a farm a short ride from Worchester. Worchester was Godric's dream and in my opinion is the greatest place on earth. The river Seven runs directly through the heart of the town and to the west of it are beautiful valleys followed by the Malvern hills. East of Worchester are some of the most productive farms in the realm. Everything is new in Worchester after Godric's wonderful building program. Worchester feels like home even without Godric. Godric Junior is only five and seems to have already forgotten his father.

Without a king I can feel the uncertainty of the people. News of the losses up north will already have an unsettling effect on the people and without their hero they now have a female queen. I don't feel up to this and wish the responsibility was taken away from me. These emotional swings up and down in mood must also be due to feeding a baby and a shortage of sleep. Now that Hereweald is back he can help me to govern the country. He is a stalwart of Wessex and now England having lived longer than most and seeming wise in all matters of state. I have already opened myself up to Hereweald while in tears, telling him that I was not up to governing the country. I broke down and I feel that I made a fool of myself or would have if it was with anyone else. My father relied on Hereweald and together they had been a successful team. Hereweald told me to get a stiff back and lift for the challenges ahead. 'You are your father's daughter in every way and Alfred is not remembered as Alfred the Great for nothing. Your love for your people and your country is known by all and they trust that you will keep them safe. I trust you as my queen and with every breath until I die, I will support you and our kingdom.'

That conversation with Hereweald was what I needed and had made me feel a little better. I have so many problems to deal with and every time I think of problems, I wish that Godric was here with me. The first of many problems is that it has been a bad harvest this season with next to no rains in the east. Winter is only weeks away and we will be relying on the western counties to supply food for the rest of the country. Worchester always has good stores of food with the best granaries in the land.

My biggest problem is the north and the activity of the Picts. They have taken Bamborough, and it looks like they will attack York. The castle walls at York are strong however against the force coming south it will not last for long. This is the assessment of Hereweald and Eadwulf. However, they say that we need to hold York as the next defensive line is Worchester to Northampton if York is to fall. Torksey and Repton still have palisade walls which could be easily overrun, and Leicester and Nottingham do not have defensive walls at all. Given what is at stake we need to raise an army and ride to the defense of York. It will be possible to raise an army however the morale is low, and a victory is essential to repair the damage of the last defeats. A council meeting has been organized which includes the commanders of the guard. I will authorize the raising of a force to ride north to support York. We will bolster the castle and use winter to train and increase our army numbers to launch a spring offensive against the Picts. Godric's dream was a united England which included Bamborough. We do not expect an attack during winter however the additional men, maybe four thousand, will protect York in case we are wrong.

With winter coming there are already many who are suffering. Requests for aid have been sent to the west and hopefully food and supplies will come before winter and be in quantities to prevent further suffering.

It is good to see old John Archer from Worcester and Earl Evan Tudor of Northampton. Both men are respected leaders and crucial for a balanced discussion and outcome. This meeting could be one of the most important in our young country's history.

Looking around the table I could see the familiar faces of the council plus the other leaders from around the realm. I started the meeting by thanking them all for their attendance. I thought it important to clearly outline the challenges facing our land. As I spoke there were lots of nods of agreement and smiles of support. The table was then opened for members to add their own discussion points.

Besides the poor harvest and the Picts in the north there is still problems with Vikings in the east of the country where integration of those who stayed behind was happening slowly. When the Vikings were conquered the residents of these towns such as Colchester and Tretford were given the option to leave or stay. Many decided to stay as the lands of Britannia were all they had ever known. They also must have heard rumors from the English and their sense of Justice and freedom. All of this did not seem to be making integration any easier and there is still ongoing tit for tat attacks.

Henry of Exeter says that there is increased pirate activity along both the north and south coasts of Cornwall. Fishermen are too scared to set sail which is having an effect of stores for the winter. They will only stay close to the land where they can flee for safety if a threat is noticed. Some of the smaller coastal villages have been raided and it feels like the days of the Vikings have come again. The pirates seem to be organized and many are reporting French accents or the Normans. We are concerned that there is something bigger coming if Europe has its eyes on Britannia and more importantly England.

The talk of the Normans seemed to put everyone on edge, and it was agreed that we needed to maintain a home guard to defend against a possible attack from the mainland. Maintaining guards on all our fronts would reduce the number of men we could send north. This is where the arguments commenced as there was no region which wanted to sacrifice its men for winter to bolster the defense of York. Wulfsige said that London was on the firing line from the Normans and even the Picts from the North. Evan and John both offered a thousand men however did not want to weaken their guards further as they were the next line of defense after York. Henry refused to offer any men as he said that he had the largest stretch of coast to look after. Eadwulf was concerned about supplying men to bolster York as he said that Wessex had lost too many at the battle of Darlington.

We debated the defense of York for hours and in the end, it was decided to leave York to its own defense. Given the recent defeats we thought it best to let the men winter at home. The council will meet again in the spring with an attempt to put together an army to march north.

This decision is a relief as it will give each of our regions the opportunity to deal with our local problems which includes the threats from aboard and the poverty of the population.

After the meeting John caught up with me and we shared supper together. John said that Worcester was ready to rise again to fulfil Godric's dream. The granaries are full, and the forges have never stopped. He told me that the alliance with Powys had been maintained and was as strong as ever.

King David's youngest son is Emrick, and he has moved to Worcester. Emrick's wife Hafina had died in childbirth. Emrick has taken up residence at the Amity farm and is engaged to marry Hilda. Emrick has four children as does Hilda although his children are slightly older. The children have moved with Emrick and filled the Amity household. Emrick's eldest is Morgan, and he is now eighteen. He has two daughters, Mary, and Jane and the youngest is his twelve-year-old boy, Simon. All children are well bred and a big help on the farm and in the forge. Hilda's eldest is Osgar who is fourteen and has joined the Worcester guard as did his famous uncle at around the same age. The other children are doing well with Elfin being a real beauty, much as her mother was and still is. Worcester is in good hands and has friends it can rely on. 'I will speak with the council, and I can assure you that we will be all in for England. 'We will continue to build the guard and recommence our training as soon as I return. Worchester's population still swells, and I am sure we can raise seven or eight thousand in an emergency.

My conversation with John was reassuring and I appreciated his confidence and support. John was like a father to Godric and John had lost as much as anyone. His two boys and daughter had all been killed in the Viking wars. John and his wife Leofflaed are respected members of the Worchester community and John is still leader of the council there. It is men like John which will keep England safe and together in the coming years. Men with cool heads which can see the bigger picture and not get caught up in the pursuit of glory. I relied a lot on men like John, Hereweald, Eadwulf, Wulfsige and Evan. Sitting back, I smiled with this reassurance. The realm would survive with the leaders we had at the helm.

Chapter 6

Starting from Scratch

I had been at the Glasgow estate for four days and was beginning to recover from my shoulder operation and imprisonment. I spent more hours awake and had begun taking short walks in the extensive gardens. Tadg had been right about the temperatures this far north as the sun set early and the air never lost its chill. The winds from the north carried the hint of winter to come. This household, like all the households around the north, were preparing for winter much as a squirrel gathers and stores its nuts. Winter came with a fair degree of trepidation for the people this far north.

With my imprisonment and emancipation, I had been living with a mental acceptance of my demise. I had got to the point where I had not expected to live. My mind had slowed, and I had stopped contemplating a change in my circumstances. Already I was now beginning to see things clearly and see the opportunity I had been given. I was once again starting to think of returning to the south and being reunited with my friends and family. It was a little embarrassing how I had stopped thinking of them during my imprisonment and even after my release. The more that I thought of them the more I longed to flee south. This was not possible in my current state as I had lost maybe fifty percent of my body weight and could still only stand up and walk for short periods of time.

At the top of my mind is Aethelswith and her beautiful long brown hair, her slime figure and ample bosom. Aethelswith is an amazing person who is an example for us all. She leads her people with purpose and compassion, and I have never seen her wavier from their concerns. She would be looking after England. Our second child will have been born and I prayed that it was healthy and strong, boy or girl. I also longed to discuss the matters of the state. I wanted to discuss the problems and spend our time together inventing solutions. Mostly I wanted to go somewhere quiet and spend some intimate time with her. It had been over twelve months since the battle of Jarrow and the south would think I was dead. This was the first time I had experienced this thought.

My death could change everything in the south. It might embolden our enemies, what did Tadg say about King Oengus and his push south. He had taken Bamborough and now maybe York? Might Aethelswith remarry out of love or for the good of the Kingdom. What sorrow would be in the hearts of my loved ones back in Worchester. These thoughts were beginning to make me miserable. I needed to get a message to Worchester, to Hilda and Aethelswith to let them know that I was well. Who could I trust with such a message? Just as importantly I needed to get my strength back and get home as quickly as I could.

I was still in my room but felt the urge for some fresh air. I did not wait for Tadg as had become the custom but took myself for a walk in the garden. There was a light drizzle however this was not going to stop me. The rush of realizations had almost overwhelmed me. The drizzle on my face was refreshing and droplets of water began to form on my hair, brow, and beard. It was paradise here, but I now had purpose and needed to plan.

There was a sudden shock as I sensed and found out that I was not alone. In an instant I was staring into the eyes of one of the most beautiful women I have ever seen. Kenner was there standing by a magnificent plane tree. Her smile was mischievous and totally addictive. Kenner spoke with that irresistibly feminine voice, 'I see that you are feeling better. I was praying for you and for a speedy recovery.' I was still stunned and suddenly I became self-conscious of my appearance. All I could think to say was to tell Kenner that she is the most beautiful woman that I have ever seen. I told her that she had hardly changed at all. Kenner laughed at that and told me that I still must be delirious and needed to get back to bed. This made me laugh and I told her that I was well although I may not look it. Regaining some of my faculties I thanked her for my rescue and treatment.

Kenner told me that she had never given up on me. She always knew I would return and that I had a magnificent son who could not wait to meet his father. It seemed like we were going to be talking for a while as we had a lot of catching up to do. I excused myself and made my way to the nearest bench, the same bench which overlooks the lily pond. The lilies are flower less yet still pretty spread out across the pond. Kenner followed me and sat next to me on the wet bench. I could now smell her and the sweet perfume which brought back more sensory memories. Kenner always seemed to have a gentle fragrance around her which was alluring in our previous life and the impact on me had not lessened over the years.

'I knew you would be leaving as you spoke with such passion about Worchester and the south. Your dreams of a united land excited me and were and are still my hope. You could not stay in the north with so many relying on you in the south. I had hoped you would stay for longer and was initially angry when you left. However, within the day I was happy for you and content that our paths would once again cross. We continued to receive news of Worchester and the English. I had all news from the south directed to me. Even before he could walk, I have been telling Godric junior about his father and what he was up to. Hearing about the battle of Jarrow had almost ripped the heart from my chest. I could not understand god or why he would punish us in such a way. Then I heard that you were a prisoner of King Oengus, and I knew that god was looking out for me. We needed a plan as Strath Clyde and Pictland have an uneasy truce and we did not want to start a war over you. We did not want to antagonize Pictland either as we thought they would just as quickly kill you. Waiting was what we decided on. We waited and kept our eyes and ears open for an opportunity. King Oengus rode south with all of his men leaving the dungeon all but undefended.'

This was an amazing story of faith which Kenner was telling me. I could not believe that this beauty before me was thinking so strongly for me, a blacksmith. 'I hear that your brother has no love for me and would as quickly run me through if given the chance.'

This made Kenner smile and she said that not everyone was pleased by my escape. 'When news of my pregnancy came out my family were angered as this only struck a bigger wedge between Strath Clyde and Pictland. Father, in all his wisdom, was able to look at the bigger picture when I affirmed my feelings for you and my belief that you would come back one day. Father was quietly pleased that I was not forced to marry Causantin as he is as cruel as he is ugly.' Kenner told me that Munro holds a grudge, and it was best I avoid him at least until I have my strength back. With that she looked at me and said that it would be a couple of seasons before my weight and strength returned. With how I looked and felt I tended to agree with

Kenner's assessment. She asked me if I could ride to which I scoffed. She gave me the look so I justified myself by saying, 'Of course I can ride however I would not recommend it for a couple of weeks.' Kenner laughed and again I was hooked. All my earlier thoughts of south, Worchester and Aethelswith were quickly forgotten. I had to get well, and I had to have this girl.

Kenner reached over and held my hand. Looking into my eyes she told me we have plenty of time and my health was a priority. Those eyes had me pinned and before I knew it, we were kissing. How could this be, me in this unkempt and fragile condition and Kenner one of gods gifts to the earth. Kenner was stunning with the wet hair draped over her head with the odd strand strung across her damp cheeks. I realized that I was now soaked through from the drizzle and that Kenner was probably the same. All thoughts were lost again as Kenner again kissed me and moved in and attempted to wrap me into her arms. Although emancipated I was still too large for her arms. I was pleased that I still had my size as at least this set me apart from most others. I closed my eyes in her embrace and felt myself drift off before Kenner woke me telling me not to drift off on her. Grabbing my hand, she pulled me up off the bench and said It was time I was back in bed. As she said this there was a twinkle in her eye and then that laugh again. 'You should be so lucky,' she told me.

With that I was put to bed and had the soundest and most refreshing sleep I could remember. Once awake I was more determined than ever to continue building my strength. I was still on stew however my portions had doubled in the space of days. The outdoors and additional food were doing me wonders.

I did not see Kenner again for the following few days which suited me as it gave me time to contemplate the future. In Kenner's presence all memories of responsibility and the south disappeared however these returned within days of her absence. It was almost like Kenner was a witch with power over me. I noticed this phenomenon when next she visited a week after we last caught up. This time I had the strength to walk the grounds as we talked and once again all thought of my other life disappeared from my mind and memory. The weather on this day was unseasonably fine and we took the opportunity to wander further then I had done since being there. Coming out into a clearing we came onto a paddock with half a dozen beautiful chestnut mares. These were beautiful animals which should not have been a surprise from what I knew of Gregor. King Gregor loved his horses and seemed to have one of the best breeding programs I have ever seen. Kenner asked me if I wanted to ride one of them however, I had to decline. I told her I needed another week as I did not want to risk my recovery with a bad fall. Kenner laughed and said she was surprised that I had lost my courage.

Feeling hurt by Kenner's remarks I was bulldozed into agreeing to go for a ride with her. There was a shed in the corner of the paddock which had saddles and all the riding equipment. I helped Kenner prepare two horses and then was gingerly assisted onto one of the chestnuts called Poly. Kenner was to be riding a horse called Trish. Together Kenner and I set off with Poly and Trish out of the clearing and through the trees. I had no idea where I was so did my best to keep up with Kenner not wishing to get lost. We continued to climb through the birch forests north of the Estate which was north of Glasgow. There was an expanse of forest which became visible as we climbed up a mountain track above the tree line.

It is cold up here as evidenced by our breath being visible in the air. Kenner took it easy on me with her pace and I was able to stay on the horse, to my surprise. At the top of the trail there is a flat rocky outcrop with views south to the winding Clyde river. We did not stay for long to admire the view as daylight was disappearing fast and we knew the temperature would drop quickly once that happened. I was not ready to spend the night out in the elements.

It was just on dark when the horses were back in their paddock and the saddles stored. Kenner again grabbed my hand as we walked back through the trees toward the house. This situation reminded me of the time years before when Kenner and I had first been intimate. The thought aroused me, but I did not get my hopes up. With some effort I changed my direction of thought. I am married and in the Christian world it is adultery to be intimate with another. Adultery is one of the sins which could send me to hell. How could something which would feel so right be so wrong in god's eyes?

Our rides became longer and further over the following week. My riding abilities came back quickly, and I noticed that my energy and strength had also returned. Each ride increased in enjoyment as I became able to push Poly and keep up with Kenner and Trish. Horses are quick to form bonds with humans they like and judging by the response I was getting from Poly our bond was strong. On one such ride we came to a glade which sloped down to the upper reaches of the Clyde. It was early in the afternoon and although cool it was a fine day.

Kenner suggested that we go for a swim as the river water looked calm and clean. It felt like years since I had swum so I agreed. We left the horses to graze and walked to the edge. I had taken off my boots and shirt when I looked across at Kenner standing before me without an item of clothing. I did not want to stare however I could do nothing but stare at her beautiful white body. Every curve looked as perfect as it had when I had last seen it. Kenner made fun of me and asked if I had had a good enough look? Kenner turned and with a couple of steps she was at the edge of the river where she disappeared with a dive beneath the river surface.

Feeling a little silly being partially clothed I followed Kenner's lead and quickly stripped off. My feelings of being silly were soon replaced with embarrassment as I stood there in broad daylight with everything to see. It was also impossible to hide my appraisal of the situation which was obviously promising. Following Kenner's lead, I also stepped to the edge and dived for the protection and shelter of the water.

The initial shock of the water was enough to have me regretting this decision. This water is freezing to a point where it is painful. Any thought of an agreeable situation was completely suppressed by the shock my body was now going through. 'Swim' was what Kenner yelled to me. 'Swim to the other side and join me over here.' Kenner was yelling from the other side of the river. While in shock and feeling sorry for myself Kenner had swum to the other side of the slow-moving river. I felt too cold to move and was tempted to get out of the water. 'Swim, come on silly, don't be a chicken.' Goaded as I was, I decided to put my head under and swim across the river. The lure of Kenner on the other side was enough to get me over the line. My ears ached and I was again wondering what I was doing. When I reached Kenner, she did not seem to be affected by the water which must be close to freezing temperature.

I was however rewarded by Kenner when I reached the other side of the river. While wiping the water from my eyes Kenner came in close and wrapped me in her arms. I could feel every part of her nakedness press against my body. I opened my eyes in time to see Kenner's mouth lock with mine. The press of her body, the firmness of her curves and the surprise of the occasion and I was every bit ready for what was to come. We played in the water for another few minutes however even Kenner agreed that the water was too cold. I believe she may have been playing tough to show me up however I did not care. We swam back to the glade where our cloths were lying in two neat piles. On the banks of the river Kenner and I came together as two long lost lovers. The occasion could not have been better if I had put days into the planning. We were completely secluded with the sound of the river and the birds in the background. The intimacy must have lasted for over an hour and I could tell that Kenner felt the same as me and did not want the occasion to end. I was thrilled being so close to Kenner again not least seeing her in all her glory. I was reminded why I had come under her spell the first time and couldn't care about anything else in the world at that moment. I was in love, and it was the greatest feeling in the world.

Eventually we had to dress and gather the horses. I am sure the horses enjoyed their freedom even though they had stayed close and looked keen to get going. The sun was already at the horizon and once again we would be getting back on dark. We were in no hurry to get back even though we knew it was reckless to be out after dark even though the weather had been fine. It was a half-moon which would just give Kenner enough light to guide us home. Riding home after dark was enough to give me the realization that I was unarmed and effectively defenseless. I told Kenner that I would like to make myself some weapons and begin training again. She was in front of me so I could not see her expression however she said she agreed that it was about time and said that I should catch up with Shug.

Later when walking from the paddock in the light of the moon I asked Kenner if I was free to go or if I was a prisoner? Following on from this I told her I wondered if they would be comfortable if I was armed? Kenner pulled me around into her arms and kissed me passionately. 'My handsome Godric, you are free to go when you like. You are also free to carry weapons of your choosing. I would recommend you do not leave until you have regained your strength and I would like you to meet your son. Your leaving would also give me a sadness in my heart for I have waited since you first left for a moment like today. God and the fates have destined us to be together and I don't believe anything can challenge this. If you leave, I know that you will return as you were delivered to me this time. Please stay with me, meet your son, and catch up with my father.' That led to further kissing and some more intimate action in the dark of the trees. Lying there soaking in Kenner's sweet smell I almost fell asleep. How could I walk away from her, she was right about us being made for each other? Maybe god was wrong and there was more than one perfect woman for each man. This could be why men kill each other so that the surviving men could love more than one woman.

The following day I went down to the forge at the back of the stables and caught up with Shug. I told him I wanted to make some weapons which included some special swords and arrow tips. I was going to construct an English longbow and offered to show him my latest high-quality weapons. I could see the immediate look of glee in Shug's eyes with the thought of seeing how I made my light but strong weapons.

Shug had plenty of high-grade iron and I showed him how to increase the carbon to reduce the weight of the blades. It was important to keep the carbon at between two and three percent as any higher and the blade could become brittle. Three percent carbon and the sword being forged in two layers is the secret to getting light blades which had the strength to penetrate armor which can be sharpened to easily cut flesh. My twin swords are feared by the Vikings, and I was now giving this innovation to Strath Clyde.

Something inside me trusted Strath Clyde and I hope it was not just the lure of Kenner. I was still to meet up with King Gregor and was looking forward to meeting him on more of an equal footing. He may still be angry about getting his daughter with child, but I hoped he would be over that by now. Strath Clyde were vulnerable to Pictland and may need an alliance with England to prevent it from being attacked. The Vikings are gone for now however we had no idea if they would be back and in what numbers. Britannia will be much stronger if we stopped fighting each other and worked together to strengthen our borders. Shug had always had a pure heart and I warmed to him almost instantly when we met again.

There was some trial and error with the weapons over the coming week but finally we produced perfection. With the prototype mastered we set about making several copies so that both Shug and I had spare weapons. With weapons in hand, we commenced practice in the yard. Shug was strong however he had never had weapons training with a master. I was able to show Shug the ideal techniques with the twin blades although the going was slow as he had many bad techniques which he had to unlearn. Shug was an enthusiastic learner and most of the difficulties he had at first were able to be overcome with practice. Archery practice had impressive results as Shug had only ever used a bow for hunting. With some lengthy practice sessions Shug was able to regularly hit a target at fifty yards.

It took weeks for me to get my strength and precision back. It had been over a year since I had handled a sword and just as long since I had shot an arrow. I found the swords were too heavy for me at first and knew it would take time to build up my strength. With determination I practiced beyond what was probably healthy with each session. Within a week of having every muscle aching I could feel that I was making great gains. My strength was returning and once I noticed this everything began to get easier. The pain and exhaustion were still there however now I knew there was light at the end of the hard work.

Shug and I kept at practice all winter and without noticing it I was back to my former self before the first shoots of spring. Kenner had been around for most of winter, and we met up at least weekly in locations where we could be alone and share each other's company.

I had still not met my son and had not pushed for a meeting earlier because I wanted to live up to what he may have been told about me. I wanted my strength back so that I could impress him. Kenner told me that he was in Carlisle with his grandparents, aunt, and uncle. As soon as the winter thaw takes place and the leaves are shooting on the trees, they will be travelling north to catch up with us. Kenner had travelled south at least twice over winter to see Godric junior and had always returned in a depressed mood. She told me that being away from Godric junior was tough however her love for me far exceeded that sadness. I wanted to get to know Godric junior and was looking forward to the day as surely it was not far away.

Spring had arrived and we got word that King Gregor and the household were on their way. Life around the estate became frantic as everyone knew they only had a couple of days. The gardeners were out in force, mowing, weeding, and edging everything. The servants were dusting the house and the groomsmen were brushing down the animals. Everything which could be done was being done and everyone, including me, was hoping to make a good impression.

King Gregor arrived on horseback with several of his commanders by his side. Gregor led a procession of three enclosed carts and a guard which must be a hundred strong. I recognized Gregor instantly from his size and the casual way he handled a horse. Gregor is a man who has grown up around horses and is as comfortable on one as he is leading his people. He is a similar size to me which is unusual for the Picts as they all seem to be smaller than what I thought was average in Worchester. Most of my time has been spent on one of the royal estates so I may not have a balanced view however the people appear to love Gregor. Strath Clyde seems to have avoided major conflicts which in turn has contributed to the prosperity of the land. Given the weather this far north the land would be difficult enough to turn to profit. Losing the male population to a pointless war would only make the situation far worse and that was if they won. I was looking forward to spending some time with Gregor and hearing what made the man tick.

Walking alongside Gregor was a boy who looked about seven. Instantly I felt the connection as I could see Kenner in his stride and the smile he casually wore. He had sandy blond hair slightly darker than his mothers and his eyes are a piercing dark blue, a color I have only ever seen when looking at myself in a reflection. This was my son, and I was nervous.

King Gregor and his entourage walked directly at me as I was standing adjacent to the front door. I was doing my best to be courteous to the King by greeting him with eye contact but was struggling to take my eyes from Godric junior. I could not call him Godric junior forever, so I had to come up with another name for him. Greeting the King I thanked him for his hospitality and said with sincerity that I was pleased to get the opportunity to meet him again. Everyone in the entourage had stopped as the king stopped to address me. 'You are most welcome Godric for it is my wish for us to be friends. I have heard of your exploits in the south and I know my daughter has great affection for you.' As if on cue Kenner appeared and ran up to hug her mother and father. Queen Lileas is nothing like her daughter but then she must be pushing fifty. She is still beautiful for her age but where Kenner is slim and curvy, she is short and curve less. I bowed to Lileas and said that I was so grateful to have been allowed to stay in her home.

Kenner had picked up Godric and swung him around a couple of times. Putting him down she stopped in front of me and told him that I was his father. I stuck out my hand to shake saying, 'Godric.' While at the same time he stuck out his hand and said the same. The three of us laughed at this and I said that this was no good. 'How do you feel about being called Rick so as we don't get confused.' Godric or should I say Rick, said that he would like that as it would be his first nick name. We shook on it and Kenner laughed at us.

'This is your son. Godric, give the boy a hug.' Embarrassed by my obvious failure in the situation I reached down and picked up little Rick. Holding him close my boy whispered that he loved me into my ear. This whisper made me hold him closer and before putting him down I held him out a little so that we were looking at each other eye to eye. I told him that I have been looking forward to this day since the moment I found out that he was my boy. I said that we had much to catch up on and I could not wait to hear what he has been doing.

Lileas tapped Kenner on the shoulder and said that it was time we all went inside. Inside the house was immaculate as the servants had been busy for the last two days since hearing of Gregor's arrival. Immediately at home Gregor invited me into the sitting room for some mead by the fire. Kenner and Rick joined us which made me think that there was not going to be some secret agreement on this meeting.

Taking a seat by the fire and across from Gregor I noticed Rick hesitate between going to sit with his grandfather and coming to sit with me. I felt a pang of disappointment as he chose to go and sit with Gregor. The advantage was that I could look at him as Gregor and I conversed. Kenner took a seat next to me to balance out the arrangement.

It was not my house, so I did not commence the discussions, as tempted as I was. There were a few moments of silence before Gregor asked me if I was fully recovered from my injuries and time in the dungeon. He told me that they knew I had been taken prisoner however they could not risk an escape attempt into the capital of Pictland. They were hoping that King Oengus would be treating me better than he had. 'It is possible that Oengus did not appreciate who he held in his dungeons. He knew you as the man who shamed his son and maybe as the King of England, but he did not know who you truly were.' This had me intrigued and wondering who I truly was.

Over my life I have often reflected on who I am and what my purpose is so hearing this phrase from the King of Strath Clyde made me curious.

'Who am I truly King Gregor?' Gregor had a glint in his eye as young Rick answered for him. Rick told us that I am his father. We all laughed including Rick however we told him that King Oengus would have known this. Gregor told me that I was written about in the prophecies from the highland witches. 'They say that a man will come out of the south and nowhere, he will tear apart Britannia and remake it as one. His line will go on to rule Britannia for a thousand years.'

This was a powerful prophecy and especially if it meant me. I am not overly superstitious or believing in the occult however I am a Christian and a believer in Jesus Christ and how different are they really? I wanted it to be true as it would give me the reassurance that everything will work out as it should. At that moment It was so far from the truth as I was at the other end of Britannia to where I needed to be to be the instrument of peace. Gregor was watching me strain as I went through these thoughts in my head. As though he was listening, he said that the witches were not specific on which country would be dominant over Britannia. 'Now you may believe it to be England and maybe it will be however it could just as likely be Pictland or Strath Clyde.'

I told him that I had always believed it was my destiny to free the land of the Viking invaders so that the peoples of Britannia could live and prosper in peace. That destiny was close to being fulfilled when the fates chose another destiny for me. However, all is not lost as the fates, or Jesus, again found me friends and freedom. My next path is unclear however I am content to regain my strength, renew my relationship with your daughter and get to know my son. I am a lucky man although at times I have despaired. Life does not appear to be easy for anyone so one cannot complain about one's lot. I have exceptional abilities and it is my responsibility to use these for the greater good of the people. As I was speaking, I could sense that all eyes were on me. When I stopped Kenner pulled me to her and kissed me on the lips. Gregor scolded his daughter and told her to leave me alone.

The King agreed with what I said as it matched with what he told us from the witch's prophecy. He told us that we cannot concern ourselves with prophecy as we needed to live in the now. King Oengus has been a powerful king for Pictland and although harsh at times he has also led his people well. Oengus is getting old and although he still leads his army, we believe he is not long for this world. His son, Causantin, is as different from his father as a bird is to a fish. Causantin is powerful in build and ambition. He has no empathy for his people and much less for anyone who is not Pictlandish. He holds a definite grudge against Strath Clyde because of Kenner's folly eight years ago. Causantin would take his country to war with us just to avenge this hurt that was done to him. He is a man who will seek revenge.

Pictland has taken Bamborough, and they may take York however for now we have heard that they returned to Pictland for the winter. It may take a year or two for their next campaign as they will have crops to sow and animals to husband in preparation for the coming winter. A delay to any push south would make Strath Clyde stand out as a juicy target. We are close to their supplies, and they could war on us and return to harvest their crops. I believe we are most exposed this coming summer especially if anything should happen to Oengus.

We have some minor castles and defensive walls. We have our islands and sections of the highlands where we can hide if forced from our land. However, we want to keep our land and thus we will do whatever it takes to stand our ground. The truth be told we would be slaughtered if King Oengus came for us with his full army. We have half their number without the initiative.

King Gregor looked at me then with a more serious look on his face. 'This is where you come in as I know who you truly are. You are the man who will unite the lands of Britannia. I do not believe it will be with Pictland so it must be with either England or Strath Clyde. Either way I would align our people with England for their protection and prosperity. In return for this alliance and for your rescue and recovery I would have you arm and train my guards so that we could at least defend ourselves against an imminent attack.'

This gave me many things to consider, and I felt the pressure of the moment. I was now considering England because of the direction of the conversation. England was my home and I needed to get back for my family and people. I felt uncomfortable thinking this and could not say it in front of Kenner and Rick. It was obvious that Kenner loved me unconditionally or at least I thought it was. I had only just met Rick and he was a sweet boy who I think would be heartbroken if I were to leave now. It is an awkward position for me to be in, but I thought that another month or two would not make any difference to England. Rather than answer I asked Gregor what intelligence he had of England and Pictland.

Gregor told me that Oengus had returned to Edinburgh with his army and that England had reinforced York and would likely meet Oengus in the field or at Bamborough. The report has said that the English are determined to see my dream become a reality. The Vikings are gone, and their old lands would become a part of the new England. Hearing this account reassured me and helped me to agree to the terms. Kenner squeezed my hand and did not seem surprised by me agreeing however I could see relief on Gregor's face and Rick just looked confused.

'I will give you two months, but I will not fight against England or its allies. You shall not raise your arms against England unless it is in self-defense or provocation of another kind. At the end of two months, I will evaluate where everything is at. I will have to return home shortly after as it is not fair having them think I am dead when I am now perfectly well. I would also have a message sent to Winchester saying that I am in Glasgow and recovering from imprisonment by King Oengus. The message should say that I will be coming home when I have the strength to travel.' Saying these words were difficult and as I looked at Kenner, I could see the hurt in her eyes. 'I must go back my darling. Going home will not diminish the love I feel for you and Rick. I am English and these are my people.'

Kenner got to her feet and left the room. I think I could sense that she was about to cry. Rick looked at me and then at his grandfather. He too rose and took off after his mother. 'It seems that the lad has good intuition,' I commented to Gregor.

'Just like his father it would seem,' said Gregor. 'I agree to your terms and agree that you will need to go home to your family and people. A messenger will be arranged immediately. You will be welcome to return and make Strath Clyde your home. Whatever you need to assist with your decision to stay can be arranged and I know my daughter would love for you to stay. Rick needs a father, and he will not find better than you.' The pressure was sure there however I now had the breathing space of a couple of months before I would have to break hearts. I intended to use the time well with getting to know my little boy. I would see what Rick knew about the forge, weapons and horses and teach him as much as he could absorb.

I excused myself from Gregor and went searching for Kenner. I found her in the garden sitting on a swing. Rick was leaning into her lap and Kenner had her arms wrapped around his body. Hurting you or Rick is the last thing on my mind. Seeing my family is important to me and will be to them. I have two other boys at home, one older and one younger than Rick. These are his half-brothers, and they deserve to see their father again. Kenner smiled at me and reassured me that she understood and would want to do the same if she was in my position. She told me that she loved me and that she was with child again. 'Please excuse me as being pregnant makes a girl a little emotional.' We both started laughing at this and this made little Rick laugh to. I came forward and pulled them too me off the swing. We hugged like a family, and it felt like I was home.

Chapter 7

Celebrations and Comings Together

It was the middle of winter, and the news could not have been worse. York had been taken and was now occupied by King Oengus of Pictland. The messenger told us that all the lands north of the Trent river were now in the hands of Oengus. It seems that the intelligence that he had returned to Edinburgh had been false and he had intended on taking York all along. There were now less than six hours of daylight, and the roads were clogged with snow so there was very little which could be done until spring. Spring was a month or two away and Oengus would be making the most of this time to reinforce his claim over these castles and the land.

Hereweald had confirmed that nothing could be done. He said that the best which we could do was to send men out to the cities of the kingdom to have them begin preparing for the Spring offensive. The forges can continue to run, and the men can train in the warmth of their homes and barns. The land claimed by Godric Amity could not be lost so easily.

King Oengus and his men must have endured the harsh conditions in the north and waited until the defenses of the castle were lowered. Eadwulf who is commander of the guard and had travelled with the army which took Bamborough noted that these men are from the extreme north where very few can survive in the open. The conditions outside of York were probably like a warm winter's day for Oengus and his men. We were outsmarted once again and needed to be ready when spring came.

I asked my council a question about King Oengus and the men from Pictland. 'If we were outsmarted in York is there a chance that King Oengus could outsmart us again? We believe the roads are clogged and nothing can be done as it is the middle of winter. We thought the same at York and look at the position we are in.' I saw lights go on in the eyes of my council. Hereweald concurred that it was possible but highly unlikely. Andras who is second in command to Eadwulf said that a warning should be sent to the northern cities of Worcester, Northampton and London. They must prepare for attack and thus must ensure they do not relax the guard on their gates. Their walls are strong, and the cities will not be easily beaten. They can send word to their fringe areas to prepare for attack and to stay behind their Palisade walls as much as possible. They might even reinforce some of these areas if they can spare the men and their families. Torksey and Repton are the two towns most at risk although they may head out to Tretford with the aim of capturing all the once Viking areas.

There seemed little else which could be done although we discussed various options into the night. Eventually the mead was brought out and the council relaxed and began enjoying the evening. I was telling Andras and Hereweald that everything seemed to be falling apart. 'Why do men seek conquest and war? Can't they see that it only leads to heartache and suffering?' I so much wished that my Godric was with me. Godric had a way of taking charge even though he did not do it intentionally. He always seemed to grasp a situation and make the right decisions at the right time. I wondered if Godric was up there in heaven watching our meeting and trying to guide me. Maybe I was not praying or listening hard enough.

'It is not your fault my lady. King Oengus has jumped at an opportunity and could have been preparing for years. From what we have gathered we have heard that the King is just appeasing his son who seems to have leadership of the army. Causantin has a reputation as bad as they come, and the commander of his forces is said to be just as evil as Causantin. The cities will be doing their part to raise armies for the spring and will not let Godric's memory down. We have the finest warriors in Britannia and will soon have our lands back and a surrender agreement from these men of the north. It is our belief that they have over stretched and could easily have their homeland taken while they are in the south. Either Strath Clyde, the Vikings or Pirates may seize this opportunity and Oengus would have to rush home with his men. If we had the boats, we could also do the same.' Hereweald had a great idea with the mention of boats. We cannot do it this year however we should commence a building program and options like Hereweald just mentioned would be real opportunities for us. If the Vikings were to attack again, we could also take the fight to their homeland and make them think again. We are an island and thus we needed to become more powerful and skillful with the waters surrounding us.

During this exchange I noticed that Andras was watching me closely. He is a handsome and powerful man of a similar age to me. I know that he lives alone with his two teenage children. He had married young and had had his first two children early in the marriage. Evie his wife had then had many miscarriages over the years and finally when it looked like they would have their third child Evie and the child had died during the birth. Eadwulf and his wife have helped Andras with the children, especially when on campaign. Andras's tale is a sad one which is probably why we have grown close. I have lost my immediate family, parents, bother and husband. I also have two children although the youngest is still a baby. Hereweald and I have discussed my situation and he has suggested I might marry again for the good of the kingdom. Part of me has resisted such talk as I am still in love with Godric and although outside the official mourning period of twelve months I am having trouble moving on. The way Andras is looking at me with his big blue eyes and the effects of the mead are helping me to clear my mind of guilt and helping me see him as an attractive proposition.

The drinks continued to flow and slowly the council members excused themselves and left to join their families. Andras was the last councilor as Hereweald excused himself with a bow and a smile. As soon as we were alone, I took the steps required to come within Andras's space. Simultaneously I reached up with my head and with a hand behind his head I pulled him down to my lips. I have been keeping Andras hanging on for months as I was not ready to move on. The gravity of the attacks up north, the mead and the late night made me want Andras even more. All that frustration was going to be released tonight and we could deal with the consequences in the morning. We stayed up most of the night exploring each other intimately and I liked what I saw. Andras was a thoughtful and gentle lover and not too unlike Godric.

We were not disturbed early as the household maids and servants had known that we had a late night with the council meeting. I woke with the first light and was able to lie awake listening to Andras breath. Eventually I must have fallen fast asleep as when I woke it was light and probably mid-morning. Andras was still in bed lying on his side looking at me. He smiled when he saw I was awake, and this removed all worry that what I was doing was a bad decision. I was ready to move on and Godric would have wanted me to move on and be happy. The children need a father, and the Kingdom needs a King.

After lunch we all met up again and confirmed the plans for the winter defense and the coming spring offensive. Messengers were sent and Winchester swung into its own preparations which kept Andras busy.

Spring arrived and the men were eager to get started on reclaiming the land which had been taken by King Oengus. A council meeting was organized for Worchester as this was much closer to where the war and battles would be fought. Andras and I were now publicly dating, and he had proposed to me two weeks before we were due to ride to Worchester. I wanted some of my close friends to attend including John and Leofflaed Archer, Hilda and her family, Wulfsige, Evan, Ethan and Wassa. If we were to marry before the council meeting, then we would need to send out invitations immediately. We discussed the planned wedding with Hereweald, and he suggested that it was probably not the best timing considering the upcoming campaign. He then changed his tune and said there was never a good time in the world they seemed to live in, and a wedding might boost confidence. With Hereweald's blessing the wedding was organized for the day before we were due to leave for the council meeting. This would enable us to travel back with our friends from Worchester.

It was wonderful seeing Hilda, Emrick and the children. Hilda is Godric's older sister and matriarch to the Amity family. They had all grown so much including Egbert who was now around eight years old and my late husband's first child to his first wife Sunngifu. Sunngifu was daughter to John and Leofflaed Archer and had been killed by the Vikings in an attacked when returning to Worchester after Godric's sister Wassa's wedding. The attacked had been avenged by Godric however Egbert had been left without a mother. Since then, Hilda has been raising Egbert along with her four children. The father of Hilda's children, Leofric, had been killed in the great Viking wars which had cleared Britannia of the Vikings. Leofric was a hero and a great friend of Godric's. Since then, Hilda had married Emrick who had come to the farm after the death of his wife Hafina during childbirth. Emrick was a skilled farmer, hunter, and military man. He had also been working tirelessly with Tata to keep the forges going every day of the year. The battle of Jarrow had ended Tata's life and since then Emrick had been working with Alun, Bevan and Bert to keep the forges working. The Amity and Archer families are the backbone of the tight knit community which is Worchester even though Worchester has now grown to be a city. Worchester is the crown in the Jewel of what is England although London and Northampton are also powerhouses of the north.

With all the guests having arrived the service was conducted in the Winchester cathedral. John Archer walked down the aisle with me, and I was finally joined with Andras Arturo. He is a fine man and I feel blessed to have found another who is like the salt of the earth. Down to earth and humble. We opened the mead and larder for the celebrations that night. The future is uncertain, and we can never be sure we will have an opportunity like this again. I was reassured by the love and congratulations given us by the family and friends of Godric. We all knew hardship and we had to move on with our pain and grief. The dream of Godric is that one day our children will grow up knowing nothing but peace. 'We want them to not dread their fathers riding off from the house with the fear they will never return. How good would that be,' Godric would say?'

The following day it seemed like there were many who were feeling worse for wear with headaches. I felt poorly however I could not get out of the trip to Worchester. I would have loved to have stayed in bed but being the Queen I had to lead by example. I rose early and helped the servants with the breakfast. The main hall was still a mess from the banquet the evening before however there were servants everywhere cleaning up the mess and preparing the tables for breakfast. Within the hour the room was once again spotless and there were dozens of us sitting around eating eggs, bacon and sausages.

Andras was going to be busy assisting Eadwulf in preparing the men for the march north. They would make directly for Repton where they would wait for the rest of the army to arrive. Eadwulf said that we had been able to raise an army of six thousand for the campaign north. This is only slightly less than we had when we were fighting for survival in the Viking wars. I was impressed with the numbers as these are more peaceful times and there is plenty of work to do sowing fields and repairing farms after the winter.

Although similar in temperament Andras is physically different to Godric. Godric has the body of a black smith with the wide solid shoulders and thick chest and arms. His legs were like tree trucks from all his work on the stone for the Worchester building projects. Even with all his size he was as fast as anyone I have seen. Godric was also a ball of passion and once he had an idea, he was difficult to stop, like a snowball with momentum coming down a mountain. Andras is tall, lean and thoughtful. He is much quieter than Godric but in a way he is more peaceful.

Godric was good for Wessex and the people and was the best match I could have made in a period of uncertainty and turmoil. I know father would have been proud of my choice and he was in the end, apologizing for sending me away to that Welsh convent. Initially I saw the friendship and match as being beneficial for my people it was not long before I had fallen in love. The way he looked after his people and the way they revered him. He was uncompromising in his pursuit of what he saw as being best for them. His smile and energy were infectious, and I ended up more in love then I thought was possible. I did not realize it however I had started crying as my maid Ebba came over and put her arm around me. 'Is everything as it should be my queen?' Brushing off her concerns I was a little embarrassed that the thought of Godric being killed still brought tears to my eyes.

As soon as our mounts were arranged the council members and I rode out of Winchester for Worchester and our council meeting. I always loved arriving in Worchester as it is one of those cities which feels like home. There are beautiful stone walls which give one a feeling of security. The cathedral is the grandest I have seen except for maybe the cathedral at St David's in Wales. The castle stands out from anywhere in the valley and the river is wide and deep. Worchester is surrounded by a mix of forest and agricultural land which creates a contrast with the beautiful stone creations. I have always felt at home in Worchester, and this did not change with the passing of Godric.

I used the journey time well catching up on all the news from Worchester and the farm. Seren had already remarried as I had now done. Seren is the younger daughter of Bledri and Gwyneth who had come back with Godric when they escaped from Strath Clyde all those years ago. Seren's older sister Riannon had been married to Alun and had died giving birth to their second child. Seren was married to Tata who was Godric's younger brother. Tata had died in the same battle of Jarrow which had claimed Godric and many other good men. Seren has now married Bevan and is pregnant with their first child. Seren and Tata already had a daughter who they had named Cyneburg in honor of Tata's older sister who was killed years earlier in Powy's. Cyneburg is now a bubbly toddler who keeps everyone on their toes.

Hilda is like a sister to me, and we could natter with each other all day. Her children are well and although she still misses Leofric her new husband Emrick is a reliable man. He is pushing to have his own children with Hilda although Hilda is not sure she wants to have any more given that she seems to be responsible for all the children on the farm. However, she understands his desire and will likely succumb to his requests if god is willing.

Riding into Worchester I was not disappointed with what I saw or my emotions with the place. The meeting was to be the following day, so I stayed with Hilda and her family out on the Amity farm. I would spend the night with them and have Bledri and Alun escort me back to Worchester in the morning. Winter had only just left this place so most of the farm is in the shadow of the western Malvern hills. There is little of the spring growth we had started to see around Winchester on the first day of our journey. I thought these colder conditions would suit our army as it was the cold of the north which is more likely to have kept King Oengus from moving south. It is easy to forget that the different regions of Britannia experience different weather conditions at the same time. Maybe it is because we are an island that the weather is so variable.

On the farm it was good to see some of the old faces again such as Egbert, Godric's first child and Hilda's children including Osgar and Godiva. I was tied and sore from the long journey so excused myself early after listening to a couple of Hilda's songs. Hilda is renowned as having one of the most beautiful voices in Worchester. It is always a treat to hear her sing however even her singing will not keep me up tonight.

The meeting went as planned and John confirmed that he had four thousand men which would join the campaign north. He apologized for the numbers as he said that the times of peace had made people less likely to take the risk of going to war. The guard was now only two thousand strong so building the numbers to four thousand was a big task. All men have been in the guard at one point, or another so will be good in a battle. Supplies of weapons were not an issue as Worcester still had the best forges in the land and all the minerals they required.

There was more good news as Evan said he would be sending his entire guard of two thousand from Northampton and he would use an emergency guard to protect the city. Wulfsige committed four thousand men from London which meant that the army going north would be the largest ever put into the field by England or the countries before it. Wulfsige was committing more men than I thought he could afford to commit so I questioned his numbers and suggested that we may not require all four thousand. Wulfsige agreed that sending four thousand would leave London vulnerable to attack. He followed that Godric had always been true and treated him as well as possible. In his name I want to crush these northern bastards and bring back the peace which we all fought for in the Viking wars.

With these words a roar went up from those around the table. John Archer raised his mug and yelled, 'To Godric.' After which we chugged down our mead. Evan and Eadwulf said that both Northampton and Winchester would be there to support London if it was required. I told them that I did not expect a long campaign as the Pictland army is a long way from their home. They will have endured a long winter away from their loved ones and with any luck they will not fancy a long campaign in the heart of a foreign land.

Hereweald and John would lead this push north even though they were both aging gentlemen. Evan, Wulfsige and Eadwulf would also take command positions and Evan's boy Ethan was already leading the Northampton guard to join up with Andras and the men from Winchester. Sixteen thousand men, wow that was a massive army. Fortunately, the northern cities were well provisioned as the south had suffered one of its worst farming seasons in living memory. Well at least I could not recall a worst one.

At the completion of the meeting, we drank to our coming success and agreed that the men would set off the following morning. John suggested a messenger be sent to King David of Powy's just to let him know that we are riding north with most of our guard and more. If all goes wrong and we call for help we really would appreciate it. At that time, we were already in a good mood, so John's instructions made most of us laugh. I had forgotten this important allegiance and its importance to victory in the Viking wars.

I was going to stay in Worchester while the army was up north. Worchester is closer to where the battles will be so it will be quicker for the commanders to get messages to me here. I have Godric junior and Albert with me, and they will have a great time playing with their cousins and brother. It will be nice to be in a less formal setting where I will be able to get my hands dirty and help around the farm.

As planned the guard left Worchester the following morning. I travelled back into town to see them off and was accompanied by everyone from the farm except for Seren, Bevan, Bert and his wife Matilda. They stayed home to keep the forges going and to look after all the younger children. Only those who were ten or older were permitted to see the guard off. This left eight children for them to mind although on a property like the Amity farm children soon learn how to look after themselves.

Back on the property I kept myself busy knowing that I may not get news for weeks and it was best to take my mind off what might or might not be happening. This was a large army, and we have an extremely experienced command group.

Chapter 8

Something is Missing

The last time we came up against Pictland they had defeated us with superior numbers and the terrain was to their choosing. We now had more men to command then I had ever seen assembled in an army. We had the weather at our backs which will only improve as spring deepens, and I can see the moral of the men is solid. They can sense a victory already and it must feel good to be out on the road, out on another adventure.

In the days with Godric there always seemed to be adventures from raids to full lengthy campaigns. Godric could never sit still and had all of us on our toes. I missed my son in-law more than I would like to admit. I know he saw me as another father however I also knew that we were close friends. I watched him grow up from birth into being one of the finest men ever born. Godric was best friends to my youngest son Egbert and together they were always up to mischief and in trouble. However, they were also adventurous, strong and loyal and if something needed doing either one of them would be first to put up their hand for the duty. He married my daughter Sunngifu and made her the happiest I had ever seen her. They were in love as much as I have ever seen a couple. They had a beautiful baby and a long future together. The Vikings tore that away from them and us as they had done to thousands of families over the years.

I wished I had Godric and my boys with me now. Leofric was strong and loyal much as Godric was. After the death of Egbert, he became very close to Godric. They were fanatical at planning everything including their endless practice. It was a powerful friendship which had really hurt Godric when it ended. I know he still blamed himself however he could not have known the ambush was coming. It saddens me to think that he took this heavy heart to his death. Leofric loved Godric and would have happily sacrificed his own life for him.

The call came down the line. 'John, John, the gates of York look open, what should we do?' I told Gerome, who is the cavalry commander that we needed to proceed with caution as it is likely a trap. We had left Repton at daybreak this morning and expected to camp an hour south of York. We have marched hard all day and the men would likely be too tied to fight although they would if they needed to. I looked across at Hereweald and he nodded that he had heard the message. I told the men around me that we will set up camp where we are and would assess the situation overnight and decide first thing in the morning. Hereweald added that we might even send a couple of men to the castle in the evening to see if they could work out how York stood. I agreed that this would be a good idea but for now everyone is to set up camp and prepare supper. Gerome you and the Cavalry are to take first watch so spread out and keep an eye on our perimeter. Make sure no one comes within five hundred yards of our camp without an alarm being raised.

Gerome went off to his business while the other commanders and I gathered around for a meal and to discuss our tactics. We did not have siege engines with us and knew that we would struggle getting through or over the York walls. Evan had the siege engines making their way up the road from Northampton however these would not make it to York for another week. If King Oengus has twelve thousand men in the castle, then we will struggle to get over the walls, even with the siege engines. It will be a blood bath trying to scale the walls with that many men guarding the top.

I suggested that we could split the men and send a force north if the castle were heavily guarded. When Oengus saw such a large force heading north he would be forced to abandon the castle to cut us off before we reached his undefended homeland. Our intelligence told us that Oengus had come south with not only his men of fighting age but his women also. The Pict women are renowned for being fierce fighters even surpassing the men in some cases. We have reminded all our men that should they come up against a woman then they are to be treated as they would any of the men. If they hesitate, they will die. This was always the case when fighting the Vikings as at least twenty percent of their warriors were shield maidens.

Hereweald seemed to think that this was a sensible idea as he said he did not have the stomach for a long siege, and he would quite like to do some damage to Pictland after what Oengus had done to England. We drank to these sentiments and continued discussing other options.

It was after dark by the time we had eaten. We allowed fires for the men as there was no way we were going to be able to hide sixteen thousand men. Oengus will know we are here so we might as well not freeze overnight.

After dark we sent a couple of the men to the castle to report on what they saw. We waited for their return which seemed to take much longer than we had planned. I wanted to have a rest in preparations for the following day however as commander I had to wait until I knew the men were back safely. Hereweald and I were about to send some additional men to find the first men when the scouts returned. They were out of breath and looked slightly ill.

We gave them a drink and gave them some moments to settle down. When they were ready, they proceeded to tell us what they had seen. They told us that the castle gates were still open so they crept as close as they dared and still, they could not see any movement. Doing rock, paper scissors the decision was made to enter the castle. 'It took some courage but eventually we ran through the opening and into the city. We were met with a scene from revelations. There were thousands of vermin which scattered when it heard and saw us. The castle was dark with only the light from the meagre moon. There were carrion birds filling the sky, rats running in every direction and probably a dozen other breeds of animal and bird. When the cacophony of noise and commotion settled, we lit up a couple of torches and began to look around. There were maybe a thousand tortured bodies. Half of them crucified on sticks, some upside-down others without limbs. There were burnt bodies and others which had obviously been mutilated. The scene is something I never wish to see again as it is the most horrific possible. God bless their souls. The men who have done this are devil's and need to be punished in this world and the next.' This news shocked us and left a sour taste in our mouths and a sickness in our guts. We all knew many men in that castle and to have the women and children treated the same way was a disgrace.

Thanking the men, we suggested they find themselves some hot food and try to get some rest. The decision was not hard to make, we would ride in and secure York. We will dig graves and give all of those deceased a good Christian burial. Hereweald and I both agree that we would go north and hunt down the scum who were responsible for this crime. I did not think that I would get much sleep that night visualizing what I had been told. I even feared that we had left the south relatively undefended and worried that the fate of those in York could be coming to our loved ones. This was absurd as Worchester and Northampton both had strong imposing castles and one word from the south and we would turn around instantly. The cavalry with numbers close to five thousand could easily be sent on ahead.

None of us got much sleep that night as we did end up visualizing the horrors inside York. Morning came and we had the gruesome task of digging graves and gathering the mutilated bodies. I had been around war most of my adult life but had never seen such acts committed. Looking at the eyes of our men I knew that they were thinking similar things to me. They would want revenge for what had been done to our people, to our women and children. We had the biggest army we had ever assembled and nothing but the head of Oengus would suffice.

It was a long day as was expected and our task was not finished. There turned out being many more bodies than we had first thought there were. We ended up counting over two thousand English. It would take another day at least to dig the required graves. It was terrible work however we knew we needed to do it and make sure the graves were deep. Everyone who witnessed what we saw wanted to make sure the deceased were given respect and a Christian burial. Father John from Northampton was with our group and made sure he said a blessing for each body. It was evident that Father John was suffering as we were with having to complete his duty. The bodies had been there for a long time from the look of the remains. Winter would have slowed the decaying process and may have kept the vermin from doing more damage than they already had.

The process took three days in all which held us up for four days by the time we had rested and headed off the following day. There was determination amongst our leadership group to get our revenge for the people of York. We closed the gates of York and left a dozen men to man the gates. They are brave men as there will be many ghosts in the place. We want to guard the castle from looters, so the men are there to ensure the gates are kept closed but not to defend the walls.

We marched north across the Yorkshire dales, through valleys and rivers. Caution was shown as we moved forward with scouts being sent ahead to look for trouble. We did not want another battle like the battle of Darlington. This time the battle would be on our terms. Our target was Bamborough, and I know I was not the only one hoping for a quick victory there. Bamborough is a castle with massive walls on a thin slither of land on a headland with one-hundred-foot cliffs on three sides. There was only one way into Bamborough and that was easy to defend and thought to be impregnable. The impregnability of the castle was proved false when Dunstan was able to breach the walls and destroy the last stronghold of the Vikings. King Oengus was then able to take the castle from Wulfsige although this was through negotiation with the purpose of saving the lives of his men.

Whenever we came to towns and villages, we found the same horrible degradation of the residence. Everyone has been killed and their bodies presented for maximum effect. The roads leading into these places were lined with crucified bodies. Eyes were missing from all of them as the crows had already beaten us. These scenes did not get any easier to stomach. I was glad I could ask others to gather the bodies as the scene kept reminding me of my children and friends I had lost to war over the years. When I knew I was alone I could not help but shed a tear. Life can be harsh for the people living in the north from the remoteness and the weather. These people demanded to be respected however Pictland had done the opposite.

It took us two weeks to reach Bamborough as we were compelled to bury the dead as we came across them. The moral and spirit of the men seemed to dip as we headed further from home and with each dead body.

Coming up to Bamborough we could see that it is occupied as there is smoke coming from the chimneys and activity on the turrets. Our army would have been spotted hours before and the men on the walls were preparing for our assault on their walls. The cautious march north and the delays with burying our people had enabled our siege engines to catch up. We would need every one of these if we were to have a chance cracking this nut. I told the men to prepare camp and set up defenses. It is the afternoon, and we will not be starting this battle today. I was wondering how many men Bamborough could hold. Hereweald called for a commander meeting so I might find out at that.

Wulfsige had been with Dunstan when they lead the men to take Bamborough. He told us that it was surprisingly spacious inside and could easily hold eight thousand men in his opinion. There are great stores as the headland had been chiseled out to create space for soldiers and supplies. This information was not reassuring as I did not want a long siege as we had already been on the road for over two weeks.

Weeks later and the siege had still not succeeded. We had attacked the walls on average every second day and each time we had lost siege engines and ladders but more significantly we had lost many men. In the first week we had lost over a thousand and feeling under pressure we had pushed harder in the second week and lost another fifteen hundred. Bamborough castle was living up to its reputation and was giving me a bad feeling about our campaign. We discussed other options although we could not think of an alternative other than marching to Edinburgh. Heading north for Edinburgh would leave an army at our back and be a massive risk.

We had not received any supplies since leaving York and our stores were dwindling rather quickly. It was strange that the supply lines were cut however we did not have the mind to follow this up. All efforts were going into getting through the gates or over the walls. We wanted to avenge our people and bring the Picts to justice.

It rained for the entire third week of the siege. We had one push at getting over the walls but gave up when men kept falling off the ladders. The ground and ladder rungs were just too slippery. At the same time the men were getting showered with arrows and rocks.

Close to the end of the third week we were attacked from our flank. It was a determined attack which came at us an hour before dawn. Fire arrows were aimed at our tents and thousands of men on horse charged the camp. Most men were cold, weary and asleep and confusion reigned in the chaos. I cannot say how many it was in the attack, and I am sure that many of our dead and injured were from friendly fire. Our men swinging in the night and hitting one of our own. As dawn arrived the attackers fled back into the northern hills. It must have been the Picts and they have probably been watching our progress and waiting on their opportunity. What a miserable day that was, counting our dead while drenched in the ongoing rain. What a miserable place the north was.

By now our army of sixteen thousand had been reduced to twelve thousand. I suggested that we send a thousand men back along the road to York to see what was happening to our supply lines. This was agreed and Earl Evan of Northampton said he would lead the men. The men were getting restless and us commanders were probably worse. It felt like we were losing this battle and it worried me. These are good men who are relying on us to deliver them victories. They have families back home and plenty of other things they need to be doing. I am sure they are still with us and want revenge for the slaughtered people, but spirits were as low as I had felt them.

The weather in the fourth week cleared up however the castle walls still stood as a barrier. We had increased the guard ever since the dawn attack although this did not make any of us sleep any better. There was no news from Evan, or his men and I was now worrying about this. Godric had been on the same stretch of road with a thousand men and had been slaughtered by the Picts. Just as I was thinking they were all around us. A massive force came at us while we were taking a midday meal.

A ferocious battle ensued with both sides fighting until the end when we all stopped from exhaustion. The battle was evenly match and consequently very bloody and costly for both sides. If we did not have our defenses and early warning, we may not have survived this attack. Our defense was a makeshift palisade wall and I thanked god that we took the time to set our camp up properly. We lost a further three thousand in that battle and without Evan and the men checking on the supply line we were down to eight thousand men which is half what we left with. We needed to decide on what we would do next. We had been too slow coming north and we were now short of supplies as a result. The men were homesick and weary of the war.

We could go back and occupy York, conceding the rest of the north to the Picts. This would be a humiliating defeat and embolden the Picts. Eight thousand lives were already too costly for what we had gained. I was tempted to go north to Edinburgh as I was sure their men were all in the field. Thinking back to Godric I know he worried about being too far from home. Without a known back up army it would be too easy to be surrounded and starved. We were already being starved and we were still in our own land. We decided to sleep on the options and agreed to meet the following day.

That night we were again attacked by what seemed like a force a similar size as ours. It was relentless these attacks and the impact was profound. The following day I was surveying the damage when I noticed some of the weapons the men were carrying looked like Worchester weapons. How could this be I said to Hereweald who was walking with me. He said that they could have been making them since they had captured Godric all those years ago. I responded that they were Strath Clyde. This could mean that Strath Clyde and Pictland were working together against us. One country was bad enough but two of them together and we were in serious trouble.

While walking around many men told me they wanted to go home. Every time I walked around the camp; I was accosted by men wanting to leave. I just kept telling them to have faith and that a decision would be made shortly. At the meeting I pushed for a retreat to York. We are surrounded up here and must get back to somewhere defendable and with fresh supplies. Looking at the faces of the command council I could see that they agreed but at the same time they did not wish to admit defeat.

We only had seven thousand men left and I did not want to lose any more to this blasted north. A show of hands and it was agreed to pack up and head home. The weapons of a possible Worchester make and style along with the possible introduction of Strath Clyde into the war only made our retreat more important.

As we came close to Jarrow we saw Earl Evan and his men. They were stacked up in a burnt-out pile of bodies. They had been left in the same condition as Godric and his thousand in the same place. What a haunted place Jarrow had become for us English. This time we did not stop to bury our dead. Nobody had the stomach for burying the charred bodies and we felt that we were being watched every inch of our march south.

Between Jarrow and York, we were harried in the rear and lost dozens of men. The injured men in the carts were particularly vulnerable. Seeing the castle at York was a relief but did not bring us peace. The gates were opened to us, and we at least had the safety of the castle walls to give us respite. Although safe behind the walls I did not think that we would get much sleep given the horrors we had witnessed. I dreaded telling Aethelswith of our failures and I know the others feel the same way.

The men in York said that supplies had been coming through, but nothing had come back from the north. They said that we were the first people they had seen from the northern road. It was obvious now that we had been goaded into pushing north while they sat back and cut off our supplies. Bamborough castle probably had the minimum number of men required to defend it while they left most of their men behind us to attack us with stealth. How affective it had been.

Chapter 9

Betrayal

Training of the Strath Clyde guard was going well. They had enormous strength and enthusiasm to learn. In a way they reminded me of the men back home which at times made me homesick. I spent an equal amount of time between Carlisle and Glasgow training up to five thousand men in total. By the time spring was getting ready to roll over into summer I felt like my job was done. I had built weapons for the Picts of Strath Clyde and had trained them with the weapons and for fighting a defensive war. I was conscious not to show them everything or teach them the war tactics I had learnt through my books. I liked these men however it pays to be prudent as I had been betrayed before.

Kenner and I were mostly living together through this time. Rick was living with us, and he was always watching and learning. Out of the blue Kenner said she would like to take me to a holiday home of theirs out on the islands. She begged me to come and said that it would only be for a week. Once Rick started pleading, I had no chance of saying no.

The reality was that I had worked virtually every day since agreeing to train Gregor's guard. I had felt alive again and knew that I was fully recovered from my incarceration. I had my strength and skill back and it was now time to make the trip home. This last week with Kenner would be a nice way to finish off and hopefully leave some good memories for Rick. Kenner is a beautiful woman and I know that I love her however I am married to another woman, and I am the king and protector of another land. Kenner now carries a second child between us and as ideal as it sounds to wait around for the birth I would struggle with my consciousness as it was time to return.

The place we were going was north in the Loch country. There is an estate there called Arrochar which is a great location from which to hunt and fish, go out on boats or for hikes in the mountains. Kenner told me that they have servants and a game keeper who maintains the property all year around. Rick was so excited as this was his first big adventure with his father. He was talking about many things and nothing all at once. I caught that he was going to catch the most fish and he would show me how it was done if I were having trouble. I was thinking back to when I was around his age and Egbert, and I would find worms and with hooks we would catch Salmon using hooks father had made us in the forge. Sometimes we would sit there for hours without any luck and other times we would catch half a dozen each. These were good days as we knew our families would be pleased and our catch usually brought on a mini celebration in each of our families. Food was not taken for granted and a feed of salmon was an appreciable delicacy. This odd success was probably why our parents let us waste so much time fishing. I thanked Rick and agreed that I might need him to show me how to catch the fish in the Long Loch.

Although we were told everything would be provided, I ensured that we had food and clothing. I was also heavily armed as I wanted to continue practicing now that I had my strength back. Six of the guard were going to travel with us as I was told there are highlanders everywhere and highlanders are opportunists. If they saw the king's daughter unarmed, they would take her with the aim of getting a ransom. This kind of kidnapping is common and when times are tough in the highlands the highlanders become more brazen. I felt ready for a challenge but then remembered Jarrow and how I was not invincible there. I had lost many good men including my brother and the son of one of my closest friends. Thinking about Tata and Swidhun broke my heart. Deorwine had also been a close friend for more than ten years as he was the commander in charge of the archers, and I often helped train his men. That experience of Jarrow meant that I needed to be more careful and to take less risks. Rather than send the six men, from the guard, away I welcomed them and suggested the company would be good. I did not know this country at all.

Although not very far the journey will take us most of the day. We would leave at daybreak and aim to get there before sunset. The intention was to take it easy with the horses and walk them as often as we rode them. A slow pace would give us time to look around the countryside.

The Journey was everything that I hoped it would be. I had a great drop in stress the minute we were out of Glasgow. Until then I had not realized the burden of responsibility I was carrying or even how much I was on edge watching my back. Out in the countryside I leant back in the saddle and looked up at the trees. Rick asked me what I was doing so I told him I was thanking god for the wonderful trees and the wonderful life I had been given. Rick asked me why it was so wonderful, so I told him that I had grown up with a fantastic family in a great supportive community. I had grown up in the wilderness with beautiful natural areas just as we are going through now. Very rarely were we hungry or thirsty and I always had love. This seemed to make Rick thoughtful and maybe a little sad. I asked him what he was thinking about, and he just said he was wondering if I was going to marry his mother as he wanted me as his father. This was a difficult question as I did not want to lie yet I did not want to hurt him either. I could also sense that Kenner was listening.

'I am already married Rick to the Queen of England, way down in the south. This does not mean I cannot be your father and always love you. A man is not allowed to marry more than one woman in our Christian faith. If I were not already married and in a different life, I would be honored to have married your mother and to have us always live together. I will have to go home and see my family and the community. I will come back one day, and I will hopefully be able to show you around my home down in the south.' There was quiet after this as Rick looked ahead of his horse and started looking around.

The journey was easy and pleasant. My conversation with Rick did not seem to upset Kenner which made me hopeful.

Well before arriving at Arrochar, we could see that there was a problem. Kenner and the men noticed that the gates were wedged open with one of them hanging by one hinge. As we got closer we could see that the house looked empty. There were no fires and there was no light from any of the windows. The shutters were open even though it was only half an hour until sunset. It was already getting cold even though we are almost at summer. I get the feeling it is cold in this part of the world all year around. The house looked deserted, and I had alarm bells going off in my head. I drew my bow and prepared for an attack.

Dismounting, I told Rick to stay on his horse and with his mother. One of the men who knows the house jumped down and joined me as I entered the house. Inside everything was ransacked. We searched around and did not see any bodies although we did see patches of blood which was a good indication that there was foul play.

We rushed out of the house as we heard a scream. I knew it was Kenner, so my heart was thumping until I knew she was unharmed. Kenner was looking in the glasshouse and had found the bodies of the servants and the gamekeeper piled on top of each other. A gruesome discovery of what looked to be a wretched end for these souls. There were two men and four women. Kenner said that she knew them all, so she was more upset than she would normally be. I turned to the men and asked them all, except for Ramsay, to get the fires going in the house and secure the shutter closed. Rick, Kenner, Ramsay and I took the horses to the stable where thankfully we found some hay. I grabbed our supplies and headed back into the house.

Seeing the house upset Kenner further as she had many fond memories coming here with her family. It now looked in ruins and she could tell it had been stripped of anything which they thought was of value. I felt much better when the shutters and doors were secure, and the fires were lit. I had brought some mead although only enough for a couple of nights. I was expecting the house to be well provisioned as Kenner had explained it would be. It was a good night for a drink and fortunately mead was something all the soldiers had thought to bring. The motto of a soldier is to be well prepared.

That night we sat around the fire listening to stories mostly from Kenner's childhood holidays. Occasionally one of the guards also had a story from a visit. The positive stories kept the mood up and stopped fear. I was worried that Rick might be scared and asked him if he was all right as I was tucking him in. He called me father and said that he felt safe and secure if I was with him. I smiled at him and told him that I would not let any harm come to him or his mother. We cuddled for a minute, and it felt like he was not going to let me go.

Finally, it was just Kenner and I looking at the fire. I had just loaded it up to make sure it burnt through most of the night. The morning would be cold, and I wanted some decent coals to make sure I could get it going again. I asked Kenner who she thought had killed the servants. She did not know but said it could have been highlanders or clansman as they are sometimes called. It was a harsh winter, and they may have become desperate. Most highlanders were outcasts from the towns who learnt how to live and survive in the deep mountains. A tough life for the best of them, scraping together a living. 'Should we head home tomorrow, or do you want to stay and tidy things up?' Kenner looked at me and categorically said that we were making the most of the holiday and were not going home. It was a strange response as I expected some uncertainty. 'You're not worried about the bandits or whoever it was which did this?' Kenner said that this looked to have been done months ago and the perpetrators were probably long gone especially now there were seven armed men including me.

Accepting Kenner's response, I allowed her to snuggle in as we quietly watched the fire. It was so peaceful in this area of the world. The only sound I could hear was the sound of the fire crackling. It felt like we were the last two people alive on earth. I had to leave Kenner but like the first time I was almost totally caught in her spell. The worry was that I would not be as strong this time as I drifted off to sleep with her in my arms.

The circumstances from the first day brought us all closer together. The men were included in our activities as there was safety in numbers. The boat was still in the boat house, so we rowed to the middle of the loch and attempted to catch fish using the snails we had gathered from around the vegetable garden. Either the snails were no good as bait or we were terrible fishermen as we did not manage to catch anything the three days we went out. Hunting was more successful as the mountains around Arrochar were filled with game. We had plenty of meat every night and Rick even took down his first dear with a beautiful headshot on a fawn. This was the moment of the holiday as I saw the utter joy in his face. 'My boys first kill,' I was almost as excited as he looked.

A week up at the holiday house went way too quickly. We had buried the servants on the first day and each day we set about repairing something which had been damaged. Hopefully, the house was not stripped or damaged again before Gregor could send some more people up there. We had not been attacked nor did we see any sign of people although on one hunting trip I did feel like I was being watched. This is a sixth instinct I have always had and one which I have trusted in battle. I am confident that we were being watched but did not tell any of the others as I did not want to alarm the others and I hoped it was innocent curiosity.

Glasgow was very quiet when we finally got back. I did not pay it much attention as I was tied and wanted to unpack and put Rick to bed. That night I told him a little bit about my home and the caves up behind our property. He made me promise to take him there so I promised and I told him I will gladly take him one day.

The following day my thoughts about the place being empty were justified as it became even more evident. There were servants and woman everywhere but most of the men were gone. I asked Kenner where they were, and she told me they were off on some exercise. Gregor was gone which was also unusual. I was wondering what was going on as I could sense that Kenner was keeping something from me. I suspected she was feeling uncomfortable in my presence as she was having to lie to me, and she did not want to.

I overheard one of the servants speaking about Munro, so I stopped her and asked if Munro had been here. She said, 'Ay, he has gone off with the King. He arrived the day after you left with Kenner.' This got me to wondering about Munro and whether he still had a grudge against me for leaving Kenner and with a child in her belly. Why was Munro up here and why now? I decided to go and catch up with Shug in the forge. There was nothing like the company of a blacksmith as they are the salt of the earth. Strong and dependable my old man used to say about the trade. From my experience I know he was right.

Shug was hammering away on another set of swords. One thing about the trade I did not miss was the repetitiveness of the job. Horseshoes, swords, knives and forks, arrow tips, gates, hinges, locks the list goes on but there is little variety when doing these things day after day, year after year. Shug looked pleased to see me and put down what he was working on straight away. Shug cooled the fire and offered me some water as he took a seat outside the forge. It was a glorious day outside, so I did not blame Shug for wanting to take the opportunity out in it.

'I have something to tell you,' Shug said in an almost conspiratorial way. 'Gregor and the guard have joined with Pictland to attack the English at Bamborough.' I was shocked as I could not believe what I was hearing. 'They left two days after you left with Kenner. Munro arrived with two and half thousand men from Carlisle the day before and then they all set off the following day. They were saying it was going to be a route of the English. It was like they were going to a party, and it makes me sick.'

The rage inside me was building as Shug was telling me about the betrayal. I could not believe that I had armed and trained these men to kill men from my beloved country. My feelings were a mixture of rage but also of sickness as I felt so ashamed that I had betrayed my people. I wanted to find somewhere to hide and die but at the same time I wanted to rush to the aid of my people. 'Shug, you have a lovely family with Liela and daughter Lily, and you have a good life here. I am going south now, and you are more than welcome to come with me. I have forges and you would be given a home back in Worchester. The offer is there although I do not expect you to take it.' I was hoping for the company and Shug had always shown me his friendship. He is open and always friendly. Shug told me that he would love to come but like I had said his life was here. He also said that it was worth me having a friend with the Strath Clyde Picts. I thought I had many friends but took the comment for what it was and that was an offer of friendship.

I thanked Shug and went back to the house to gather some provisions for the trip, including all my weapons. On the way to my horse, Austin, Kenner came flying out and demanded to know where I was going. I ignored her at first and commenced loading my saddle bags on Austin. Austin is a large brown mare who has now been with me for close to three months. I love her strength and willingness and would need it all if she were to get me back to Worchester.

Kenner was pestering me, so I turned on her. 'When did you know your father was going to attack the English? We had an agreement, and he has now broken it. Your father has betrayed me, and I feel a broken man for it. You knew about the betrayal, and this is the reason for our trip to the holiday home. Even with the dangerous situation we found ourselves in on that first night you were certain that we had to stay. You are complicit in the betrayal.' I was surprised that she had let me speak as normally she would have cut me off. She dropped to her knees and began to cry. She told me she was sorry, but she wanted to keep me safe. Kenner told me that she did not want to lose me, so she had gone along with her father's request. She hoped that I would not find out about it and life could go on.

Ignoring her pleas, I mounted my horse and commenced riding south out of Glasgow. My only regret was not saying goodbye to Rick. He was a darling boy who could not be blamed for the sins of his family. I had to get home to make amends for my mistakes. When I left Kenner was still on the ground sobbing. The magic had been broken when her loyalty had not been transferred to me. She claimed to love me, yet she could so easily betray me. I was confusing myself as I was about to leave Kenner anyway as I was married to another woman. Aethelswith was back in England waiting for my return. I had a large family waiting for my return and three of my own children down there. I was blaming Kenner even though I did not feel much better for my own actions. Now it suited me to blame Kenner for everything however part of me knew that this was because I felt so guilty. I am responsible for my actions, and I had armed and trained a country which is hostile to my people. I had been blinded by a beautiful woman.

I had reached Kilmarnock which is only an hour south of Glasgow when Kenner came riding up at pace. I had calmed down a little as I had allowed myself to be manipulated so was doing more self-loathing rather than Kenner hate. Kenner rode around in front of me and begged me to stop. She told me that she was sorry and that she loved me. I explained that it was too late, and it was well past the time that I got home. There was nothing which could stop me now.

Kenner then shocked me again. 'Tata and Swidhun are alive. They are in an iron mine outside of Aberdeen, up in the north country.' I was looking at Kenner in disbelief. She was telling me now that my brother was alive. She must be lying to me and I said as much. 'We found out that they were kept as prisoners in the mines. The guards told us this before their throats were slit. Tadg told us when he returned. You were in bed nearly dead and in need of major recovery. There is no way you could have gone after them, so we allowed you to recover. When you had recovered, I was having so much fun, totally in love, that I forgot to tell you. Please forgive me my love. You are my everything Godric, you have to know this.' I was still stunned and again my anger grew.

'You knew about my brother slaving away in an iron mine and you failed to tell me. He is my flesh and blood and knowing me you must have known how important he is to me.' I wanted to head home and could not wait to be back on the farm but the chance that Tata was alive was worth fighting for. I had been like a father to my little brother and if I did not try to rescue him, he would die in that mine. 'If you mean what you say, take me to the mine so I can bring Tata and the other survivors home.' Kenner started to say that it was too dangerous when she closed her mouth. I guess she could see the look of rage in my eyes, so she trotted past me heading back towards Glasgow. In Glasgow we would grab some additional supplies and maybe one or two other men and horses. The quarry was sure to be guarded. Following along behind Kenner I still raged but I was also getting excited by the thought that my little brother was alive. How I longed to look onto his face. I would hold him and never let him go.

My anger toward Kenner was not going to go away but I knew I needed to tolerate her if I was to find Tata. Kenner knew Pictland well or at least she had told me she did. I guess she had visited on many occasions when courting Causantin, the Kings son. Rather than let my feelings be felt I thought that it was best to keep quiet. As a child I would keep to myself if something had upset me and at that moment, I had no interest in being nice or talking to Kenner.

I was already packed and provisioned so once back in Glasgow I had to wait for Kenner and our escort to prepare for the journey. We would take an extra two horses to assist with our supplies and to use for Tata and Swidhun should we be successful, and they both still be alive. Ramsay, McGregor and Bran would come with us which suited me as I liked all three. We had spent the week together up at the holiday house and they had shown themselves to be resourceful men.

We would be heading deep into Pictland and had choices to make. The coastal route would take us east through the most populated regions. Travelling through these areas would be easiest as there would be places to sleep and get meals. The roads travelling this way would be mostly flat and easy going. This way would be risky as we could be spotted and arrested. However, travelling this far north should be safer than if we had to go anywhere near Edinburgh. We do not know if King Oengus has issued a warrant or reward for my arrest. It could be a dead or alive warrant. He has probably heard that I was rescued by the Picts of Strath Clyde. Who knows what conversations have gone on between the two Pict kings as they attacked my homeland?

The second option is to head through the highlands which will be a more direct route. We will come out at a fishing town called Dundee and travel up the remote stretch of coast to Aberdeen. The journey through the highlands should be quicker however there will be no comforts and it was not without its own risks. The highlands are full of brigands and clans all struggling to survive in the harsh conditions which they live. We would take the central pass which will enable us to take our horses as it is relatively flat once we are up the mountain pass. There will be no Pict lander's in the highlands which is a positive. Either way has its risks but being arrested by King Oengus could be fatal as I do not think he will make the same mistake of keeping me alive twice.

'We take the highlands,' I instructed the men. Bran grumbled and noted that it would not be his choice, but he will go along with consensus. McGregor said that he knew them well and was looking forward to showing me some of the most breathtaking views I have ever seen. Ramsay simply said, 'well let us be off then,' keeping his opinion to himself. Kenner was silent as I guessed there was no point talking to me. My attitude was not going to change, and I felt sure about that.

We set off in the early afternoon which was probably not the best time to be setting off. We would only just be through the pass and into the highlands when we would lose our light. McGregor was already telling us tales of the highlands and mentioned how cold it will get through the night. 'Throw in some rain and you will never feel more miserable. Then wake up to a full day of rain and by the time you close your eyes on the second day you will wish you were dead.' McGregor's stories were miserable, and I hoped just tales. I was now praying for clear skies although I knew that clear skies were colder nights with possible frosts. McGregor loved winding people up and I could tell he was doing a good job of getting on Bran's nerves.

Highlanders were on my mind, and I considered them to be the greater risk. I was alert to ambush as I did not know the land or the paths. McGregor and Bran had both travelled the mountain pass and central highlands road however this did not make me feel any better. We are all heavily armed so unless caught by surprise we could put up a decent fight.

As expected, we had only just come out from the steep mountain pass when we were losing our light. Kenner, McGregor and Bran had all brought a tent. Ramsay was going to share with McGregor, Kenner was on her own so it looked like Bran and I would share one. We put the tents side by side and looked for wood for a fire. Up here wood was scarce and difficult to find. We were fortunate that there is a fallen silver birch tree not far down the track and plenty of dead hawthorn bushes which can be used as kindling. Ramsay got the fire going while the rest of us found some food to put in a pot. I went hunting with my bow intent of finding some game. As I got further from camp all remaining light seemed to disappear. A shortage of light would make hunting very difficult and eventually I had to give up. I was following the light of the fire back to camp when I disturbed some nearby pheasants. I fired off three quick arrows and heard two of them hit their targets. Finding the birds and the arrows took me a good half hour. By the time I returned to camp everyone was sitting around eating soup. 'Where did you get to,' enquired Ramsay?

I told them I was off looking for some meat and I held up the two pheasants. They laughed and said that they had found a couple of squirrels living in a pine tree down the pass. McGregor had gone back and taken both, perfect for squirrel stew. I thought it must have been vegetable soup, but a meat stew had my mouth watering. Ramsay reached over with a bowl and fork for me. The stew was delicious and warmed me up where the highlands was draining my warmth. Over dinner I asked McGregor if we needed a watch. McGregor said that this pass was so close to Glasgow that it should be safe. People usually came thirty miles up the valley as they normally set off at the start of the day. This variation to the norm should keep us safe enough.

Feeling slightly safer I decided to drink my mead and go to bed early. I wanted to make good ground the following day and my enthusiasm grew about seeing Tata again after so long apart. Oh, how I now prayed that he was still alive. My brother is almost as strong as I am, and he is tough. It will take a lot to destroy Tata so I held out hope that he would be alive. Like me Tata had worked the forges from a young age and there is nothing like being a blacksmith to build up your strength.

The following morning, we were packed up and away an hour after sunrise. The tent was not comfortable and not really designed for two. Bran had tossed and turned all night which I only noticed after I was woken mid-way through the night. From then on, I was constantly elbowed or bumped into. It did not matter too much as my first sleep had been deep and satisfying. As morning approached the air and the ground under me got extremely cold. Thinking of McGregor's story, I thanked god that at least it was not raining.

Along the way we were confronted by a dozen men around midday. They wielded swords and demanded our possessions. It felt unfair to be so unevenly matched that I suggested they turn around and leave us be. They laughed and asked us why they would be turning around and leaving. 'I am a better warrior then all twelve of you put together. It would be unfair for me to hurt you and it will not help your people if you are dead.' As they scoffed and laughed at my cheek, I stepped toward them drawing my twin swords. 'I am not kidding as I am trained to the highest standard. I will not die this day, but you could if you do not leave us be.'

The men attacked me just as I was finishing speaking and as expected I easily accounted for them. I do not think any of them had been formally trained. It was a horrible loss and waste of life, but I did warn them. Even when the first three were cut down within seconds the others still came at me. I just hoped they had not left a family hungry somewhere here in the mountains. The men were dressed in rags and looked as rough as they come. McGregor spat on them and said brigands as he walked past. He said that he could tolerate the clans as they had codes and standards, but brigands were the pirates of the land. They did not follow any honor but lived off the suffering of others. I suggested that the only suffering seemed to be their own. These were not rich or well men.

That night we camped at the other end of the central highland's path. Still the weather held out and this time we stopped early enough to bring down a deer for supper. The cooking meat smelt delicious as it was turned over the fire. I was still not talking to Kenner, and she had still not attempted to speak to me. I did my best to avoid eye contact as I could not stand the sight of her.

Kenner had colluded with her father and his betrayal to attack my people. My brother and other countryman are slaving away in an iron mine in the northern town of Aberdeen, yet she only told me this when she thought she was losing me. Kenner is an evil woman who had tricked me into staying in the north. Many would call her a witch and that could be fatal for any woman. A claim of witch was enough to have any woman burnt at the stake. I hated Kenner but I did not wish for her to be hurt. My anger was subsiding, but I did not want to be bewitched by her beauty and charm.

The others had known we were fighting before we set off. They did not know the cause of the fight and on more than one occasion they had made fun of us and made jokes about lover's tiffs. Kenner would often laugh and make some dismissive comment however they never received any recognition from me. I either ignored them or told them to leave it alone. I knew they were only trying to be helpful, and I am sure they hated travelling with two people who were ignoring each other. We are a group of five so it would have been making what was already a tough trip miserable.

Apart from that small group of brigands we did not come across any other humans even though we were travelling one of the most well-known tracks across the highlands. The highlands are so vast and sparsely populated which was evidenced by what I had seen.

The following day we made our way down the Dundee pass and into Dundee. This fishing town is not much more than a village. It would have a thousand people if it were lucky. We did not hang around in Dundee as we did not want to attract attention. We replenished some of our supplies including picking up some whisky and headed north. There were more people on this stretch of road however everyone seemed content on their own business. Travel was faster as we were now able to ride. Travelling over the highlands we spent most of the time walking our horses. It was getting late when we at last came to a village called Stonehaven. We decided to stop the night at an inn called "The Greatest Catch". This was appealing as it had more than one fire going and plenty of light from candles. The inn was not far from a low headland looking down over the boats.

After two nights out in the open it was great to have a roof over our heads again. The inn was quiet which was a little surprising given it was summer and the season when people move around. Talking to the publican we heard that it has been quiet since Oengus has taken the men south. The publican introduced himself to us as Orloff. Orloff has a very big head with a smile which almost reaches the sides of his wide face. His face is mostly covered with hair in what could be described as a handlebar's mustache. Orloff is wide but not tall as he looks to be a head shorter than me. He is dressed in leathers which look to be foreign. He said that there were not enough men and women to complete all the work. Half of the fishing boats cannot go out; nets remain holed, and buildings are falling into disrepair. It was a good night for catching up on what was happening outside my sheltered existence. The inn still has travelers, and they talk and tell stories.

Ramsay and I sat at the bar and talked to the publican. The others took a table by the fire well away from us. The distance suited me as I was still avoiding contact with Kenner as best I could.

Orloff told us that Oengus had crushed the English with some help from Gregor. He said that the army was still in the south and he thinks they will push to take York again. York was apparently left for the English in a plan to lure them up to Bamborough. Bamborough was where the English army was defeated. There was also a second battle at Jarrow where Earl Evan and a thousand men were slaughtered. The mention of Jarrow sent a chill up my spine from my own experience in the first battle of Jarrow. I confirmed that it was Earl Evan who was leading at Jarrow which only brought me sorrow and Anger. Evan was a close ally in the battle to defeat the Vikings and in the process create England. Evan is the father in-law to my sister Wassa. Wassa would now be countess of Northampton and its regions with Ethan becoming Earl. I so hoped that Ethan was not with the defeated army and was unhurt. The last I saw Wassa she had two beautiful children, and I did not want to contemplate heartache for them.

King Oengus is thought to be in poor health and be back in Edinburgh. Causantin is now leading the army and would crush the remaining English army or, so Orloff boasted. I questioned where Orloff was from as he sounded foreign. He told me he had settled in the north with his family when he was ten. They came across from Bergen, a northern village in Norway. I asked if they were Vikings, but he said they were simple fishermen from a fishing village. There is too much war in Norway with the continual battle to be King of all Norway. There are many Viking chieftains who want the title. His father had wanted to get away from all of that and have a simple life. Many others from their region had migrated with them as they sort a better life. Until recently the decision had worked out as their region had always been free from conflict. Orloff had been in Stonehaven for thirty years and had found peace. Fishing the north sea was dangerous work and had claimed the life of his father and an older brother. Orloff had chosen a different career to stay clear of this danger. Being a publican suited Orloff as he has a cheerful disposition and seems to have an energetic demeanor given his age.

We did not stay up drinking for long as tomorrow when we reached Aberdeen, we would find the Mine and hopefully Tata and others. There would likely be some fighting which means we need to have our strength and whit's. When I looked around, I noticed that Kenner had left. McGregor and Bran were discussing something by the fire. We booked two rooms with the four of us men in one room and Kenner by herself.

Kenner had been trying to break the ice with me by catching my eye and asking me the odd question. Each time I had looked away or ignored her. I knew I was being childish however I did not want to be manipulated by her charm. I needed to sever this relationship and I would not have a better opportunity. She had deceived me on more than one occasion and each one broke my heart to think about.

There were two beds in the room, and I offered head to toe with the men, but they said that I could have one of the beds and as McGregor was the oldest in the group he could have the other. Warriors are used to sleeping on the hard ground, so I did not think twice about the offer. I wanted a good night's sleep to be alert in the morning. A good sleep is exactly what I got.

I was downstairs having breakfast when Bran came bursting through the doors of the inn. 'There are Vikings in the quay, raiding the village. They have taken Kenner.'

As soon as the abduction of Kenner was mentioned any shock, I felt at the mention of the Vikings was gone. I was up the stairs in an instant and a moment later I was fully armed and out the door. McGregor was not far behind Ramsay and me even though he had been lying on the bed when I entered the room. He reacted straight away even though he did not know what the commotion was.

Outside the inn we could see the chaos growing as men, women and children ran for their lives. The inn was overlooking the quay and I could instantly see the two Viking boats along a jetty. There looked to be up to a hundred Vikings moving along the waterfront going through every house and business. Some were carrying off women while any man or child they saw was being run through. I was still running to the quay scanning around me as I descended the hill to the jetty.

It was as I entered the quay that I saw Kenner being dragged back to a boat. Up until then I had not been confronted but that all changed suddenly when I did well to avoid a blow from a sledgehammer and another from a broad sword. Every one of my senses was now alert as I moved into my battle zone. My first thought was to free Kenner, and I immediately released two arrows which took down her assailants. As the men fell, they took Kenner to the ground with them. She knew this was her chance as she bounced to her feet and ran back in my direction. As Vikings made moves to grab her, I took them down with arrows. A couple of the arrows were less than an inch from her face but credit to Kenner she did not even flinch. Kenner ran past me, and I knew I had been deluding myself. I loved Kenner even with all the hurt she had caused me. Turning I saw that Kenner had reached the hill to the inn and was being protected by Bran and Ramsay. McGregor was now by my side as we set about taking on the Vikings.

I was now in my berserker frame of mind where the battle is like a slow-motion dance. I moved from Viking to Viking cutting them down as if they were children. I should have known this was a fight we were not going to win but the adrenaline was pumping, and I felt invincible. I had first felt the superior thrill of the zone or berserker when my first wife Sunngifu had been killed many years ago. Since then, I had trained myself to be able to slip in and out as required although there was nothing better than a crisis and a loved one who was in danger to trigger it. Kenner was a loved one and I would do my best to make up for being so miserable when this was all over.

McGregor and I were making a mess of the Vikings, but we were quickly being surrounded and I saw McGregor take a blow across the back of his head and a thrust through his middle. With my attention distracted I also took a blow to the head and felt myself falling to the ground.

Chapter 10

The Normans

A rider came out to the farm and alerted us that the men were returning from up north. We were all eager to welcome them as we had already heard that there were many killed, and the campaign was a failure. Hereweald had sent riders home to warn us of the defeat and that they would be making their way slowly with the injured. This was a grim message which had devastated us all and left me with great fear for the future. The army had been the biggest to ever leave on campaign, so the loss was unexpected. Moral was high when the men left even though there had been previous losses in the north. I had not been informed that Andras was killed so I expected he was either well or one of the injured. I felt anxiety and I know that the others on the farm were feeling the same. Alun was the only warrior from the farm, and he was also in our thoughts.

Regardless of the outcome we all wanted to be there to welcome our hero's home. It was critical that they get rest and care so that they will be ready for battle when it comes. I do not expect that the Picts will settle for their victory but will be emboldened to come deep into England to increase their land grab. As queen it was important that I put emotion aside and look at the longer-term security of the realm. Hereweald had said they were resting up in York castle so at least this was a minor victory.

The turnout from the town and region was outstanding with more than ten thousand friends and family cheering their loved one's home. Most of the men were not from Worchester however they were English, and they were treated like hero's none the less. John Archer was leading them through the gates and immediately ordered that the store be opened for the mead and a feast. John would understand how important moral was and he did not want anyone thinking they were losers, even though they were.

John looked tired and old, but he was not the only one. Hereweald came into view, and I was a little shocked by how he had aged. The campaign had lasted months, and the men looked exhausted even with the weeks in York. There were far too few men even knowing that some had been left in York. There were dozens of wagons carrying the crippled and mutilated. The sight at York would have been heartbreaking considering what they looked like after some rest. Our beautiful army had been reduced to this. There are approximately four thousand men with most of them from London and Winchester. It seems that the men from Northampton and Worcester had volunteered to stay and bolster the York castle until a replacement garrison could be organized.

The firsthand account given to me my Hereweald, Andras and John told me that we were in a lot of trouble. I remembered conversations I had with Godric years earlier about tough times. Godric would say you must fight for your life and defend your ground when the world was turning against you. He would talk about defense as being our greatest weapon. Thus, Worcester had built the most impressive castle and city walls. Godric would be training the women and the men to defend their homeland, not just the men. Security had brought prosperity and that had brought extra support. Each life was valuable, and Godric had ensured that a life was never wasted. His thinking was not universal among the other leaders around Britannia, so Worcester had prospered and grown strong on its defense. His words were ringing in my head as I asked John to organize a council meeting with the remaining battle commanders.

At the meeting John gave us a summary of the campaign and the remaining resources including people. Outside there was still much sorrow for the loss of loved ones even though a lot of the Worcester men were still in York. The greatest losses had been from Winchester and London although seventy five percent of the men from Northampton had been killed. Out of the two thousand men sent only five hundred would be returning. I told the council and the commanders that the mourning would go on for days and that I understood the pain of the people. God was testing us with these hardships as surely, he could see the righteousness of our cause and how uniting the land would support him. I explained that I did not know why we had been punished as we had but we would use this adversity to become stronger. Before giving them time to consider my words I quickly moved on. Some might oppose my holy optimism and I did not want to face that at this time.

Everyone agreed that the men should be allowed to rest for a day or two. We also agreed that they should return home to their communities. A relief garrison would be sent to York to relieve the men there. The garrison would come from Worchester and the surrounding areas as all the other regions had been so badly devastated.

A delegation would be sent to Earl Henry of Exeter to request fifteen hundred men to help hold York castle and its region. Henry would not like it as he liked to keep out of trouble whenever he could. Henry would not decline the request as everyone knows that the English came to his defense to free Exeter of the Vikings. Worchester would request two thousand volunteers. John noted that priorities for Worchester would go back to the pre-English days where every male would be obligated to join the guard and practice weekly unless they were exempted. Since defeating the Vikings, the northern cities had allowed their Guard numbers to drop and families to get on with business. The world was again at war and Worchester would once again be fighting for its survival. The meeting went on without argument as nobody had the stomach to argue or be obstinate.

Andras and I stayed in Worchester with John and Leofflaed as I wanted to be close to the people. The men wanted to be home with their loved ones, so all started leaving in groups the following day. I had thought they would want to rest but was mistaken. It was obvious moral was low and this continued to drive a dagger into my heart. Andras was unhurt although his ego had taken a battering. He mentioned the miserable conditions with the cold and the rain. 'We were infested with fleas and lice which drove us mad every waking hour. There were times when I wished it would all end and I prayed for an arrow in the heart. The Picts knew the land and had comforts while the only comfort we had was each other and even that was miserable before long.'

I pitied Andras and the men and hoped they could bounce back as I was sure that the Picts would be at us again before long. They may campaign before winter or wait for the new season.

The following day my world got decidedly worse. A rider came into the town and said that King William of Normandy had landed an army at Hastings and was marching slowly toward Winchester. The timing could not have been worse as the survivors from Winchester were in clusters making their way home. Hereweald had told me that of the six thousand to leave from Winchester there were approximately two and a half thousand survivors and some of those with crippling injuries.

An emergency meeting of the council was called with all the remaining council and commanders. It was grim news, but the energy was immediately back. It was impressive how these defeated men rose to the challenge. An unknown threat had arrived, and they were willing to put all on the line to meet that challenge. Gerome was to ride with his cavalry, although depleted, to Winchester. He was to notify all the men they came across on the road that they were needed for the defense of Winchester. At Winchester they would notify the guard and ensure that all the harvest was brought in even though it was early in the season. The walls were to be prepared for defense and we want all the forges going day and night. Wulfsige would leave with his remaining men for London as London was as exposed as Winchester. London had also lost more men than they could afford and Wulfsige prayed to god that they had enough men to hold off an attack.

The relief guard for York was put on hold and men would be organized to bolster Ethan's defense at Northampton should it be required. The delegation for Exeter would now be requesting fifteen hundred men to support Winchester against the Normans. Andras would ride with them to make sure Henry gave us the men we needed.

There was not a lot known about the Normans although talk in the coastal towns was that they are feared warriors who call themselves knights. They fight with heavy armor which cannot be pierced by the common arrow or sword. In my head I lamented being told these tales as they just made me more fearful. My world was slowly falling apart, and I was now being forced to heed my own words about god testing us for the better.

The following two days were hectic as we made our way to Winchester. King William was already stationed on the battlefield outside of the city. He had banners flying across the field flying the colors of his different knights. The banners made William appear even more threatening. Our men will not have time to rest and recover from the battles up north. I was thankful that they at least got the weeks recovering in York otherwise we could have been doomed to defeat. As it stands the men look exhausted from their three-month campaign. Andras and Hereweald would have to get them up for this battle.

As we arrived at Winchester, we saw that not only were William and his men ready to meet us but the guard under the command of Albert, were making their way into the field. Albert had command of the Winchester home guard and in the absence of instructions had thought to defend the city by meeting King William in the field. As we neared the gates some of the men recognized us but none of them looked overly happy to see us. A queen must take responsibility for failed campaigns and maybe they were thinking I brought bad luck. I would not blame them as the kingdom of England was unravelling before my eyes.

I thought it best not to enter the castle as most of the men were now outside the walls. If I had my way, I would have brought everything inside and sealed the walls. We have some of the best castle walls in the land and we have come into the open to fight. Thinking back to Godric his words about defense and saving lives so that you can fight another day keep coming to mind. Meeting William seemed like suicide, and I said as much to Hereweald. He agreed however he noted that the size of William's army was such that if it was not stopped it could take or destroy large areas of England. Hereweald said that he expected that Kent had already fallen to the Normans and if we hide in our castle, they will simple go around us and take what they want. 'How many men do you think they have,' I asked Hereweald? From where he was, he said it was hard to see but expected it was more than us. Besides half of our men being exhausted from war we were also outnumbered. We did not have the time to wait on Andras and Henry from Exeter.

Joining the command, I acknowledged Albert. 'How many men have we?' Albert said that he had six thousand including the ones returned from up north. 'Have the crops and harvest been recovered and stored in the castle?' Albert said that they did not have time to complete the harvest although the women and children were all safe within the walls. 'How many have been left to defend the castle should this battle go poorly?' Albert looked at me with annoyance but thought better then to voice it. He said that there were maybe only two or three hundred old men left to defend the castle. This did not sound promising as a place of refuge. Luckily Godric and Albert were back in Worcester although many who I grew up with were within those walls.

I suggested that we retreat from this battle and get the men behind the walls. Start pulling back the rear ranks and get as many men safely behind the walls as we can. Albert asked me if I was mad and Hereweald told me that it was too late. 'The heavy horse will ride us down and cut us to threads.' I told them that my suggestion of stripping the ranks from the back left the front defenses to protect their retreat. Hereweald said that we would be sacrificing up to a third of our army on this retreat. 'As soon as King William sees what we are doing he will send his heavy horse at us.' It seemed like my advice was falling on deaf ears and rightly or wrongly this battle was going to be fought in the field.

The battle commenced on the morning of the fifteenth of September in the year 869 AD. William was thought to have five thousand infantryman and three thousand knights in the field. We were outnumbered but fought for our lives. The battle ebbed and flowed over the day where at times it looked as though we were going to win and at other times we were getting beaten back. Our longbow was able to inflict heavy losses on the Norman infantry however the heavy armored knights made light work of Gerome and our cavalry. Our cavalry is skilled but without armor we lost two for every knight we brought down. Late in the day it was obvious that we were going to lose the day. Hereweald and John came back to my position and said that we must flee for our lives. They asked me to give the command for the men to stop fighting and escape if they could. John said we were down to less than two thousand men. With tears in his eyes, he said that it had been a massacre. I did not think it that bad until I considered the numbers of men who had lost their lives. Nodding my head, I gave the command to sound the retreat.

As I turned toward Winchester Hereweald grabbed my reigns. 'No, my Queen, we have too few men to defend such a large castle. If you go in there you will be caught. You are the Queen of England, and you must not become prisoner. We must head for London as that is our closest castle and more easily defended. The city may fall but the castle can hold out for years.' This would be abandoning Winchester to fate and likely the Normans, however I could see that Hereweald's advice was sound.

We alerted as many men as we could to follow us. Hopefully the rest of the men would make it into Winchester and onto the walls. I could see the knights running down and slaying our infantry. We lost many men in the chaos which was the retreat. I was now riding at full speed so did not see what was to become of Winchester and the men. Hereweald and John urged me to ride as fast as I could so that the knights did not catch up and cut us down. We had a guard of maybe a hundred men however a few dozen knights might take care of them. It was after dark when we reached the gates of London which were closed. On seeing who we were the gates were quickly organized to be opened. Inside we were met by Wulfsige who was desperate to hear the news. Before telling him about the battle John instructed him to have all the produce and resources which were outside the wall brought into the city and castle. 'Once inside the castle we will take the luxury to tell you about the massacre.' Wulfsige looked at us with worry and gave some commands to his men.

Going through London we could see a city on hard times. London had committed four thousand men to the northern campaign and had lost half of these. Families and communities were already suffering from having their bread winner away for so long. With the death of so many the community would suffer further on top of the existing heartache. There was now a hostile enemy on their doorstep and a Queen to defend.

We were recognized and again the look in the people's eyes told me that they in-part blamed me for the loss of their loved ones. How had my father coped for so long with these looks? They were already affecting my self-esteem and soul. I did not want the responsibility, yet at the same time I knew that I did. I was born for this, and these are my people.

Once inside the castle we were at least able to relax for a few moments. Food and mead were ordered as we entered the dinner room. I took the opportunity to question London as our destination. John said that if it wasn't for the dark, we would have seen the knights not two miles behind us. We had kept ahead of them but if we had of travelled any further, they would have run us down. They stayed in the dark as there was no use attacking London without their full force. They will now guard the roads into and out of London. We are as good as trapped until we can be rescued by Northampton or Worcester. I nodded to them that I understood. 'if we could have ridden to Worchester then we would have, suggested

Hereweald.' I would have preferred this as my children were there and I believe that to be the best Castle in the land.

Chapter 11

Rescues

Ramsay and Bran were dragging me away from the quay. 'We have to go Kenner; we cannot stay here.' That was Ramsay over and over in my ear. It was no good as I was in shock. Godric had just been netted and hauled onto one of those boats. My Godric was gone, taken and we could not do anything.

Regaining some sense, I looked around and still the Vikings were all around. Bran and Ramsay were doing their best to fend them off while assisting me. Snapping back into the moment I regained my feet, drew my blade, and said to the men that we needed to get out of here. Ramsay laughed and said, 'About time.' With a cheeky grin.

At that moment we were rushed by four Viking men and a scuffle broke out. While two of them were grappling with Bran I had my opportunity to take one from behind. It was a neat right thrust straight through the ribs. I put all my strength into it as I was not sure what resistance I would get from the material. There was plenty of emotion with that jab as I was still feeling the battle frenzy.

The horses were behind the inn away from the quay and still unaware of the commotion in the village. The village would be ransacked and anybody still in it would be killed or carried away. We had only been in Stonehaven for the one night however it seemed like a picture-perfect fishing village, isolated and self-contained.

That morning I had decided to take a walk to see more of the village. The sun was not quite up but the sky was starting to get some light. It was a grey morning with a gentle breeze. I did not realize that I was walking into a raid. Looking on the different houses overlooking the quay I was intent on walking down to the jetty to see what the early morning fishermen had brought in. I started to hear noises and looking around my alarm bells started ringing in my head. Something wasn't right. I had heard of raids before as our homeland had often been raided along the coastal settlements and even along our length from Carlisle. Turning back to the inn I had commenced running when I was grabbed by one of the Vikings and then a second. Kicking and screaming seemed to be doing no good however I did notice that Bran had been trailing me and could see what was going on. Bran was still on the hill overlooking the harbor. He had either thought the same or was chaperoning me to make sure I did not come to any harm. In that glance I could see his shock and that he was unarmed. As I was getting dragged to the boat Bran turned and went back into the Inn. I continued to resist however it seemed futile as the two men who had me were like goliath. Settling a little I had looked around me and there appeared to be hundreds of them. I remember thinking that If Godric and the others tried to come to my rescue they would be killed. A sense of dread came over me as I had thought of this situation. I knew that I needed to get away but could not think how. I had a blade hidden in my leggings, but I was being carried as a sack of potatoes and did not have the opportunity to reach it. All my thoughts from that moment became clear to me. There was nothing I could have done.

It looked like the horses had sensed something as they seemed pleased to see us. We led all seven out of the yard and west back towards to the highlands. On this track we noticed many of the villagers were making for the hills to hide out until the raid finished. Maybe this happens to them regularly and they would go back to their peaceful ways. I doubted it however I knew that humans have a way of dealing with adversity and surviving. Thinking about where we are, I could see that this stretch of coast would be vulnerable to raids. I have seen crude maps of the waters around Britannia and the mainland of Europe. The Viking lands always seemed to be across from this stretch of the north sea. This could be the Vikings last opportunity for some looting before winter stops their boats. I was on the back of my chestnut mare, Royal Blood, and my mind was wondering. We were slowly making our way west and it seemed that we were now safe.

Ramsay dismounted and said that we were safe and should stop for a rest. He began tying up the extra horses. Bran helped me down from Royal Blood and went to help tie up the horses. I followed and thought to grab some breakfast from the saddle bags. We were all silent as I think we were all digesting what had just happened. McGregor was dead and Godric as good as dead. Nobody ever came back from the sea, and we all knew it.

Sitting around with some dried bread and jam I began discussing the raid. 'Why would they take Godric as they normally don't take males?' Ramsay said that they also have slaves to work their pits. They might also know who he is as Godric is the bane of all Vikings. He is a legend down south and responsible for killing their King Knut, his son Eric and famous leader Halfdan. If this is so he will be a big prize for them back at their home.

'Did you see him fight, asked Bran? He cut down dozens as he created a path for us to get you out. It was a sight to remember as he was in the berserker zone which he had told us about. Time must have slowed for him as he went from Viking to Viking. I have never seen anything like it and apart from being distracted I doubt that they would have taken him down.' I could sense that Bran was pouring out his heart as he is a sensitive soul who builds close relationships.

It was then that I lost control and broke down into tears. I was used to putting on a brave face as I was daughter of the king. My father had taught me to be as tough as my brothers. He would scold me if I cried and send me to my room. Ramsay and Bran were looking at me not knowing what to do. They would not know, and I did not know either. I hated myself for I was the reason Godric had to come to the quay to fight. I hated our last few days together where he refused to talk to me. He was angry that I had not told him about my father's plans or about his brother. Truth was I had forgotten about Tata by the time Godric was healed and had his strength back. Father had ordered me out of Glasgow with Godric and told me I must not mention the alliance with Pictland. Father told me that Pictland had grown strong, and that the alliance was needed as insurance. Strath Clyde had to join in the campaign against the English as part of the agreement. I was miserable then and I am even worse now knowing I would never see Godric again. He is a good man whom his people needed. His brother and the other English slaves need him. When he wakes, he will hate me even more as he will be even further from his dream of a united and peaceful Britannia. My misery could not get any worse.

Later that day Ramsay noticed that the people were making their way back into town. Orloff and his wife came down the path close to where we were camped. Orloff saw us and directed his wife over to us. 'I saw one of your men go down and another taken to the boats. They fought bravely and should be remembered for their sacrifice. I have never seen anyone fight like that man I met last night in the Inn. It was like he was dancing as he moved through the enemy. Both of his arms worked in harmony, left to right as he swiveled and circled around cutting them down. Please meet my wife Avalon and come back to the inn to recover. The Vikings will not be back again this year, we can be sure.' My tears would be obvious to Orloff and Avalon and they might suspect my relationship to Godric. It was late in the day and shelter and a warm fire would be welcome, so I graciously accepted their offer, wiping away my tears.

Orloff told us that they get raided every three or four years however they had now been raided twice in the one year. They had heard how the English had forced the Vikings from the land and suspect that this second raid might be retribution or a chance to grab some resources before winter. Whatever the reason, the attack could change things for Stonehaven for good. Avalon promised us some soup and warm mead when we were back. I gave her a questioning look and she smiled and said that they always had something aside which the Vikings would not find. This improved my spirits marginally but only for a short while.

Back at the inn I was drowning my sorrows as Bran and Ramsay chatted with Orloff. They had all decided to leave me alone with my thoughts. I was going over my time with Godric right through to when he freed me from the Vikings and was knocked unconscious. He looked relieved when he saw that I was free. He even smiled when we caught each other's eye. Godric had fought like a madman for me, to free me from the Vikings. He still loved me and had met his end for that love. Godric had also shown me his true feelings which were that he loved me even though I had broken his trust. I was at that moment elated to have discovered Godric's true feelings yet devastated that I had lost my true love. I took my hands away from my face and saw the others had stopped talking and were looking at me.

'Are you all right' asked Bran, with concern on his face? I told them that I was getting better but was still shocked by the loss of Godric and McGregor. It then occurred to me that Godric's loss should not be for nothing. We were riding north to rescue his brother and countryman from the iron mine. Just because Godric was lost we could still rescue his brother. This is what Godric would have wanted. If I could do anything to honor his memory it would be to continue our mission to rescue his brother. I said as much to the others and they both smiled and nodded their heads. Bran added, 'That this is exactly what Godric would have wanted if he were up in heaven looking down.'

Orloff, who was following the exchange asked if that was the Aberdeen Quarry. 'They mine all manner of blue metal stone and iron. It is less than a day from here between the Moure mountain peaks to the west of Aberdeen. I have never been there however I have heard that it is a harsh place where they send prisoners. There are regular transports of prisoners which come north through Stonehaven.'

Although what Orloff told us was depressing it was also reassuring that there is such a place. If Tata was made from the same cloth as Godric there was a good chance he was still alive. We asked Orloff for a map or clear directions, so we did not need to raise suspicions when we reached Aberdeen.

Orloff was able to help us as he had family up that way. With the map and the use of Orloff's knowledge we were now in a much better position to rescue Tata. Planning the rescue had revived my spirits and given me purpose. I was no longer in the doldrums and was looking forward to achieving the aim of our adventure. Orloff gave us some additional provisions as it seems that most of their stock is secured in a secret room which the Vikings have never found. The room is below ground in the odd chance that the inn was torched. Apparently, the Viking know enough not to destroy the village as a destroyed village would have nothing to plunder the next time.

We set off north the following morning as none of us wanted to hang around. The turn off for the quarry was just before the road dropped down into Aberdeen. Orloff told us the quarry was an hour ride from this intersection, so we were getting close. I so much hoped that Tata was still alive. I had never met Tata but the fact that he was Godric's brother and that Godric loved him dearly made me so wish for a positive outcome. The world needs men like Godric and Tata sounded like one of them.

It was not obvious that we were coming to the quarry as there were no signs or landmarks. However, when considering the distance, we had travelled and our time on the road we knew we must be close. It was time to be cautious as we were not sure what to expect. Bran signaled that he could see some sort of gate house on our road. We stuck to the edges so that we were under the canopy of the trees. Our intent was to stay out of the line of sight to the gate house. Ramsay signaled for us to stop, and we came up to where he was positioned. From his line of sight, he could see that there were two men at the gate house. From here we could see that there was a wrought iron gate and walls running either way from the road.

Ramsay suggested we should go through the bush a little to see if we could find a low spot in which to get over the wall. This sounded like a good plan to me as fighting with only the three of us would be risky. We must have tracked the wall for half a mile before we found a hill crest where the wall was little more than two meters high. Bran boosted Ramsay to the top so that he could have a look around. Ramsay said that it was all overgrown and there did not seem to be anyone around. Bran then boosted me onto the wall. I jumped down on the other side while Ramsay reached down and helped pull Bran up onto the wall.

The bush was thick which gave us excellent cover. We made our way in the direction of the sounds we were hearing. The sound was that of metal on stone, metal chipping into stone. As we got closer the sound was almost continuous. There were soft chips and loud chips but either way there was a hive of activity not far from where we were. Nothing was yet visible for the trees, but it could not be far.

Next Ramsay shot out his hand to stop us walking any further. We were about to step to the top edge of the quarry with what looked like a forty-yard drop. Ramsay was on the edge, so he took a step back for safety and to be under the cover of the trees. It would have been very unlucky if someone had of been looking up at that moment and noticed Ramsay.

Creeping to the edge enabled us to look down at the activity below. There were maybe a hundred men that looked about the size of sheep. Some were chipping at the face while others were breaking up the larger boulders which had been loosened. It looked like back breaking work, man against rock. The men were only clothed from the waist down and I was certain if we got closer we would see the sweat glistening on their bodies. Bran pointed out two guards however this was all we could see. The men were connected by a chain so we would need to find the key to the lock. We had a few choices. We could wait until dark and find out where they slept. With an opportunity we may be able to speak with the prisoners to find out if any are aware of Tata or Swidhun. Another option would be to take out the two guards with arrows and expect that they would have the keys to the locks. Even if they did not have the keys the prisoners would surely know where they are. The other options seemed too risky including that last one. It was agreed to stay under cover and wait until the men finished their day. We would follow them to where they eat and rest.

As I watched them work, I began to consider the likelihood of Tata and Swidhun surviving. The work was physical, monotonous, and endless. I shuddered when I thought of these poor men working through winter. This far north it would be as miserable as I thought it possible. Ramsay, Bran, and I were all somber by the end of the day. Bran noting that he thought it unfair that these men should be treated like this. 'They have no chance of survival as they are expected to keep working until they drop dead. Working in a quarry in the middle of nowhere these men would all have been forgotten. Only their loved ones would remember them.' I could see Bran understood the enormity of the human misery. One day if I am in a position of leadership, I needed to remember this lesson.

An hour from sunset the men downed tools and the ends of the chain were unlocked and handed to the men on the ends of the line. The men shuffled out of the quarry toward the only entry and exit point. The shuffle was slow as some of the men were in poorer condition and the men in the lead looked to be considering the health of these men. The guards walked along beside the men and seemed to be chatting with some of them. They looked to be armed but also at ease. We made our way down from the high wall so that we were close enough to see where they walked to. It was unlikely they would get away from us as they were moving slowly. They were a bit like a slow-moving snake.

The accommodation was only a hundred yards from the entry path into the quarry. There was a tree lined track linking the quarry and the barracks where the workers slept. The barracks were surrounded with a palisade wall and gate. Seeing where they were going, we quickly moved to a position where we were hidden by the timber walls of their accommodation. Keeping an eye on events we watched them as they were unlocked and given their meals. There were prisoners who had prepared three pots of food. The prisoners lined up and were given scoops of mash and a choice of one of the other pots. From where we were, we could see that both pots were probably filled with stew. If they were given meal options, this would be at least one positive amongst the hardship. They were all given a mug of something hot to go with their food. After receiving their meals, the men lined up along one of the benches. I was looking for someone who looked like Godric however from this distance I could only look for broad shoulders. Unfortunately, there were dozens of men of this size all helped by the nature of their detention. We were left to wait until dark and the guards left and locked up the gates. The men were left to themselves inside the locked compound.

Ramsay stepped forward as some of the men were still at the table. Many of the others had started making their way into the barracks. It was a dark night as the sky was thick with cloud. The silhouette of a full moon could be seen through the cloud. I was watching as Ramsay approached the men at the nearest table. None of the men even flinched as they looked up toward Ramsay. He asked if he could be taken to Tata. I could see heads shake and then one of the men stood up and shouted rock splitter, you are required to solve a riddle.

We all waited for a few moments, and I realized I was holding my breath. Out of the furthest barracks came a large athletic man. It was too dark to see his face clearly, but I could see some resemblance to Godric. This was our man; I had that feeling. Tata came up to Ramsay and they exchanged some quiet words. Ramsay pointed in our direction, and I could see he was asking Tata to come and talk with Bran and me. Tata nodded and followed Ramsay to where Bran and I were waiting. In seconds I was looking into the eyes of my beloved Godric, only it wasn't him. I broke down into silent tears.

With my hands over my face, I heard Bran introduce himself. 'I am Bran of the Strath Clyde cavalry, and this is Princess Kenner. You must be Tata Amity, brother of Godric.' I looked up from my hands in time to hear Tata's reply. Tata acknowledged who he was and followed that this was an unexpected visit. He wanted to know the nature of the visit as he said that it was late.

I regained some composure and told Tata that I was Kenner of Strath Clyde and that I had loved his brother. Tata suddenly looked at me with those piercing eyes. 'I have heard of you Kenner. My brother spoke highly of his time with you. Some of the men here talk and sing of your beauty and I can see why they do. I figured that Godric was killed by Pictland at the battle of Jarrow. However, from the tone of your voice there may be another story.'

'Godric survived the battle of Jarrow and there is much to tell you of the events since. We have come to rescue you and any of your men who survived Jarrow. Godric was with us however he was taken as a prisoner of the Vikings in a raid two days back. We do not know if Godric lives but if the Vikings have their way with him, he will wish he was dead. Godric wished to see you rescued so we have continued with our mission even without him. Godric wants to see you and the men back home with your families and we will do what it takes to make this happen.'

With fading light, I could see that Tata was thoughtful. 'I have had nothing but time when thinking about Godric and home. The only way of surviving this life is to keep the faith that one day we would see home again. I have dreamed of this every night and in my dreams my brother arrives to rescue me. How many nights this has been I cannot recall but I had never given up hope. My brother would come, or I would die with the dream in my heart. With this dream I have been able to inspire the others to survive and dream with me. There are thirty of us in all. This is a big number and close to a third of the workers in the quarry. With such a strong core number we have survived longer than any previous group, or so we have been told. That Godric survived gives me hope as he does not die easily. I would hear the tales since that day, and I would hear of England and how she fares. We have so much to learn but first please know that we are two years past ready to leave this place so we could not be more prepared. Let us sleep as we have slaved all day and the men need rest. If we can wake an hour before sunrise then we can leave with strength in our legs and back.' Wow, he was so much like his brother, decisive and without fear. I had goose pimples thinking of the similarities. This man was powerful, I could see the arms and the muscles through his shoulders and chest. I said that we could wake them an hour before daylight. We will get through the walls as we have swords which could cut the door fastenings. 'We will organize this as there will be two guards on the outside and we have never caused trouble before. We will call Braun or Walter and tell them that Thomas is sick again.

Thomas is struggling with the work and has been suffering of late. We will say he needs some food or water and beg them to bring something. If the doors are not opened after this rouse, then you can use your swords. I would prefer that you do not kill the guards as they have been fair with us. They have a job to do, and they have done it without being cruel which is all a prisoner can ask.'

Tata went back and we could hear him whispering to the other men. I felt thrilled to have met Tata and I was sure we would be free within hours. Although I had lost Godric I was as happy as ever that we would be freeing his people. I almost felt that these were my people such was the closeness I felt to them at that moment. I prayed to our mighty father that all would go well in the morning. Ramsay and Bran both said they would stay awake to make sure we did not miss this opportunity. I was so grateful to have two such wonderful companions who were resourceful and empathetic.

At an hour before sunrise Ramsay woke me and we woke Tata and the others. The other prisoners had agreed to come with us as they had no love of the Picts and if they did not come with us, they would die in the quarry. A third of them were Vikings and some had been in the quarry for longer than the English. Everyone grabbed the small possessions they had as we prepared for the long journey away from the quarry.

Tata called out to Braun and told him that Thomas was bent over with cramps again. Thomas needed some food or water, something to try and sooth his pain. I could hear a man on the other side of the gate swear and say that he would grab something. A short time afterwards the man returned, and he and the other guard opened the gate to enter the compound. This was our opportunity so Tata and Swidhun took it by quickly overpowering the guards and taking their weapons. Swidhun, who I had just been introduced to, is another powerful man with a leadership presence. I can already see that the others look up to these two. With regards the two guards, Ramsay and Bran were heavily armed but were not required. The guards were tied up against the barracks and had rages shoved into their mouths so that they could not speak. Tata apologized to them, and I could see that he was sorry that it was required.

There was no hanging around as the men started pushing out the gate. Without the chain holding them and their legs together the men could move at what would be considered a normal walking pace. Instead of the path back into the quarry we took the path up the slope toward the mine gate. This was Bran and Ramsay's chance to race ahead and deal with these guards. I thought they would not take any chances and would silence them quickly. These guards could raise the alarm and we could have guards swarming the roads looking for us. We did not know what happened at the gates however the gates were open, and we just walked out without being accosted. Bran and Ramsay were waiting for us on the other side with broad grins on their face. It was evident they were enjoying themselves just as I was.

I walked with Tata as he enquired about his brother. We had hours together, so I was able to tell him what I knew from when we rescued Godric to when we lost him to the Vikings. I told him what I knew of the south and what had been happening to the English. Light was just starting to appear as a slither across the horizon as we came to the Stonehaven to Aberdeen road. Our pace was still good as we had put the injured or slower walkers on the horses. We had six armed men and then of course I was also armed.

Tata asked me about my plan and how we were going to get them through Pictland and back to English land. He could see me struggle with the answer and in the end, I had to admit that I had not thought that far ahead. I told him that It had only be a dream that he had survived, and we were expecting to rescue maybe him and Swidhun if that dream came true. As evidence of this I told him that this was why we had brought two spare horses. We now had four spare horses however this was a result of losing McGregor and Godric to the Vikings. We did not expect to be rescuing thirty English and certainly not all ninety-five prisoners. By the end of this day we would make it to the central highland road. Once up in the highlands we would be safe for a day or two. I would like to think we would be safe going to Strath Clyde and heading south however I did not trust my father or brother. Now that they had an alliance with King Oengus he would not want to be seen aiding and abetting escaped convicts.

We continued walking south like a returning army from a battle. Passersby were allowed around or through un-accosted. All would know we were prisoners however it probably looked like a prisoner transfer as Bran and Ramsay were leading the procession and they were dressed as soldiers and were heavily armed. Ramsay took a dozen men with him into

Stonehaven as the rest of us turned west and up into the highlands. We would need supplies to help us over the highlands and Ramsay knew where to get them. He would pay as we did not want to enforce any more hardship on Stonehaven then they had already experienced.

Camp was set up at the foot of the highlands. It had been a full day's walking which looked to have taken its toll on some of the men. All the men looked happy despite the rain beginning to set in and the obvious discomfort of the days walk. It was looking like it would be a miserable night in the open if the rain did not blow through. We found a forest filled with spruce trees which would give us adequate shelter for a while if the rain did not get strong. Fires were lit for warmth and light as it was very dark in this forest. The men were resourceful and looked elated with their freedom. I could see that they were trusting or faithful men. There were very few questions from the others as they seemed to leave the questions to Swidhun and Tata who seemed to be the natural leaders.

Taking the weight off my legs was welcome and sitting around the fire gave me a chance to think of what to do next.

Going south was going to be fraught with danger as we were a threatening force, and we could not hide that we were escaped convicts. Tata suggested we might be better off going south in boats. We can go around all the forces if we can find suitable boats. One of the men called out to Tata. 'Rock Splitter, if we can find the boats, we could take you south before going back home, across the sea.' This was one of the Vikings and it seemed that they longed to see their families again also. Why wouldn't they I thought? Tata was shaking his head and smiling. I could see he thought it a good idea and admit that it was starting to grow on me also. My distrust of my father was enough to have me worried.

Chapter 12

Allies

William has consolidated his hold on Southern England and the Picts have York under siege. I was praying to our lady Mary the mother of Jesus. The current situation had me reaching to heaven for any advantage. Thus, I am spending hours in the London Cathedral every day. All my efforts have helped little as England is getting sandwiched and strangled between two superior forces.

London has been taken and we are trapped in the Tower of London itself. There is plenty of food and other supplies and we have enough men to hold the walls or at least make it very costly to break through. The Tower of London is not large and with moat and fifty-foot walls it would be the most impregnable castle in the kingdom. News from outside had stopped coming weeks ago as all access into and out of London was snuffed out.

The last correspondence to make it through said that Exeter was still holding out but would not last much longer without support. Andras is there with Henry leading the resistance against the Normans. They are apparently doing well however this seems to have only prolonged the inevitable. I hoped that Worchester would ride for Exeter as England could not afford to lose this critically strategic location. Exeter protects the southern flanks of Worchester and is the gateway to Devon and Cornwell. Exeter protects a third of southern England. There is some fertile land in this region which the Normans would love to get their hands on. I also worry about my Andras as he was not shy of a fight and would be out amongst the fighting.

York was still holding out however they were short of supplies and needed reinforcements and the blockade to be broken so food could get through to the soldiers. Winter is coming and it is thought that they may make it through to then but if the Picts do not retreat then the garrison in York would starve. King William had himself led the army at Northampton and was repelled. They had set up a siege however Worcester had been able to push the Normans back from the wall. Emrick had led the army and had a significant victory.

Emrick is now Godric's brother in-law having married Hilda. Emrick and Hilda had both lost their spouses and had children which needed caring for and raising. I am not suggesting that they did not love each other however their union solved many problems while at the same time cementing the alliance with Powys. Powys was crucial to the English in the defeat of the Vikings and would be again if we were to have a chance of surviving our current situation.

Further good news had come that our cities had been bolstered by refugees and these additional numbers were being trained to join the city guards. Defense was all that was possible for now as our survival was currently on a knifes edge.

If we can make it through to winter, then there was a chance we could survive the following summer campaigns. Worcester was still key to our survival as it had the resources needed to fight the Normans and the Picts. It also had the people and the manufacturing to keep an army in the field protecting our borders. I prayed that these rays of hope and wins on the battlefields would lift the overall army moral.

I hated having no news and complained about this with Hereweald. Hereweald is well read and said that he had read of a solution only it was now too late to put this into practice. It seems that there are homing pigeons which can be trained to take messages between cities. All we would require is to train a pigeon or two from London. The pigeons would be taken to Worcester and when they needed to get a message to us, they would strap the message to the pigeon's leg and release it. The pigeon would then fly back to its home of London. Likewise, we could attach a message to a Worcester pigeon's leg and when released the pigeon would fly back to Worcester. Then the Worcester rookery would have pigeons from different locations including London. Messages could be sent backwards and forwards using this method. This sounded intriguing and Hereweald assured me that it works. The problem with the system is that it would have been required to be established before we were trapped in a siege.

John and Wulfsige walked in on our conversation just as I was highlighting the problem. John enquired what the latest problem was and looked ready to jump to a solution. I told him that it was too late to set up a pigeon communication system once we were in a siege. John slapped himself on the forehead and looked around at Wulfsige who suddenly looked at his feet and looked a little sheepish. I had to know what they were hiding and insisted they tell me. 'We are not hiding anything my queen only we have been forgetful. When Godric heard of such a system he asked John and I to set one up between the major cities including London and Worchester and between Winchester and Worchester. Obviously with Winchester in the hands of the Normans it is now useless however we did get a rookery set up for both London and Worchester. With the siege and everything else we had forgotten that it existed.

I was furious with the men for being such dunderheads. After scolding them I told them that I was thrilled and insisted we get down to business and send off a message. The men seemed hesitant although I did not see the problem. Hereweald voiced where he had a concern. 'Why hadn't we received any messages from Worchester? Is there anyone at Worchester who knows how the rookery works?' John answered that there were people looking after the rookery and if we sent a message then the message would reach the council. With this reassurance we did not waste any time and commenced dictating a message to be sent to Worchester. We needed to know what was happening and if there were any decisions which needed making. Information was the key and we have been in the dark for the last four weeks. I was excited that we may have a solution to the dilemma.

Wulfsige said that it was important that they are aware of our situation. The queen is safe, and we are a tough nut to crack, here in the castle. The priority should be protecting the lands north of the Themes and our three strategic cities.

Chapter 13

Captivity to Freedom

I woke up, vomited, and then coped a kick all within a few seconds of being conscious. My head is throbbing like never before. Death would have been welcomed at that moment. I was now lying curled up with my face half in my vile vomit. The floor was moving up and down and I guessed it wasn't my head causing this motion. I was in a Viking boat on the sea. The fight and then this. That's right, I was fighting the Vikings in that fishing village. I must have been captured and was now captive. It made sense that they were taking me back to their stronghold which was probably in Norway. The pain was more than I could handle, my head and the nausea from the motion of the boat. I could handle being stabbed, bashed, and left for dead but not this endless torment. All I wanted to do was escape the pain no matter what the cost. I even contemplated making a run to the side of the boat. The nausea and then there, I had vomited again. The kick was swift as though he was waiting to deliver it.

The motion sickness would go away as I got used to the motion or so I had heard in the stories. I had to use this information as a ray of hope. Apart from being alive it was the only ray of hope I had. Did the Vikings know who I was became my next thought? If they knew I was the king of England I would meet a cruel death. They would know what I had done to their armies and King Knut, his son Eric and their famous warlord Halfdan. I was sure they would want revenge if they were given the chance.

Now that I was awake one of the slaves on the boat offered me some water. I lifted my head to drink. Every movement as painful as the worst I had experienced. I needed the water so took the pain and the water. Moments later I vomited again, and the water was wasted. Another kick welcomed me with the vomit. The water sloshing around the bottom of the boat was like sewage. I was sure it was not just my vomit which made up the soupy mess. In my head I started telling myself that I had to survive this.

I had to get home to England to see that the land survived the attack by the Picts. I know I passed out again after that thought as when I awoke it was to moonlight. Sleep had been a blessed relief and I was not going to begrudge my fortune.

The sea was now much calmer than earlier, and the boat was drifting as most of the men at the ores were sleeping. My head still throbbed but my stomach nausea had subsided. I looked around to see if there was anyone awake as my throat was so dry it was sore. I saw one of the slaves resting near to me, so I shuffled over and gave him a nudge, pointing to my throat. He knew what I wanted so reached over and gave me a drink from a water skin. The water did not help my throat all that much however I knew it would save my life. I kept the portion low as I could not afford to vomit it back up.

It was a big boat with what looked to have fifty or sixty men on it. I was not the only captive lying in the mess at the center of the boat. As I looked around, I notice a man at the front of the boat watching me look at him. My hands were tied behind my back, something which I had only just noticed. The man did not respond to my recognition and ignored me as if I were nothing.

I was not awake for long as I could not remember anything else from that time awake and I was next getting rolled from side to side in heavy seas and what looked like a midday sun. Looking around for my servant, as I was beginning to think of him, I motioned toward my mouth. He knew right away and was over to me with the skin at once. My throat was dry and sore and again the water did not appease this dry soreness. It was what was needed and helped fill a growing hunger gap. I must have been getting my sea legs as I did not feel as sick as I had every other time, I was awake. The rest had done me good, and I noticed that my head was hurting less than it had. My arms were still tied and would likely remain that way, so I had no chance of feeling the wound on my head. I suspected that my skull had been broken given the pain I had been in. There was plenty of blood in the boat soup however I did not know how much of this was mine.

It now came to the time when I needed to take a leak. This was going to be difficult lying in the bottom of the boat with my hands tied. I called out to one of the men and told them I needed a leak. With my head I tried to point toward my manhood. He followed my lead and looked where my head was pointing and suddenly, I could see a recognition on his face. He said something to the man at the stern of the boat. The man at the stern said something to my guard and the guard came over to the water boy and told him something. The next I knew I had the guard and the water boy helping me to my feet and to the edge of the boat. I was propped against the boat edge where the guard held my shirt at the scruff of my neck and the boy dropped my breeches so that I could piss over the side. It felt humiliating however my dignity did not stop me from emptying my bladder into the sea. It felt so good to have been for my wee and even better to be standing upright again. My breeches were pulled up and the guard pushed me back from the edge. I was grateful that I was being held as I would have gone over several times without that support. The sea was rough but still I felt better than I had since being captured. Rather than lying back in the boat slop I was well enough to sit against the side of the boat.

Sitting upright gave me the opportunity to survey the boat. There was no doubt that it was a Viking longboat. I had seen plenty of these in my time and most no different to this. The next thing which I noticed was that I was the only one who was still tied up. There were other prisoners however they were all either sitting up like me or asleep on the floor. The Vikings were taking no chances, and this made sense given what I had done to them back on the shore. Watching the Vikings work, taking it in turns at the ores, I began to admire their endurance and commitment. It would not be easy work rowing across the sea and these men looked almost cheerful to have their chance at rowing. I also understood why they were so strong and fierce in battle. These are hardened men and looking at the age of some of them they started young and kept going until they died of old age. There were men who looked to be sixty and boys who looked fifteen.

In a seated position I noticed there were two other boats trailing ours. The boats looked to be the same and although still Vikings it was good to know that we were not the only ones on this lonely sea.

I slept regularly and was at last given some dried bread. My stomach devoured the bread as it was my first food since capture. From that point I was given a lump of bread daily which my water boy assisted me with. He was feeding me as if I was a bird. I had given up being humiliated and was grateful that the Vikings had stopped kicking me. The water boy, who I had started calling Life, stuck close to me and began anticipating my needs. He was still helping the others and jumping to the call of the Vikings however I could tell he had feelings for me. Perhaps he felt sorry for me, I do not know. Life was probably twenty years old so not really a kid. He had short hair and looked to be Pict. My guess was that he was also captured in the raid. I wondered why he had not spoken to me but did not push it as there was obviously a story there.

We went on this way for another week until we sighted land. The Vikings suddenly relaxed and began joking around and back slapping each other. It was still a risky business to cross the North Sea even for these experienced sea farers. These men did not lack courage and could work as hard as any men I had known. I was not sure my appreciation of their feats would help me however I was now so used to appraising men for one role or another. The land we were travelling past was steep and covered with forest. It looked like some areas of Strath Clyde, especially around Arrochar.

This was the first time I had thought about Kenner since being captured. I realized I had not thought of anything from back home since regaining consciousness. Kenner and I had parted on bad terms as we had not talked for days. I had been angry that Kenner had betrayed me so had refused to talk to her. I could excuse that she had forgotten to tell me about Tata however she should not have deceived me about her father's plans. Thinking this aloud I realized what I was saying. It would have been extremely stressful and almost impossible for Kenner to go against her father. I now felt worse about how I had acted. I had been the one who had trusted Gregor, King of Strath Clyde, and trained his men. I had even shown them how to make superior weapons. I had been the one who had built the army he had used against my kinsmen. I was blaming Kenner for what was my own failing. I had realized how shallow my anger was when Kenner was being kidnapped by the Vikings. Seeing her in trouble had immediately triggered the berserker rage where time stands still, and I can pulverize an enemy. It had worked again for a time, and I had been able to free Kenner. Then I had been distracted and here I now was, a prisoner again.

The eye contact before I lost consciousness was enough. Kenner loved me and was searching my face for a hint at my feelings. I remember smiling at that moment before the world went blank. Kenner would have seen this, it would be enough for her, I knew that.

I began to wonder what they would do now if they got away. I hoped they would pursue Tata and Swidhun although I would not blame them if they turned around. It had been two years since the battle of Jarrow and the chance of surviving that long as a quarry slave would be low. When I get free, I will still look for Tata as a brother should. I will keep searching until I am sure that he is dead.

When I woke the following day, the boats had slowed considerably. Looking ahead I could see we were coming into some long jetties. There were other boats on the jetties but still enough room for our three boats. I could see that the man at the stern was watching me as I looked around. My hands were still tied behind my back, so they were still taking no chances. The ache in my arms had finally gone away as I suspected the nerves were probably now dead. My water boy had been a big help and I hoped that he would be treated well. He was a captive like me and would end up doing what he was told. I was not so sure that I would end up in slavery and that worried me.

The boats docked and one of the Vikings came over and lifted me up. I would have fallen except for this Viking, as the boat was moving about with all the commotion of people getting off and onto the Jetty. There was a lot of excitement on the Jetty as goods, including the captives were off loaded. Many were there to greet their family members and it was evident that there is very little difference in the value of the family within the Viking or English families. I had not communicated with the Vikings and hoped that there was someone who spoke Saxon or English as it is now known. I could understand and speak basic Old Norse from my interactions with Vikings while growing up. Life could understand what I said however he did not talk back to me. I was sure he could talk as I had heard him mumbling to himself on occasions. Something had scared him from communicating with me.

Once on the Jetty I was steadied by the same Viking as I was having trouble getting my balance. I was just thinking that I was grateful for his support when he turned me and pushed me off the jetty and into the water. The shock of the ice water had all my senses on high alert if not already. As I came to the surface, I realized that I was not the only captive pushed in as it seemed like they had all been pushed off the jetty. The others at least had their arms free which meant they could swim if they knew how. With my arms tied I flailed around in my best attempt to keep my head above water. It was no good, the weight of my clothing and my tied arms were too much, and I began going under and accidently took a mouth full of water and commenced choking to add to my dilemma.

I was hauled from the water just as I had given up. Once air was available, I was immediately coughing and spluttering. I noted that it had taken three of them to get me out of the water and onto the Jetty. Two in the water and one on the jetty. I felt so relieved for having been in the water even though I was now coughing and spluttering. One by one I saw the other captives being dragged out of the water. The bystanders on the jetty looked amused and rather innocent.

The large Viking from the stern of the boat grabbed me by the upper arm and commenced dragging me with him, up the jetty and to land. The crowds of people parted as the Vikings from the boat came through. Several people came up to my Viking and had words only I could not work out what was being said. My Viking needed a name and since he had sat in the stern of the boat, I thought to call him Stern. Having my arms tied behind my back is an inconvenience however it is minor compared to being unable to communicate with anyone. I could have tried however I wanted to keep my basic understanding of Old Norse as a secret.

Stern led me through most of the town to a large wooden and tent like structure. Inside it was dark although still light enough to see around. There is a throne at the center back of the room. The room is empty apart from Stern and me. Just as I thought we were alone these four men came in carrying a large timber cage. The cage was placed in what looked to be the true center and then fastened to the timber floor boards with large, curved hooks. Stern and I watched this taking place without a word being exchanged. As soon as they were finished, I was taken to the cage and shoved through the open door. Once inside Stern locked the door. His release of stress was obvious once the door was closed. I was obviously a prize, and I was starting to think this was a disadvantage. Thinking that at least I was now clean made me chuckle. Stern was watching this, and I could tell that my laughing had confused him. I think that he was probably frustrated that he could not communicate with me. At least the purpose of being thrown into the water was now clear. We must have smelt terrible when we were removed from the boat. At least this is what I thought was the reason for them tossing us in.

Chapter 14

Unexpected Surprise and Hope

Ramsay and the others returned with some food which was welcomed as I for one was starving and could eat a horse, as the saying goes. Once the food was distributed Ramsay joined our fire where I was with Bran, Tata, Swidhun and the Vikings Eric and Ivan who had also just come over. We were starting to explore the use of boats to make our way south. Eric was the older of the two men, but both seemed to know this stretch of coast well. They told us that we had two options for finding a seaworthy boat and that was going back north to Aberdeen or going south on the coast road to Arbroath. They said it would be too dangerous to go any further south as there will be a fort and garrison at Dundee.

I suggested we head for Arbroath as at least we would still be heading south. Ramsay and Bran both agreed that the overland track south could be hazardous with such a large conspicuous group. Tata then added that should the Vikings be heading home with the boats that he would travel with them and seek out Godric. He asked the men where he thought Godric would be taken after explaining to the men that Godric was his brother and the king of England. These men seem to have a strong bond and are thus very open with each other. They seem to respect Tata even though he is not Viking. Ivan said that if the raiding were this far north and this late in the season the boats would be from Bergen. Most of us are from Kaupang which is much further south, but we could get you close. Tata smiled and said that he would accept their offer but would appreciate their assistance getting all the way to Bergen if it was not too inconvenient. Everyone smiled at Tata's request as it sounded lighthearted and like he was having a little fun.

Everyone then laughed and some people from the other fires looked around at us. 'You are right young Rock Splitter. If we do not take you to Bergen, you will not find it as there is no clear path to it but by the sea.

Norway is a series of Fjords and the route around them is dangerous and long. Therefore, we laugh, and I guess why you say such a funny thing. You will be taken to Bergen where we can support your request for the return of your brother. We are, however, from Kaupang and may not be welcome. The mission is dangerous as alliances change regularly and we are not sure who is supporting who.'

At that moment I thought that I had never felt happier. I never believed that there was an option to rescue Godric. I had thought that he was lost forever. Continuing with the mission to rescue Tata had opened an opportunity to find him. Once again following our instincts and doing the right thing looks to have been beneficial. It was agreed that we would go south to Arbroath where we would look to acquire some seaworthy boats. Dundee would be our next port of call if Arbroath did not have what we were after. We would require weapons if we were going to venture into Dundee however if Arbroath did not have the boats we knew it would surely have some weapons we could acquire. By acquire I knew it would be by force however we would have no other option. We were now on the run from the law and would be killed if ever we were caught. There did not seem to be other options and there were no disagreements. The plan was passed around to the other groups to discuss.

Tata then asked a little more about my relationship with Godric. I opened my heart up including how I had betrayed him with regards Strath Clyde attacking England. I had felt pressured to comply with my father's request and was scared that Godric would do something stupid and get himself killed or locked up. I should have trusted Godric and told him what was being planned.

With the chaos of the rescue I had forgotten that I was carrying my second child with Godric. I was three months pregnant and starting to show. Tata had commented on my stomach and that was when I was hit with the reality of what I was doing. Campaigning while three months pregnant would be considered reckless but we had little choice. I told Tata about his little nephew Rick who was similar in so many ways to Godric. He adored his father and they had spent a wonderful two months getting to know each other. Tata said that he looked forward to meeting his nephew.

Arbroath looks to be twice the size of Stonehaven and the harbor matches this. We can see that there are many boats as it is the afternoon and most boats fish at first light and are thus back in port. The sea looks rough out beyond the sea wall. Although I know I have very little knowledge of the sea it was then that I felt out of my depth regarding this knowledge. I would have to rely on the others for this campaign and could contribute very little. The thought of going out into that sea scares me in every sense of the word. The boats I have seen look far too insecure for such fool hardiness.

We decided it was safer for most of us to stay outside town and hidden. Ramsay, Bran, Eric, and Ivan went into town and down to the harbor to scope opportunities. I prayed that they could find the boats we needed as I now dreamed of seeing my beloved Godric again.

The men were gone a long time and it was on dark when they did get back. We were hiding in the forests northwest of Arbroath and were just eating supper when they showed up. They came and joined the fire I was sharing with Tata and Swidhun. None of them seemed overly pleased, which put me on guard instantly.

'There are no seaworthy ships', said Ramsay with a hint of sarcasm. Bran was shaking his head from side to side while both Eric and Bran were nodding. I repeated what Ramsay said back to them to confirm I had the message right. Ramsay threw his hands down in disbelief. 'Of course, there are seaworthy ships as the harbor is full of fishing boats. The problem is with Eric and Ivan as they do not agree that any of the boats are seaworthy.' I could see that Ramsay and Bran disagreed with Eric and Ivan. I would have to play this carefully as I needed Eric and Ivan if I were to have a chance of finding Godric.

'The boats, they are not safe to cross the sea. They will be fine to fish along the coast but in the sea, there are storms and big waves. We need a Longboat or what we call a knar. To take those boats out will be a suicide mission.' I could see that Ramsay and Bran were frustrated however what Eric and Ivan said made sense. There was no point in us going out in a boat to our deaths. I was thinking of the sea I had seen earlier in the day, and I got the shivers thinking about going out into that. There was nothing to do but to thank Eric and Ivan and give them leave to find a fire and some warm food.

Ramsay and Bran stayed with us and were handed bowls of soup by Tata. I told the men that I understood their frustration as I wanted more than ever to rescue Godric. None of us have crossed the sea so we must trust the Vikings. There is no point us throwing our lives away in a storm on the sea.

'What do we do now, questioned Swidhun,' as he looked at each of us? Tata was already thinking of a solution as he said he might have an idea. We shall stay here where we can watch the port daily. This is when Ramsay tried to interrupt with disagreement to the idea of staying put.

Tata looked annoyed as he patiently waited for Ramsay to present his objection. 'Now that you have finished you might give me a chance to finish. In the meantime, we find out who wants to stay with the group and go on our rescue mission to Norway. Those that do not wish to come on our mission can easily take one of the boats in port and head south. We all heard the Vikings say the boats were seaworthy enough for going up and down the coast. While all this is going on, we need to arm the men. Our best chance of achieving this is through theft. The theft must be done with stealth as we do not want an army on our tails.' I could tell that Tata had more to say but again Ramsay said that these were good ideas, but they were not going to get us any closer to Godric's rescue.

Tata answered by telling Ramsay that as leaders we need to consider what is best for the group. 'I agree with you Ramsay and I believe that the rescue of Godric is what is best for not just our group but all of Britannia also. We will let the group decide what is right for them. While this is going on, we will commission the Vikings to commence construction of two longboats. There must be at least one of them who knows the art of ship building or at least I am hopeful. If a suitable ship does not arrive in harbor, we will use our own boats to cross the sea.' I put my hands together and smiled. I liked Tata for his creative thinking and the natural authority he possesses. This sounded like an excellent plan so I said that we should sleep on it and if it is still the best plan come morning, we will put it into play. The first stage will be talking to the Vikings and finding out the intentions of the entire group.

The following day we had all agreed to follow the plan as set out by Tata. Tata said that he would address the escapees including the Vikings. He began calling them to gather around before any of us even had the chance to object.

Looking around he found himself the highest rock on which to stand. The rock was maybe a yard high and wide, so it was not overly impressive however if helped him to see all the faces. Tata told them what we had discussed last night. He told them that most of them had never seen or met Godric. However, he is the first king of England, and he is what this land needs if it is to heal. Many of us are going to cross the sea to rescue Godric. Now there are no suitable boats so while we wait and watch the harbor, we will commission our Viking friends to build us two suitable longboats.' As he said this, I was watching Ivan and the other Vikings and could see this made them a little uncomfortable, as they shuffled in their spot. 'Everyone here is free to go their own way. There are suitable fishing boats in the harbor which will take you down the coast to England. Those who are staying will assist you in acquiring these boats, even if force is necessary. Please have a think about it as I would like a show of hands from those who wish to stay and those who want to leave.' The crowd started nattering amongst itself as they were coming to a decision. Tata gave them up to five minutes before asking them for their answer. 'Will you stay and come to Norway, or will you leave for home?'

When a request was made for those wishing to leave to put up their hand there were approximately forty who put up their hand including Swidhun, to my surprise. Swidhun is one of the commanders and seemed to be inseparable with Tata. I think this surprised Tata as he was quiet for a little while after counting. I interjected that this would work well as Swidhun can take messages south to update the English. They will already know that Godric is alive however they will not know that Tata and thirty others had survived. Ramsay and Bran drew my attention. Ramsay then said that the south will not know that Godric had survived. All messages and messengers were intercepted and not allowed to go south. Gregor did not want the English knowing there were any survivors from the battle of Jarrow. This left me speechless, and I felt my eyes fill with tears.

There were twenty who would go south on a boat and a further twenty who would make their way across the highlands to Strath Clyde. I could not blame them for wanting to go home especially when their homes were so close. These men agreed to travel together and would leave on the following sun rise.

Tata took control and told the group that their best chance of survival is to stay together. 'We will give you messages to give to the queen and our families. A lot could have happened in two years, and I only hope the messages are not too late for some of us. We can start now as it is only morning. We will go to the harbor and find a boat capable of carrying twenty. We will also scope the town for as many swords and bows as we can find. Eric and Ivan, we will need you to find the tools you will require to commence building the long boats. We will help with the labor as much as you want it. It is going to be a long day and the coming weeks also promise to be busy. It is best that we get a good start so we can confirm our plans when we return later today.' With that everyone broke into groups and each group was allocated a task. I was with a group which was to acquire as much portable food which we could find. Others were after tools for the boat, weapons for all, a suitable boat to travel south and water and mead to drink.

The rest of that day was spent with each group on their own missions. My group included Ramsay and Bran with seven other men from Pictland or Strath Clyde. It is interesting how groups tended to split into racial groups. Due to language and familiar customs this made sense, but it was still interesting to watch.

We had good success with the food as I still had some silver and was able to buy most of what we needed. Some of the men had successfully stolen some barrels of mead and a load of fish without arousing suspicion however I was too uncomfortable stealing from these people. I was given a good price anyway as we are away from the cities where everything seems to cost more. When I left Glasgow, I brought some gold and silver coins which I knew were valuable. I have them stashed in a pocket of my boots. Nobody knew they were there as it was not safe carrying around such portable wealth. It is still best to make sure nobody knows about my coins, so I let the group think that I had stolen the food. The group seem pleased that I am an accomplished thief, making me one of them.

Most of us were back at camp well before the sun was due to set. We got the fires going and the leaders all met around our fire to report on their success. It seems that a boat had been identified and would be acquired overnight and brought around to the bay below where we are camped. There was an armory in the sheriff's office which the weapons group were able to clear out. They also found plenty of weapons around the properties which they looked through. There was little trouble as everyone assumed, they were thieves and they looked too threatening to confront. A man called Ox then put his hand to his head and said that the sheriff was still tied up. This made us all laugh.

At that moment, a young man ran to our group and said that there were men riding from the north. These were likely the guard from Aberdeen coming to Dundee to see if they could organize a search for us. Tata said to everyone that this was our chance. 'Those who are bowman grab the bows and head to the road immediately. We cannot let these men through, or this place will be swarming with more guard than we will know how to handle.' At that Tata grabbed a bow and went with twenty other armed men to head off the guards heading south. I considered going to see that it all went well but checked myself as Tata had everything under control. I felt like I was back with Godric again.

We could hear the fighting through the trees, and it made me nervous not being in control of what was happening. Tata and the others emerged from the trees with a dozen horses in what seemed like an hour. Tata said that they had put up more of a fight than was expected and he said they had to make sure that there were no survivors. The bodies had to be hidden so that a passerby would not come across them. The horses could be traded for more weapons and food if required. Eric put in that the horses could be used for meat. He said the meat was good for boat trips as it lasted longer than deer and the smaller animals.

I knew that other races ate horse however I did not fancy eating one of these fine animals. There was going to be no objection from me as killing a horse meant little when compared with surviving to rescue my Godric. I saw his smile which reassured me that he loved me. He was hurt and I understand that. I had betrayed him but when the Vikings had me his true feelings came out. My Godric loved me, and we would be together again.

The following day Swidhun left with the nineteen other men who were heading south. The boat was in the bay below us as it had been successfully acquired the evening before. He was going to make for Colchester. They had word that a Norman army had landed in the south and had taken Winchester and London. We do not know the truth of this and things could have changed further. In the meantime, Swidhun was instructed to take precautions. We hoped that the northern cities still held and that this was where Aethelswith and Hereweald were. Swidhun said that he dreamed of seeing his father and younger brother again. He hoped that they were still both alive.

Eric and the Vikings commenced construction of the boats. They started by felling some of the old oak trees which were littered through the section of forest we were hiding in. They told us that this was perfect wood for their construction. They said that Leif was a boat builder back home and had made many Viking boats. They told us that we were lucky as there are not many men who build longboats, not many masters anyway. We continued to visit the harbor daily and we watched the road to ensure we were not going to be ambushed. Our days were spent helping the Vikings and practicing with our weapons. It felt good to have a purpose and to still have so much hope.

Chapter 15

Unexpected Friendships

My prison looked solid and was anything but private. My hands were still tied behind my back as I was still apparently a threat. The timber used to build my cage was thick with each piece at least as thick as my forearms. If my arms were free, I would at least give breaking out a go. The gap in the cage was just big enough for an odd shaped privy pot. I was still to work out how I was going to make use of the pot with my arms tied.

There were many visitors to the room over the course of the afternoon. Some were servants or slaves cleaning, preparing meals and loitering while others were there simply to look at me. It was clear that I was on exhibition for their amusement. I did not know where I was, however, I knew enough that it was a Viking settlement across the sea.

Home was even further away now, and this thought was a little despairing. Apart from being despairing it was also a little exciting if the Vikings did not decide to kill me. It was interesting to be in the heart of a Viking settlement on the other side of the world. These are the people who have terrorized Britannia for what seems like forever. This is where that fearsome warrior comes from. Although I was concerned for my life, I held out some hope as they had kept me alive this far. In future I would have to avoid being distracted when fighting. Distraction is the reason I was caught this time. I had got lucky in Stonehaven however next time I might not be so lucky. I would love to learn more of the language and explore the lands on this side of the sea. The Viking language is known as old Norse. I had responsibility back in England however I now felt a sense of freedom as nothing could be done as I was a prisoner in Norway. It is not that I do not love my homeland however my duty could now wait as staying alive was a clear priority.

My old Norse is very basic, and I can only follow the simplest of conversations. I can speak a little more than I can hear however this is common. In England there are many who have lived across the frontier and even many Vikings who have made England their home. We did not kick them off their land when we vanquished the Vikings as I wanted to show that we were fair and wise leaders. Many of the English could also speak old Norse and I had picked up bits and pieces while conversing with them on campaign or around the fireplace. I have kept my level of understanding to myself purely on instinct that it could come in handy being ignorant.

One of the visitors was my water boy, Life. He did not speak much however at least we spoke the same language. It seemed that he also spoke old Norse and was not aligned to anyone. He told me that he was to assist me should I need help relieving myself or eating and drinking. I felt it right to apologize to him for the task he was being forced to perform. 'It is not my wish to humiliate you and would want the circumstances to be different. We are in a pickle and please understand I appreciate all the support that you have given me and will give me. If there is a chance of escape, I will look for you and bring you with me. For now, can you please bring me some food and water if it is available.' Life, was able to find me some water and meat. The meat would be a big change from what I had been getting since I was caught.

Some of the women ventured into the tent and over to inspect me. It was getting dark outside, so the fire had been stoked to bring warmth into the room. The women were mostly young and attractive however they all seemed to have a tough edge to them. Most carried weapons openly or concealed which made me think they were warriors. Some of the comments they made to each other were flattering while others were less so. I picked up that they knew that I was the king of England and a great prize to have for Gunnstein, their Chieftain. Gunnstein and most of the men were away warring with a rival Chieftain. He was expected back any day now and the debate lingered on what Gunnstein was going to do with me. Most of them thought that I was going to be burnt in retribution for the death of his famous brother Halfdan. At least this is what I pieced together from all the conversations over a period of at least an hour. After that, the room started to fill with men and women drinking and children coming up and surrounding my cage. The sound was too much for me to hear anything further.

The boys seemed to think I was funny looking and one of them found a stick and commenced trying to poke me. Although my space was small, I was having to dance a jig to avoid being stabbed by this lad who was a similar age to Egbert or Rick. Every now and then I caught one in the ribs and my how it hurt even though the stick was blunt. Each time they got me the boys would slap each other on the back and fight over who got the next turn. None of the others in the room seemed to care and some even encouraged them. One of the men told the boys to go for my nuts, a most unwelcome suggestion. The night was filled with some dancing and fighting but mostly drinking. The noise went up as the night went on and the voices were raised.

Sometime through the night I noticed Stern at the back of the room drinking quietly. As was our relationship he was staring at me, and I began watching him. Men started coming to the cage and abusing me with words and spit. There was nothing I could do so I took their abuse. I could see it for what it was and that it was false courage. Men get drunk and then they can take on the world. It was interesting how restrained they still were considering my disadvantage. The tales which preceded me must have painted a fearsome picture. Halfdan is a legend in this part of the world, and I am the man who took him down. There was a small amount of reverence which went with the hatred.

I was in the cage for a week and still Gunnstein had not returned. My body continued to ache all over as I was without true exercise or movement. During the day I had many visitors who wanted to inspect me. They would ask Life questions as they knew he could speak English. In this way I had some basic communication. I was able to confirm that I was the King of England and that our armies had defeated Halfdan, Knut and Eric. One of the visitors was my equivalent of a blacksmith and he was holding my sword, bow and quiver. Even though he is a Viking he is very likeable with his large pleading smile. He wanted to know the secret of how I made this superior metal. Questions kept being fired at me including about the shape, casts, heat and burning material. I felt bad that I was denying him this knowledge however my mistake with Strath Clyde was enough to scare me away from that same error of judgment. I apologized and said that it was not my knowledge to share. He confirmed that I was a blacksmith and I had to smile and admit that I was. I asked Life to tell him that I would tell him if I could. However, I am a prisoner to a Chieftain who is hostile to my people. It would be better to die then to betray England. The man nodded on hearing this. I could see understanding in his eyes as I had added that I would have loved to be able to share this knowledge.

The nights went on in a similar fashion to this with the drunkenness, fighting and dancing. All I ever seemed to do those days was wait for something to happen.

Chapter 16

Surprises

The communication system with Worchester was up and running and we were up to date on the war with the Normans. It seems that William has been consolidating his gains and would have taken Exeter if the Worchester guard had not arrived to repel the attack. The guard was also assisting Northampton against the Normans. The report is that the Normans are getting more desperate as winter approaches. Emrick seems to think that there must have been some promise made by King William to his lords. Our strength still lies with our archers and the English longbow.

Most of the English Council is now stuck in London tower with pigeons being our only communication with the outside world. I worry about the birds falling into enemy hands however for now they seem unaware of our little birds leaving the tower. We release them from the very top room so that if spotted and suspected of being for communication they should still be out of range of the Norman archers. We are all in agreement that we must last until winter without the loss of any more land. Worchester is doing a good job defensively and is also building their forces every week. We have seen many foreign ships arriving at the London docs almost daily. These ships are full of knights and their horses. This has turned into a major invasion force. Quietly I wondered if there were any men left in Normandy given the numbers I had seen arriving.

York is still holding out although it is thought they are desperate for some respite. Winter was going to be their savior.

Andras was alive and still fighting from Exeter. By all accounts he was doing his best however I doubted he would inspire the people. Andras is strong and steady, but he is not a risk taker and lacks impulse. This situation would be making him very uncomfortable. I longed for Godric as he would know how to handle the intelligence and the situation, we find ourselves in.

Godric always had plans and the people willingly followed him. Emrick has said that he is now remembered as Godric the Great in Worchester and a sculpture is being chiseled out of stone. I thought that it would be nice to see it one day if ever we got out of the tower. Our supplies are still plentiful however we are rationing to ensure that we can last months and even the year. My council consists of John, Hereweald and Wulfsige. All good men with close to a hundred and fifty years of experience between them.

A week after our first message from Worchester we were told of another pigeon arriving. As was custom we all met in the council room at the top of the tower to go over the message. The message this time was large as it covered over three pages, both sides. We were all intrigued as the pages were handed to me. I had first privilege to read the message as I am Queen and probably the strongest reader although John Archer is also accomplished.

The message said that survivors had arrived from up north, from the battle of Jarrow. My mind raced as I thought which battle of Jarrow. I could see the look on the men's faces as they must have had similar thoughts. 'Read on,' they insisted.

Swidhun and nineteen men from Godric's army have turned up at Worchester. Hereweald's hands went to his face and his eyes were instantly filled with tears. 'My son,' he exclaimed. 'My son is alive. This feels like the greatest day in my life. I thought that I had lost both of my boys but now god has given me one back. I wish I could have seen the look on Cynefri's face. I am sure it will be the happiest day in her life also.' I let Hereweald have his moment as I knew it was special. However, I really wanted to know more as if Swidhun was alive then maybe there was a chance that Godric had survived. They had come south by boat to Colchester and from Colchester they travelled across land to Worchester. They stayed on the north road to avoid any potential trouble.

They have news from the north and the news is that Godric and Tata had survived Jarrow. I was overwhelmed when I read this. Could this be true, my Godric was alive. Oh no, I have gone and married Andras. I broke down as I thought of the implications of what I had done. Tears were now escaping freely as I was so happy that Godric had survived and now felt filled with regret. John came over and comforted me but also insisted that we continue with the letter to find out if there is more news. John began reading as I comforted myself by wiping away my tears.

Godric was held prisoner in Edinburgh castle by King Oengus and Tata, Swidhun and the other survivors had been taken to work in an iron mine outside of Aberdeen. For two years they toiled in that quarry with the only rest being given when they were snowed in. Rain hail and shine they slaved producing Iron for the Pict's. Godric was on his way to rescue them when he was captured by the Vikings at Stonehaven. Godric has been taken over the sea to Norway. Friends of Godric had continued with the rescue plan and were able to free Tata, Swidhun and the others.

Outside of Arbroath they split their numbers and went their separate ways. Twenty or so went to Strath Clyde and their homeland. There were twenty who went south and fifty or so are building long boats to head across the sea to rescue Godric. It says that there were approximately twenty Vikings who were also prisoners in the quarry. It seems the Vikings are helping Tata and the others.

I could see all their faces were full of emotion. The man that they all loved and respected had managed to survive and somewhere in the world he was alive. God would find a way to return him to us. I knew it in my heart just as the three men who were with me knew it. Godric would return to England, to his England. We must think like Godric and prepare England for him, defend her cities and prepare her armies. England would rise again. We at least had to make sure there was an England to return to, especially now that it was not guaranteed. Men were arriving by their hundreds and thousands. Each of these men would have to be defeated and soon that may not be possible.

The rest of the letter was about Worchester and the guard although it seemed to be in code. The four of us knew what the letter meant when it said that the farm never stopped, and the cook is on her toes. We knew that meant the forges were all running flat out which means the mining is in demand for the iron, tin, silver and gold. The cook is on her toes means that the guard is increasing in size and is putting pressure on the cooks to feed them. The code was not prearranged however we all agreed that it was an important precaution. Worchester was doing what it did best and that was to build wealth and an army. They are never impulsive and play the long game better than anyone. The Normans are a major threat to our land, more than the Picts. Being from the north the Picts will always be limited with men and resources. From what we know the Normans could have an endless supply of both. Some of the land they have taken is the most productive in Britannia and certainly in England.

We discussed the letter well into the night. There was so much that we wanted to know such as how many friends we have in the north. Someone had obviously rescued Godric and then assisted Godric in the rescue of Swidhun and Tata. We all wanted to know where Godric was and would Tata be able to rescue him. It was uncertain to be sure as we had never heard of anyone coming back from over the sea that was not Viking. It was a trip that very few British had ever made, if any. In the south the channel is narrow but up in the north it is five times the width. I have seen maps which show the crossing, and it makes me weak thinking about it.

Hereweald suggested we may have a problem with Andras now that he has started calling himself King. Surely as we have heard the news of Godric, Andras will soon hear that he is still alive. If Godric was being remembered as Godric the Great, when they thought he was dead, you can only imagine the euphoria of the people on hearing that he was alive. They will have doubts and questions, but they will now have added moral and hope. Andras will feel threatened at best and at worst he could make some poor decisions to try and confirm his position. I did not agree with Hereweald's assessment of Andras and suggested he would not be foolish. Andras has always been calm and measured. Wulfsige, who also knew Andras well, suggested that the old Andras would not have gone around calling himself King. 'We all know what the Earl of Exeter is like and to me It sounds as though the Earl has got into Andras's head.' Wulfsige made a good point especially about Henry the Earl of Exeter. He is an arrogant man who was difficult to control. Even at risk of defeat he was always reluctant to leave his castle and city. Only with defeat by Halfdan had he ever ventured to Winchester to pay owed respects to my father. When handed back Exeter he did little in the way of thanks but took off at the first opportunity for home. When the Normans turned up, he did not come to help Winchester. We had ridden from Worcester and arrived in time, yet Andras was unable to get him to mobilize his army. Maybe he thought there was no point as Winchester should be able to handle it. When your queen asks for your support you should drop everything to obey.

Andras was now king. I guess he figured that the queen was as good as imprisoned, so the people needed someone to follow. A problem for Andras is that he was quite possibly imprisoned in Exeter if he continues listening to Henry. In my opinion the northern cities will be reluctant to follow Andras especially now that they know Godric is alive. Emrick and Powy's will be supporting the north holding a place for Godric. They have always been loyal friends and now that they are linked through the marriage of Hilda and Emrick the bond between England and Powy's could not be stronger.

Here in London, there had been a dozen concerted attempts to get over and through the castle walls. We are too well armed and have all the men and provision we require. The last attempt earlier in the day had been different. We could see that the Normans no longer cared if we survived or not and they cared little for the castle. The castle was bombed with boulders the size of a pony and some of the rocks catapulted into the castle were laced with burning oil. William was getting more aggressive and with his frustration we could see he was getting ruthless.

As a result of the recent raid, we had ordered that every water bucket be filled in case of fire. We are overcrowded so any fire could be devastating. At the first sign of attack the women and children must seek shelter in the tower. The tower was still a target however the tower sits in the middle of the castle and is a solid defensive building. The morning attack had killed over fifty English and caused major damage to some sections of the wall. John believes the only reason why they stopped was because they ran out of rocks or suitable projectiles. 'The catapults which they are hitting us with are more powerful than I have ever seen in Britannia', said John. He was right and this was a big problem for us. There was always the option of surrender although this would not bode well for us. Surrender should at least protect the people. Now that we know that Godric lives there is a chance we could prolong our death and give Godric a chance to push the Normans back. However, with winter on our doorstep it was unlikely we would see Godric until the middle of next year and even that was a slim chance. God would be watching out for Godric but seeing him back leading Worcester would be a miracle and a dream.

John suggested an alternative is for us to get a message to Emrick and Swidhun and ask them to send their full force to London to break us out and force the Normans back. John seems to think that Worchester could put ten thousand in the field with the aid of Powys. Hereweald was shaking his head while Wulfsige suggested John look out the window. William must have ten thousand outside the walls with the numbers growing every day. We are less than a day from Winchester and we can only guess how many men he has down there. We know he has been harassing Exeter and Northampton. Sending Worchester against William now would be risking everything in that one battle. They need winter to continue to build and practice. Winter will also be uncomfortable for William and his lords. They are away from home and their families, and this cannot be making them happy. Time and delay are our greatest friends although it could lead to our end.

    The only real alternative to surrender was to hold out for as long as we could. If the casualties from the attacks became too great, we would raise the white flag. Every day would at least buy our countryman time to prepare and bring the protection of winter closer.

Chapter 17

Death and Disaster

Work on the boats was going much slower than I had thought and hoped it would. There were just over fifty of us, so we needed two boats for comfort. Two would also give us security should something happen to one of the boats. There were many parts to a boat which I had not considered in the past. There were the oars, sails, shelters, ropes and you name it the boats needed it. Everyone had jobs to do however none of these jobs were easy. I was tasked with making sails so I sewed sheets together which I had acquired from the town. We were still stealing at every opportunity and doing our best to remain hidden.

    I was concerned as winter was getting closer. The nights were already cold and without the sun the days were also cool. Ivan had said that it was already too late to cross as the winter brought great risk with storms and rough seas. Eric told him that it could be done and had been done before. 'Everyone would prefer to travel during summer. Summer is when the warm gentle breeze blows you to sleep in the evening and wakes you in the morning. Summer is when every time you put a line in the water you pull out a fish. Yes, we would all prefer it to be summer however we must do what we must do. Godric is a great man and yes, we know what he did to our people, but would we have done anything different if we were in his position. I have labored with Tata, his brother, for two years and there is not a man alive who I would trust more. Tata speaks for the virtue of his brother, and I am in agreeance that the world needs men like him. I was destined to die in that quarry so any freedom I get is a blessing from the gods.' Ivan and Tata patted Eric on the back and told him that he was right and to not get so worked up. They told him we all wanted the same thing and with how hard everyone was working I believed him.

The day finally arrived, and the boats were ready for launch. We had paths cut and layered with logs of equal size. With the use of rope and plenty of muscle the boats were maneuvered down to the water. Surprisingly, each of the boats made the water without incident. I say this as this is the first time, I have ever seen such a major operation carried out. In my head I could picture so many things which could go wrong including the boats going over onto their sides. The men with their ropes were incredible and there were at least two on each rope.

It was midday and the boats were in the water and moored to the beach. Ivan spoke about the tide and wind direction however most of what he was saying was going over my head. Fortunately, Ramsay and Bran understood a little and assisted me with understanding that what they were saying was correct. We needed to wait until we had a westerly wind to take us away from land. The westerly would also smooth out the waves and give us the best chance of getting out safely. Making it through the break was apparently the most dangerous part of the voyage. At the other end we would put up in a Fjord which would be sheltered from most waves and wind. They said that we would wait until the right wind as the risk would be too great otherwise. It made sense when explained to me. I did not like the idea of heading out at night as they told us that we needed to be ready to leave at night if the conditions were right.

Everything looked calm to me when I compared it to some of the seas I had seen since we had arrived. I would follow the advice of those more experienced than I as I could see the wind was from the north, northeast. Every now and then the swell would lift and waves would crash the boats and the coastline. The sea was lolling me into a sense of security before it came alive and destroyed those who did not respect it. I would wait, as I needed to get across this sea to my Godric.

That night we celebrated the success of the boats. Building two Viking longboats from scratch was no small feat and it is one I am proud to have been a part of. If I was asked how it was done, I would have no idea where to start however I feel proud none the less. The boats have been provisioned and we are expecting to be away in the next day or two. This gives us a chance to indulge with some of our additional supplies such as the mead.

Being the only woman among fifty-four drunken men was not my smartest move although up until that night I had never felt threatened. Our camp was just up from the beach and on this night, we only had one fire going. On this night we were all sharing in the joy of our success. During the night it was evident that the Vikings were keen to return home and to stay home. This got me wondering about how we were going to return home however with the mead my mind quickly moved onto the next thought.

Ramsay and Bran were debating with two other men from the quarry about which was the best wood for arrows while I was in a deep conversation with Tata about his and Godric's homelife. Listening to Tata made me homesick as life on the farm in Worchester sounded so ideal. He was talking about his wife and child and the hope that they had waited for him. He would not blame her if she had remarried as he now knew that they had thought everyone had been killed at Jarrow. I could tell that this made him sad and although he was performing the duty of rescuing his brother his heart was pulling him south.

Everyone in Worchester seemed to support each other and work for the common good. Godric had been leader but not by his choice rather by the choice of the people. They have a council which welcomes newcomers, and the council elects its leaders and the leaders for the army. The motto seems to be continuous growth and by using this motto there are always jobs and people do not go hungry. It is up to the council to decide what area needs bolstering from agriculture, the forges, the buildings required right down to the social events. From Tata's account the council seemed to be getting this right. He said that it was from Worchester that England was formed, and stability was created in the country.

A bit later in the evening a lute was brought out and there was some singing and then the offer to dance. Ramsay took my hand and pulled me up to dance the jig with him. After Ramsay it was Bran and then Tata who was followed by Swidhun. Many of the other men were up and dancing and soon I felt like I had danced with all the men. The night was jolly, and the atmosphere was light. Unfortunately, this all changed when a group of men deflected me away from the main group. I could still hear the music and we were still dancing but the light from the fires was blocked by their bodies, and it had got a whole lot darker.

I was grabbed by one of the men who I knew as Ox. I thought he just wanted to close dance for a bit, maybe throw me around. I was shocked when his hand went straight up my skirt. I tried to slap him and push him away, but Ox was way too strong for me. With one arm still around me under my arms and another around my waist with his hand up my skirt he picked me up and hidden by the group of men we moved further into the darkness. I had been angry however I was now scared. I was worried that the others would not notice, or that they would not notice in time. His fingers were also hurting me as they dug into my flesh and privates. All my fears from childhood came back as when still a young girl I was nearly raped. On that occasion my brother Munro had come into the hay shed and seen what was happening. I had been in tears not knowing what to do however Munro, who was much older than me had pulled the man off and ran him through. All those fears which had been repressed most of my life started coming back to me. There were now five men egging Ox on as he pulled my pants down.

I heard Ramsay say to the men to let Kenner go so she could have a dance with him. One of the men told him to go and have another drink. 'Kenner is dancing with us for the time being.' I could hear the anger in Ramsay's voice as he tried to push his way past the men. One of the men had his hand over my mouth and Jaw so all I could do was shake and whimper. I attempted getting free, but the men were too strong from years in the quarry. I heard one of them say it had been years since he had had a woman. Looking around I could see this man had his pants down and he was preparing himself for me. My pants were off, and I was being held too tightly to move. I sensed that Ramsay now knew what was going on as I saw a couple of the men begin fighting and the sounds of shouts and grunts of anger. I could see what was going on and one of the men drew a blade and ran it through Ramsay from behind while he fought with two of the other men. I caught Ramsay's eye just before he dropped to the ground dead.

Ramsay had been one of my closest friends. His death made my fear even greater as I resigned myself to what was to come. Then came the booming sound of a voice with authority. The voice was like heaven and at first, I thought it was Godric. 'What's going on here,' he said with some authority. One of the men shouted for Rock Splitter to leave it alone and go back to the drink and fire.

Tata did not listen and pushed his way through the men. They jumped out of Tata's way apart from the two who were holding me down. However, this time he was not alone, and he also had Godric's strength. I saw him throw the men off with ease and then when someone tried to knife him in the back a friend was there to snap the man with the knife's arm. The men holding me were forced to let me go although my fear kept me from running. I pulled my pants up and curled my body up into a ball and cried. The fight grew as people picked sides. In amongst the fighting Bran came to me and picked me up like I was a sack of barley. Bran moved me away from the fight and over to the fire side. He was concerned for my welfare and held me tight and whispered that I was safe now and it would all be right.

The fight did not last that long as most of the men got involved once they saw what was going on. Slowly they started coming back to the fire, concern on most of the faces I saw. Tata was direct just like his brother. 'Were they trying to rape you Kenner?' I commenced crying again but was able to shake my head to confirm they were. The emotion in Tata's face did not change as he said right, and he turned and went back over to where the fight had been. It seems that this was enough for Tata to end the life of the remaining two men who were still alive. In all there were nine men killed which included the six who had attempted to rape me. I don't know when it was but at some time either that night or in the morning the bodies were thrown into the sea.

Ramsay, Thomson, and Anderson were the three who had died saving me. Ramsay was one of my closest friends and thinking about this brought me to tears. These men were given a Christian burial albeit without a priest. Others were injured in the melee however they would be fine to journey with us. Until they heal, they will be unable to row however we still have good numbers so it will not change our plans. This entire situation had shaken me up and I now relived the horror of this and the reminder from my childhood. There was little time for recovery as the following night the conditions were perfect. Ivan was saying that they cannot be better, and we must set to sea. The problem as I saw it was that it was early in the evening and dark. We had a waning moon and light cloud cover however setting off now in the dark scared me and I could see most of the non-Vikings felt the same way.

'The wind is a gentle westerly, and we must take it,' concurred Eric. 'Sometimes it can be weeks before the conditions are ideal and coming into winter it can be months.' I knew he was right however I had not realized how scared I had been about going out onto the sea and out of sight of the land. There was no choice however as I was one of the people pushing this voyage.

I could sense all the eyes looking at me, waiting on my decision. 'It is time we left, pack your things and get this journey started. We will have an even number of capable men on each boat, and we plan to keep the boats close throughout the voyage. We need to get out beyond the land while the conditions are what they are.' With that everyone was all action and within an hour the boats were being launched. There was a thrill but still trepidation.

All went well with the launch, and we were soon out beyond the waves. We knew the boats were well sealed as neither had leaked while being moored on the beach. Ivan stayed with us along with seven others of the Vikings. Eric led the other boat which had the remaining Vikings including Tata who decided it best he spread our leadership. We had Bran, Ivan and I in our boat and given the trouble we had the previous night it was a wise move to have an equal weighting across both boats.

Once out on the open sea it was surprisingly light even with only a half-moon. As time went by the wind dropped off and most of us took our turn at sleeping. While we rested, we made sure the boats were fastened together. Bran and Eric took watch over the boats and the sea, looking out for each of the boats. Although sleeping in an awkward position I had no problem falling asleep as I had hardly caught a wink the night before. With the attempted rape I was so shaken up and I know there were others who struggled as I did. I woke when the sun was already above the horizon. The wind had picked up, but the sea was still a gentle undulation. I said a little prayer that the sea would remain like this. Almost everyone was awake and eating some of the food we had packed. The boats must have been separated as they were no longer together.

After breakfast the rowing crews were organized and the slow slog across the sea commenced in earnest. It was at times like this that I was glad that I was a woman. I am not very fit and rowing for hours on end would be beyond me, I am sure. Everyone, except for the injured and me would have their turn at rowing. I almost think the men relished the opportunity to row to improve their fitness and strength. I was told we should be able to get across in six days but with favorable winds this could be as quick as three days. Given our westerly had died I suspected that this would not be considered favorable. Each boat had enough rowers however our boats were short on manpower with only twenty-three on each boat. I was told that Viking longships could have up to fifty rowers and the bigger boats could transport up to a hundred warriors on each.

I was happy that everything was working out better than I had dreaded. A sheet was erected across the bow of the boat giving me privacy to relieve myself. Everyone was treating me kindly and I think they all felt a little guilty from being related to the male species given what had happened on shore. There was no need as I felt completely safe and loved by most of the remaining men. They all knew I was the daughter of King Gregor, and they also knew that I was this fabled Godric's mistress.

Late on day three the swell on the sea was beginning to get heavy as our boats cut through the peaks of the waves. Many of the men began getting seasick as it felt like we were in a washing tub. My stomach was nauseous but for the time being I was holding its contents. The waves continued to steadily get worse as the afternoon wore on. On the horizon we could see a storm coming down from the north where the sky was black from the sea to the sky. Ivan was shouting some instructions to drop the sails and erect the weather sheets. The intent of the weather sheets was to give us some shelter and to try and keep most of the wash out of the boats.

The fear was on everyone's faces as our boats were thrown around by the power of the storm. Lightening lit up the sky however this only assisted in showing us the size and strength of the storm which was hitting us. Everyone hung on for dear life as the wind and waves tossed our boat around.

Our boat was hit by something extremely hard as the side of our boat dipped under water and was then thrown upright again by an opposing wave. It then dawned on me that only the other boat could have caused such an impact. Several of the men had been thrown overboard by the impact and they were now being helped back into the boat. A short while later I noticed Tata being helped into the boat. I now dreaded what had happened to the second boat and what was going to happen to us.

Tata made his way over to me and told me that the other boat had gone down. We would be fighting for our lives until this storm passed. I have never known fear as I felt then. I was hanging on for dear life as the boat continued to be thrown around. We were caught up in an angry sea which was doing its best to sink us. My only comfort was Tata who was also pinned in the bow of the boat. Both of us had a rope wrapped around a forearm which we were clinging onto to stay in the boat.

Still the storm raged on and still the boat did not go down. Some of the men were using pales to toss water from the boat. These were brave men as they looked to be in precarious situations trying to stand and work while our boat was thrown about. With time I noticed that my fear had also gone. I must have accepted my fate and when one does that the world around them seems to slow and things do not seem so bad. I watched as the men worked and I admired them for their bravery and strength.

The storm began to recede although the sky did not lighten up. Some stars began appearing and I remembered it had been coming into night. Eventually the storm left us alone and the clouds cleared. We had beaten it and all its fury. The storm did all it could to sink us, and we had resisted it. The men were all pitching in to remove the weather sheets and pale out the rest of the water. In the light of the waning moon and stars we could see the sea calm. There was no sign of the other boat, not even any wreckage. Tata had made it to our boat, and it seemed like Sven was the only other survivor from the second boat. Eric and the other twenty had gone down.

That night I believed we all rested well as the storm had taken a toll on us. I was exhausted even though I had only clung to the boat, praying for my life. Those that had fought to keep us afloat must have spent every ounce of their energy. I was emotionally spent as I had watched the horror which was the storm. I thanked God when I woke to find a beautiful morning sky with a gentle breeze and light swell. It was a cool morning however the fact that we were alive and could breathe the fresh air was a blessing.

We all prayed to our respective Gods and ate some sodden breakfast. Everything had been drenched however it could dry. Our lost boat and friends were gone forever. With Tata and Sven, we now have twenty-five on our boat. Originally, we had fifty-five on the rescue mission which is a formidable force when fully armed. We will need to be more careful now that we are down to less than half that. Making it to Bergen was still the priority and we prayed that there were no more storms.

Chapter 18

Friendships

Gunnstein had at last come home from campaign. I knew this as there was a flurry of activity around the room in preparation for his return. Blankets and rugs were getting dusted, cushions and pillows were being fluffed up, fuel for the fires was being topped up and the tents were opened to freshen the air. I had seen this all being done over the past week but not to the extent it was being done now. I was also listening to the conversations and the people were genuinely nervous of Gunnstein. The gist of what I was hearing is that Gunnstein is erratic and dangerous. They were more worried this time as too few of his boats had returned. There is a belief that he was defeated in this campaign so would be even worse than before.

Stern came into the room with two other men. The man in the middle is a head shorter than Stern but about the same age. I place them as being maybe ten years my senior. The third man was similar in statue to Stern and indeed me. He looks tough and if I had to guess he was one of the commanders while the man in the middle is Gunnstein.

All three were deep in conversation and were not aware of my presence. Gunnstein was telling Stern that Kaupang had the support of Harold and the Danes. It was a slaughter and they had to flea for their lives. Stern spat on the ground and cursed the Danes. Stern asked the other man, naming him as Sigurd, how many he thought there were. Sigurd told him there were thousands and continued by saying they were being pursued right up the coast. The muscles in Stern's neck tensed as he said how many and how far back. Gunnstein said they had seen a dozen boats so maybe twelve hundred at best. Stern said he must secure the defenses and call in all available farmers. With this Stern left the room and it was now just Gunnstein and Sigurd.

They were soon joined by some women who may have been their wives. The men took seats at the table to drink, and food was brought out for them. More men arrived and the room began to get rowdy again. The women pushed the conversation as they probed for details of the battle. I decided it was best to sit and face away from the table as I did not want them to think I was listening in. If they saw me listening they would know that I understood old Norse. Listening to the conversations was beneficial as I was finding out a lot about the Danes and Kaupang. Kaupang is where the Capital of Norway is situated, and the Danes are from Denmark which has its Capital at Roskilde. I had seen maps and studied the great campaigns of Alexander the Great, the Persians and the Romans. I knew that the world was much bigger than Britannia however it had never really dawned on me until that moment. I needed to learn all I could about this world as there might be something which will help me to secure England and help make it a powerful and forward-thinking nation.

At that point Gunnstein noticed the cage and must have seen me as he asked one of the women about me. 'He's the king of England. He has been here for two weeks.' This seemed to excite the king and the other men in the room as I heard them rise and I guessed to come over for a better look. Hearing them approach I stood to confront my captors.

Gunnstein noted that his luck must have changed. 'At last, my brother's killer can be brought to justice.' I could see the glint in his eye. 'Godric the King of England, my captive,' he laughed. He came to the cage and put his face between the rails, baring his teeth. It felt like he was almost daring me to strike and strike I could have although I did not want to reveal my strengths until I was desperate. The others who were gathered also began their abuse which started with verbal insults but soon progressed to being spat at and then one of them even pissed on me. They may not have realized that I was now used to this behavior as many of the children and others had been taunting me since my arrival.

Sigurd asked me if I understood his language. I did not change my look portraying that I could not follow what he had said. Gunnstein then shouted, 'Is there anyone who can speak Saxon?' One of the women said that Bjorn could speak Saxon. The king demanded that Bjorn be brought to the cage to interpret for him. While this exchange was going on the taunting continued. It turned out that Bjorn was my water boy whom I had started calling Life. It was reassuring they had called for Bjorn as Bjorn and I had developed an understanding which included looking out for our combined welfare. Bjorn was brought to the king who abruptly hammered him across the face. 'Kneel before your king you scum of the earth.' The knock across the face was enough to have Bjorn on his knees. 'Now tell this prisoner that he will be treated well if he tells us what we want to know. Tell him that he will be tortured and burnt alive if he fails to share with us his knowledge of Britannia. Confirm that he is going to die but let him know that his compliance will grant him a merciful death.' The king waited for half of the message to be translated however he soon lost interest and went back to the table and his drinking. Some final spit and taunts and the others left me alone and returned to the table.

It was a strange message as it demanded that I obey their demands, yet they did not wait around long enough to make any demands. The king seemed an impatient man to me, and I disliked the way he had hit and treated Bjorn. I decided that I did not like this King and made note that should I get the chance I would like to hurt him. It was also evident that the King wanted to celebrate and fornicate after his long campaign. From the sounds of it he did not deserve rewarding as he had lost many men and the campaign was a disaster. The king seemed oblivious to the hurt of his people and those who have lost loved ones. These were Halfdan's people and from my knowledge of Halfdan he would not have wasted his men on a useless campaign. I could not believe what I was witnessing considering that the enemy had been at their backs. Stern had not returned, and I guessed he was preparing for the defense. Stern was made of the same character as Halfdan, with a serious disposition and a strong sense of duty.

The attack came that night and I would guess it was around midnight. The king had already bedded his wife and mistress and rejoined the party to drink and boast about his prowess. He was a loathsome man, and I pitied his people. There were shouts from outside the tent and the sound of steel on steel. There was a palisade wall around the town however the attacking force seemed to have already breached this. Horns were being sounded everywhere so I guessed the attack was coming from all around the perimeter. There was chaos and pandemonium all around me as the king and his men jumped into action. They were all drunk and would be found to be wanting if they encounter anyone who knew what they were doing.

At least the women were more sober as they too went for their weapons. I was impressed by the physical strength of the women including their attitude and independence.

The fighting was going on all around our tent as I could hear the shouts and screams outside. I was trapped where I was, and I only hoped that the invaders thought to free me not knowing who I was. Suddenly men started falling through the walls of the tent and some of the material from one of the central poles ended up in one of the fires. Within seconds the throne room was going up in flames. Some of the invaders came through the door and went for some of the women who were still inside. The fighting was fierce however the women were no match for these Vikings as they quickly cut them down. Stern came through the door and met the advance of the attackers. The roof was now on fire and there were flames springing up all around. The heat was becoming unbearable the longer the fire went on. It was now time to use my strength to try and break this cage. Stern cut down the attackers using moves I was familiar with. Stern was used to the ways of Britannia, and it made sense that he had learnt some of our sword techniques. Stern looked at me as I pleaded in old Norse that he release me so that I could help. Hearing me speak his language stopped him momentarily before he was back out the door.

My skin felt like it was starting to burn as I found my fury and began smashing the cage around me. Side to side I kept hitting the cage hoping to splinter and break the upright timbers. My strength was having zero impact on the cage as the uprights had not splintered at all. The pins holding the cage broke and the cage went over onto its side. This still did not make any difference to the walls. I was impressed by how strong the cage was however this was a fleeting thought as I was burning up and beginning to panic thinking that I was going to die. The entire room was now on fire and many of the cushions and pillows around the floor were little islands of fire.

I felt like I was at the end when I notice Bjorn had arrived in the tent and he was carrying one of my swords. With the sharp edge he began cutting the fastenings which were holding the timbers together. It was hard to believe that this boy, maybe eighteen years old, twenty at most, had entered this inferno to attempt to break me out. I already thought highly of Bjorn, but he was now elevated to a status almost equal to family. If I survived this, I would see that he was looked after. Bjorn was struggling with the weight of the sword as he tried to work the strappings. The fire was closer and the heat even more intense. How could Bjorn stand the heat. His face was dripping sweat and his clothes and hair were already dripping as were mine.

From behind Bjorn, I saw Stern come back into the remains of the throne room. We were surrounded by fire and in the middle of an inferno engulfing all of Bergen. It was so intense that I could not see any of us surviving. Stern and I locked eyes and I pleaded with all my emotion for him to help to free me. For once this seemed to work. This was the first time I had been successful in my appeals to him, or at least it looked like it. Stern charged through the fire and within seconds he had shoved Bjorn to the side, picked up the sword and chopped away the strappings holding the door. I was on my side along with the cage. Once the strappings were away the door fell back to the ground and I was at last able to roll out of my cage. Stern freed my hands as I stood. Finally, I was able to feel what it was like to properly stretch.

There was no time to enjoy this feeling as my skin felt like it was about to catch fire. Stern threw me my sword and told us to follow him. There was no point pretending I did not understand old Norse now as this was my chance at freedom. Although out of condition from my captivity I now had a weapon, and I knew how to use it. My arms are very weak, and I struggled to hold my sword properly. I had no doubt my strength would come back if confronted with a life and death situation. I thought there was chaos inside the tent however outside was ten times worse. There was frantic fighting everywhere I looked and as we moved, we were stepping over many dead or dying bodies. Stern was heading away from the quay and out of the town. Everything got darker as we moved away from the fires. On the way we were confronted by a group of men who were ransacking the various living quarters. They attacked as soon as they saw us, and this gave me the opportunity to repay Stern for setting me free. Together we were able to cut them down. There had been five in their group, burly men who had underestimated us. I was surprised at how accomplished a swordsman Stern was. He danced his way through three of the attackers.

We reached the palisade wall and saw that the gates were open. Stern did not look back as he led us through and up a slope and deep into a forest. We were not the only people as there were others we passed who were also making their way up the hill. The people we passed did their best to hide and be silent. Those fleeing had no way of determining if we were friend or foe. I noted that they were mostly women and children.

As we walked, I asked Stern about the fight and whether he thought Gunnstein had a chance. Stern spat on the ground and said that there was no chance. The men were already exhausted from their campaign, and they were now drunk. We could not have been more vulnerable. Bergen was once the power of the north back when Halfdan first took control from his father. We could call on ten thousand men if required. Bergen were the king makers as only with our support could someone rule Norway. Everywhere we travelled in Norway we were greeted with open doors and given respect. This continued while Halfdan lived even though he was mostly in Britannia. Halfdan won many battles and expanded our lands. He never forgot his roots and continued to send wealth back to our town. The people worshiped Halfdan and his family. His brother Gunnstein was always jealous of Halfdan and was already ruling Bergen in the fashion of a tyrant. He was cruel to the people as the people had loved his brother so dearly. Gunnstein became worse and sort vengeance on those who had been most loyal to Halfdan once he heard about Halfdan's death. Kaupang had appointed a new king of Norway and Gunnstein and his ego took offence that he had not been asked to approve the new king. Gunnstein coveted the position of King and as Bergen had been the king makers, he thought he should also be King. The war with King Leif Erikson was the beginning of the end. Bergen is doomed and Gunnstein is already dead.

I could hear that Stern had no love of Gunnstein and was saddened by the outcome for his people. Stern said that he had continued raiding as he could not stand being idol and refused to follow Gunnstein and his men. Stern laughed when I told him I had called him Stern as he was always at the back of the boat. He told me that he liked that and could live with being called Stern however his real name is Sigvald. I would try to remember this as Stern was now stuck in my mind and it may be difficult to change.

We pushed on up the hill which seemed more like a mountain. We caught glimpses of Bergen burning at different stages as we made our way around the mountain path. Bjorn was walking quietly beside us and had not said a word since we had left Bergen. He then asked me to confirm that I could speak old Norse. I affirmed that I understood some old Norse and could speak a bit less than I could understand. I told Bjorn that I had not disclosed my understanding as I had hoped it would help me to find out what my fate was going to be.

Sigvald said that we are making for Kaupang to present ourselves to Leif Erikson. He told me that he was intending to offer Leif his service. Bjorn asked Sigvald if he was free and if there was any chance, he could go home. Sigvald seemed to consider this and after a few seconds he told Bjorn that he was now a free man. 'Going home will be possible if my service is accepted. Leif might just as well sacrifice me to the Gods. I am a commander from Bergen so there is a chance it could go either way. I had heard that he is a wise leader and from what I understood from the war with Bergen this seems correct. I am hopeful our arrival in Kaupang will be an opportunity for all of us to reach our destinies.' As he said this, he was looking directly at me.

I remained silent on the issue as I did not want to lay my plans out for review. I wanted to get home to rescue Tata or at least confirm that he was dead. I also needed to get back to England as I know they have lost large areas to the Picts. The opportunity to get one back on Gregor or Oengus is appealing. I also wanted to see Kenner again if only to apologize. She would be getting along with her pregnancy and our second child. Rick may also be concerned about my wellbeing, and I also missed his smile and bright eyes. I began thinking about Kenner and Aethelswith, Egbert, Godric Junior and Rick and how they would view each other. The relationships were complicated, and I do not think they would appreciate the situation as I knew it. Kenner knew I was married to Aethelswith however Aethelswith did not know that I had been in a relationship with Kenner. I would deal with the relationships when I got the chance but for now, I had to stay alive. My one regret from escaping Bergen was the loss of my sword and Bow. I still had one sword but would need to make a new bow when I got the chance.

Sigvald told us that we would rest on the crest of the ridge. He said that it would take a week to reach Kaupang so we would need to hunt and provide for ourselves along the way. Sigvald was also without a bow so I hoped that he had some secrets about how we would find food. A benefit of being a captive was that I was now used to only small meals. However, a big dear would be welcome.

Chapter 19

Despair

Our boat pushed on through the open sea. The rowers took it in turns and rowed for half hour sessions. I stayed in the bow and watched them row feeling guilty that I was unable to help. Everyone seemed to have forgotten the storm and had moved on with the business of achieving our goal.

We were heading to Bergen and should be only a day or two away. It seems our prayers for better weather were being answered as we had a westerly pushing us toward Norway and I hoped Bergen. Although I had seen a map of all the waters around Britannia there was vague detail of what was on the other side of the water. We knew about Ireland but very little about Norway. There was a chance that the storm had pushed us off course however Ivan kept saying the stars were right and we would land near Bergen. The plan was not to enter the Fjord at Bergen as we would be seen and would likely be captured. We would land outside the mouth and walk across the ridge where we would have a good view of the town. The walk would take the best part of a day however it could not be avoided unless we were to quietly sneak in under the cover of darkness. Ivan thought that the towers would be manned day and night to protect against such a move, so the first option was agreed.

I was still thankful for the miracle which took place when the second boat sunk. Everyone from that boat should have drowned however two men had managed to find our boat in the dark. Tata and Sven had found the edge of our boat in the largest waves I had ever seen. Tata and Sven had pulled themselves aboard in that sea while being tossed about like a pair of dice. If Tata had of died all the effort to rescue him would have been for naught. Tata was critical as part of my reconciliation with Godric. I could not face telling him that we had rescued him only to have him die in a storm.

The following day we sighted land which was a day earlier than expected. Maybe the storm had worked in our favor and pushed us closer to the land. One of the men with Ivan was from Bergen and knew the headland well. Bjorn had been on early raids when Halfdan first landed in Britannia. Bjorn would be in his late forties now but still as fit as anyone on the boat. Years of slavery in the quarry had not worn his muscles down. Bjorn was excited to be at last coming home and seeing his kin again. He told us as much however he did not need to mouth it as the expression on his face told us his feelings. Bjorn is bald with a great beard, a head shorter than Tata. With Tata back on board he had naturally taken over command. Ivan was his confidant with all matters regarding the sea and the voyage as I suspected that Tata had never been on such a boat as was the case for all of us from Britannia.

Ivan called for the rowers to stop and the sail to be dropped. I was wondering what was going on when I saw Ivan pointing to the horizon. Tata was staring out in the direction Ivan was pointing so I did the same. In the distance there were a dozen or so longboats following closely to the coast. The flotilla was heading south and were just dots on the horizon. Given the distance I hoped that they had not seen our sail. Ivan and Tata came up to the bow and Ivan said that we would lay low for the rest of the day. Once the boats are out of sight we will continue north. We cannot see any colors however it is not worth the risk being spotted as we will be treated as foreigners either way.

It was maybe two hours later that Ivan asked the rowers to prepare to start rowing again. The sail was left down just in case. We were told that we would make landfall just after dark which would suit our needs. Bjorn suggested we make our way a little up the Fjord so that the break water does not crash our boat. 'It is a long Fjord so it would be bad luck if we were spotted.'

The boat came in nicely to the shore and we were all able to step off and onto solid ground. I fell over as I lost my balance, and my legs were unsteady. Arms shot out to help me up and besides a little embarrassment I never thought such a simple thing as solid ground could give me such pleasure. The boat was pulled up the beach and lifted out of the water. Ivan suggested that we all have something to eat and get some rest. 'In the early morning we will set off up the ridge and make our way up the Fjord. If we make good time, we should be able to reach Bergen a few hours after sunrise. The going will be slow in the dark but we just need to follow the steps of those in front of us.' His advice sounded good, and I was ready to sleep.

A waning moon meant that although a clear sky there was little light reaching us through the canopy of the pines. Although there were a couple who still sported injuries, we were all capable of walking a solid pace. It was only a couple of hours, and the terrain was taking its toll on me. I was starting to struggle and had to ask that the walking rate be slowed a little. The response from Ivan was quick so I suspected that he was thinking the same thing or at least he knew others would be.

Light started breaking through the trees as we continued along a well-worn mountain track. The view down to the water and across the fjord was magnificent. The view made me homesick as it was not all that dissimilar to the locks back home. We stopped for a short break once the sun was above the mountain range to the east. I could feel the anticipation with the group regardless of their reason. What had started as a thought outside of Aberdeen had almost been accomplished. We had built and provisioned two boats and now, although only one made it, we have crossed the sea and are about to be looking down on our destination. I prayed that Godric was still alive while others were looking forward to seeing their kin and home. Despite the trials of our journey the mood was lighthearted and required Tata to remind us to be on our toes. 'Remember you are in enemy territory and too much noise or any other false move could see our deaths. Bjorn this is no reference against you or your people.'

I knew we were getting closer as I could smell and then see the smoke. I was missing home even more, the home cooked meals and the long winters in-front of the fire. Those thoughts were tarnished due to the betrayal by my father and brother although I still longed for that simpler period of my life. We were stopped when Ivan came out into a clearing and we could all see Bergen. Ivan had dropped to the ground and crept forward to the edge. Tata followed and I pushed forward to make sure I could see what they were looking at.

Bergen was a ruin, this much was evident immediately. The walls and the buildings were either levelled or still on fire. I could see that Bergen was a large town which wound around the base of the mountain on the plains before the water of the fjord. Those ships which we saw must have just sacked the town and raised it to the ground. Tata looked at me and said that Godric will be fine, he is tough, and this could work in his favor. I told them that there was no point in delaying now as we needed to get down there to see if anyone needed our help. Tata and Ivan agreed, and we went back to tell the others what we had seen. Bjorn was in obvious distress as this was his hometown. He was as eager as us all to help if possible however it was a good hour before we reached Bergen due to the length and steepness of the trail.

For all of us the sight before us was a nightmare but especially for those from Bergen. There were bodies everywhere and piles of smoldering structures. As we made our way over the town, I noticed that there was very little which could be salvaged. I was looking for Godric as I know Tata and Bran were. There were crows and eagles in amongst the bodies already working and fighting over their favorite bits. There was a distinct shortage of woman or children although they were part of the carnage. Many of them must have been either captured or fled to the hills.

Bran came over holding one of Godric's swords. We knew it was his as he has spurs which come out on either side of the blade. These are just as sharp as the central blade and enable him to chop his opponents with force. Godric is the only person known to use such a blade. Tata being a blacksmith knew the blade and how it was made. Bran said that he could only find the one although it looked like there were the ruined remains of what was most likely his bow and quiver. I was guttered as what this really meant was that Godric was likely dead. We continued searching through the ruins as I did not want to give up and accept that Godric was gone. Others helped however there were too many completely charcoaled bodies to be able to identify if one of them was his or not. The rest of the day was spent in this fashion and the odd survivor was able to be found although most needed to have their life ended due to the extent of their burns. It was horrible and sobering work going through the bodies of the deceased.

We made camp deliberately outside of the eastern walls as a sign of respect. The eastern walls were the least damaged. We would need to give the bodies some sort of burial or ending. Many of the bodies had been piled up in the center of Bergen so that we could burn them. The Vikings wanted to give them the ceremonial burial so that they could go to Valhalla however

I was thinking more practically that we needed to dispose of the bodies so that the vermin and larger predators did not get a taste for human flesh. The fire was built and started at the same time as the sun went down beyond the horizon. There was tons of material to burn which enabled us to create the largest bon fire I had ever seen. I carefully inspected all the bodies and could not confirm any of them were Godric. This does not mean that he was not one of them as many were unidentifiable.

All was quiet in our camp that night. Oh, my Godric, have we come all this way only to find we were too late. If only we did not need to build those boats, or we avoided the storm. I cried quietly too myself aware how quiet everyone else was. I did not wish to draw attention to my misery. Tata was fondling Godric's sword, turning it over in his hands. I was wondering what was going through his mind. I wanted space and I guessed Tata was the same. I did not wish to break his thoughts so sank back into my own miserable thoughts.

Even though I was mentally disturbed I still had no trouble sleeping. Tata offered to keep first watch to make sure we were aware of any ambush and Bran said that he was happy to be on the second watch. Bjorn said that there would be many who would be in the forest and hopefully they would make their way back to town over the coming days. We had an additional dozen badly injured men who we were now caring for. Some were badly burnt, and I did not think would survive but they had done well to get this far so time would tell.

Many people started returning to the ruins the following day. Mostly women and children with the occasional old man. They avoided us at first but soon came to accept our presence. We entered the ruins and continued our search for bodies. The pyre from the previous night had all but burnt down. There would need to be another pyre with the new bodies we were uncovering. Still there was no obvious body which was Godric's. The Viking's from our boat started conversing with the townspeople and soon we were working together to clean up the town and stack the bodies for burning.

That evening Tata suggested we stay and help the people to rebuild. He said that we should start with the walls. We had the eleven Vikings from our voyage concur with this sentiment. The others including Bran and I wanted to move on or get home. I have been away from my boy for too long and I must now be six months pregnant. It already felt as though winter had set in at Bergen. The icy wind felt like it was only days from bringing snow. Tata wouldn't hear our objections and insisted that it was too late in the season to be attempting to cross back to Britannia. Ivan agreed saying it would be a suicide mission. He also said that the Vikings would not be returning before winter so we would struggle to find a crew. The following season would be different and there will be boats heading over to continue raiding.

Tata then spoke about the value of service and how it was good for one's soul. 'The benefit we will get from rebuilding Bergen will far outweigh the cost. It will build us physically and spiritually. We will get the opportunity to experience a new way of life and to learn a new language. There will be the understanding of the hardships these people experience and what motivates them to raid Britannia. It will also provide our sanctuary for winter as without this community we would likely perish over the long dark winter.' I knew he spoke sense and it would mean that my baby would be born here. We have the only able-bodied men in Bergen, so the locals needed our support. I could not speak old Norse however I knew I would need to learn. I will need these women to help me with my delivery and to care for my baby once it came.

I agreed with Tata telling those from Strath Clyde and the Pict lands that our best hope was to fix the walls and start rebuilding some accommodation. We will need to gather the boats which have not been destroyed as these will be needed to net fish. Food stores for winter were now critical along with the building. Tata is wise and we should see this as an opportunity. God has presented this opportunity to us, so we need to take it and be grateful. I looked around and there were many people nodding in agreement. They had now had time to consider our situation and it made sense to stay. The hard work would only make us stronger.

Bjorn introduced us to some of the local women who were part of the leading women's circle in the community. Helga was Gunnstein's ex-wife as he had been killed and burnt in the razing of Bergen. Elgar is their daughter and about the same age as Tata, maybe early twenties. It appears that her husband and child were also killed on that night. There was much hardship however these people seemed to have moved on. It made sense as survival was the number one instinct, and these people would now have a challenge if they were to survive the winter and possible future raids from rivals. Within days we were all working together and although we did not understand them those of us from Britannia worked hard to learn the language and rebuild Bergen.

There was a lot of rebuilding to do, and the conditions began getting worse almost immediately. There were twenty-four of us from the boat and within a week over fifteen hundred women, children, elderly and crippled had returned. It was obvious that this had been a major settlement when at the height of its powers. From the stories the decline started when Halfdan left with the better men. His brother led the decline and put the icing on the cake when he decided to attack the king of Norway. The female leaders accepted me into their group, and they seemed to be very aware of what was happening and who was to blame. Fear and misplaced loyalty were near the top as Gunnstein was left unchallenged. Sigurd and his bullies were so feared that nobody wanted to cross them. Sigvald may have, however he was always away raiding. This was simple escapism rather than dealing with the problem. In the early days some had tried standing up to Gunnstein, however they were burnt alive as an example.

Helga was relieved that her husband was dead. It seems that the fires also killed two of his mistresses which made things even better. I found her to be a warm and loving person and thought how horrible it would have been for her living under the hand of Gunnstein. We soon became close friends and worked together rebuilding the inside of the main accommodation. Rugs and blankets were in high demand given the changing season. Winter is on our doorsteps, and we will need decent shelter and clothing for Winter.

Ivan confirmed that over five hundred bodies had been burnt on pyres. Most of them were from Bergen however up to twenty percent could have been from the attacking force of King Leif Erikson. There was no sign of Godric however we had to assume that he was among those dead. Up to half of the bodies were too burnt to identify, and Vikings are large people so we could not identify the bodies by size alone. In another life Godric would have fitted in nicely as a Viking, sort of like Tata was now. I had hoped Godric may return with those who had fled. This last hope had now dwindled, and I was resigned to losing Godric after all of this. My unborn child was my new priority. The child will be my reminder of Godric and what I have lost.

Chapter 20

Resignation and Defiance

Nothing was getting better for us as the bombardments increased and more and more of our people were getting killed. Pressure was mounting on me to concede to William and give up the castle at London. We had no intelligence on what would become of us if we surrendered. If the situation was reversed, we would imprison the leaders and maybe even allow them to go back to their country. We would be dangerous to keep alive and I know this. I could try and hide as a peasant woman, but they must know that I am here as they followed us all the way from Winchester.

I was heading up for another council meeting as news had arrived from our usual source, the pigeons. I was surprised that there were still pigeons remaining from the other cities as nearly all our pigeons from Worchester had been sent. It was late as I had been praying in the chapel. God was my main hope now. I prayed that God was watching Godric and that he could be returned to us. My thoughts are a betrayal to Andras however since learning that he was alive somewhere in the world I longed for the simpler time with Godric out on the farm. I also knew Godric viewed things differently than other men and only he could get us out of this mess. My prayers gave me hope however since learning he was captured by the Vikings hope is all I have left. Godric was most likely tortured and dead or rotting in some dungeon in a city far away. I hoped that Godric prayed and knew that he was not alone. He is still in the thoughts of his people and me.

Coming into the room at the top of the stairs I was met by the usual suspects. First there was Wulfsige our once fearless and powerful leader of the Winchester guard before he was promoted to Earl of London. Second is Hereweald, commander of the Wessex army and now commander of the English forces along with last but not least John Archer, commander of Worchester's forces and now joint commander of the English forces.

Unfortunately, these decorated men are trapped like I am in the castle of London. Hereweald greeted me as I arrived in the room and the other men stood until I was seated at the table. The letters were passed to me so that I could get the first opportunity to read their contents. The men did not need to keep up this custom however they seemed happy to stick with it.

The first letter was from Emrick, and it discussed the progress at Worchester with regards to stores and preparations for winter. Everything with Emrick was in code although we knew what was intended from the messages. Prince Causantin of Pictland had withdrawn his forces from the siege at York under harassment from Worchester. The plan had worked, and it seemed the length of the campaign had worked in our favor. Provisions have been sent to York and all required supplies have been topped up. The guard has been switched out giving the men who had suffered many months of siege a chance to return to their families. The news from Emrick in this first letter all seemed to be favorable.

Emrick was a good steady commander much as John and Godric were before. Powys and Worchester have a lot in common including their ability to take good, calculated risks. His second letter had some more disturbing news although it was full of possibilities.

Andras was offered a truce by William if we surrendered London. England could still exist in the lands which were mostly Mercia with Exeter and the southwest included. The Normans would get hereditary title over the lands which were predominantly Wessex but included London and the eastern coast up to Colchester. It was disturbing that Andras had been in a parley with the Norman king. Andras is a good man however he should not be signing agreements without the high councils say and my approval. If he was negotiating the surrender of London and our borders, then what else was he negotiating. We were really isolated and although we have contact with Worchester events are spiraling out of our control and have been for two years now. Winter should bring some respite and give us time to see which way events fall. The Normans may face trouble at home and be forced to retreat home however judging by the numbers landing at London this force is here to stay.

After I had browsed the letters, John Archer read them aloud. There were some deep breaths from around the table. Apologizing to me before he spoke, Hereweald then said that he had liked Andras as a second however he had never fully trusted him. 'Their negotiations are ill news for us as it leaves us in the dark and without any say. In his capacity as a free leader of England he is making the negotiations. King William will be seeing and treating Andras as king of England as he is married to you.'

It was my turn to speak. 'King William has given us an opportunity to free our people from this siege and to keep some semblance of our country. With this treaty we have time to see if Godric can be rescued. With this treaty we can rebuild our army including our defenses. We will lose some of our most fertile lands and better ports, but we will live to fight another day.' I went on to say that I don't think Godric would be signing a treaty with the Normans unless it was a last resort. A negotiation by us to free the people of London is one thing however we would not be negotiating Worchester and its allies to stop fighting. It will take a determined force to take Worchester especially now that they have had some time to build their guard. Northampton was also building and along with Powys they have the strength to resist this invasion, or so I hoped. As I was speaking I was looking around at the eyes of my trusted council. My council of wise brave men who had been with me through the whole process which was the forming of England. England, the dream of Godric, for a united and secure land. Look at us now, a newly fragmented land with mistrust and no security for its people. It seemed that the fifteen years of fighting had been for nothing.

Wulfsige thumped the table and said that any treaty or surrender must come from us. 'Andras must know that we survive and are in contract with Worchester. What is Andras up to I wonder? If Andras knows we have communication, then King William will also know. The Normans could be trying to trick us into surrendering as they may not realize how close they are to getting through our walls. This knowledge could be a positive and an act of desperation from William. Therefore, his offer of treaty might be genuine, at least until the end of winter.'

We all agreed that Worchester should not agree to this treaty. Regardless of what happens to us England and its ideals should live on. A return letter was written to Emrick which told them to act independently of Exeter depending on the actions of Earl Henry or Andras. Be cautious of their decisions and actions as they are in negotiations with King William. Time is a friend is what Godric used to say and it would be again. The letter also included our predicament and that we were thinking of surrendering London to save the people. We thought that if we surrendered those in the council would be executed. This may be unavoidable, and no decision should be made to rescue us. This could be a trick and we may end up dead anyway. Everything was written in code as now there seemed little doubt William and his Lords will know about our Pigeon communication system.

After composing the return letter, we had a drink and ate a light meal. There were so many considerations. John suggested we needed another ally however the Picts have shown themselves to be hostile. Could any of the other countries in Wales be convinced to fight for us? 'We should add a letter to Emrick to get intelligence on Deheubarth who had always been neutral. The only blight on our relationship was your abduction from the convent although an entire country can hardly be blamed for that. Other countries should also be considered including the traditional enemies of Powys. There have been many battles over the years with Brycheiniog and Morganniog however these were with Powys and these countries may wish an alliance with England. We should emphasize that no alliance would jeopardize or replace that between Powys and England.' Once again, I thought Johns words to be wise and a second letter was added to the first. It was getting late, and I did not think we would achieve anything further that evening. With regards Andras and the negotiations with King William they would be aware that we have received the message. They will be watching to see what our next move is. If there is no visible change, I expect they will request an opportunity to parley. Winter will be a miserable time for their men due to the weather and with them being so far from home. To at last claim London will be a great victory for King William and he will be able to return home with glory.

Bombardments of our walls continued for the following week as snow and sleet sheeted the countryside. Direct attacks on the walls and gate were repelled easily however the catapults were starting to break through the ramparts in large sections of the walls. Along these sections we could no longer traverse so these exposure sites were protected by archers. The piles of rubble also made it difficult for the attackers due to how unstable the rubble is. Deaths were few as most of the people were staying inside the tower and out of the weather. Our guard were doing a wonderful job of defending the walls and the castle.

My steward came with a message that there was a delegation outside of the gates under the flag of a truce. I was looking out a window and there was a light drizzle. This would be considered good weather if compared with the past week, so it seems they are taking their opportunity. 'Dexter please pass on this message to the rest of the council. Request that they meet me in the gate house with twenty from the elite guard. Prepare the hall in the gate house with table and chairs and send a message that we accept their truce and offer them the shelter of the gate house to discuss matters.'

I prepared myself for the negotiations, which is what I hoped they were. For months we have been discussing this situation. It was much better if they instigated the parley then if it was coming from us. If we were seen to be wanting a parley, then they could assume we were ready to surrender. I armed myself with my short sword and my concealed daggers and most importantly my raincoat. John, Hereweald and Wulfsige were already at the gatehouse when I arrived. I could see from the looks on their faces that they felt the nerves and tension which I also felt. The moment we had been waiting for had arrived. I wondered if there would be any concessions and how we would end this day. I could be dead or in a dungeon, but such was the sacrifice of a leader. Whether our people be allowed out and given freedom was my main concern.

Dexter came in and said that the delegation refused to come into the castle to parley. We understood this precaution however we had thought that the opportunity to get a look inside might have been enough to get them inside. We would now need to expose ourselves by leaving the security of our walls. Hereweald said that he and John would go to the parley session. However, I refused to accept his offer. 'John and I will go with an elite guard. Should we be captured or killed we all know what that means. There is to be no negotiation to get us back. The war continues and we will stick with the current plan and wait for news from Worchester.' John agreed and grabbed his coat from the coat rack. I could see that he was carrying his longsword and two other short swords. It was good to see that John was also willing to go down fighting.

We left the castle with our escort and crossed the cobbled zone between the castle and the coach house. The distance from the castle to the nearest buildings was approximately one hundred yards. The castle sits in the middle of London town on the north bank of the Themes River. The closest building is a coach house where people could rest after a long journey and find a coach to wherever they wanted to go onto. Given the existing circumstances the coach house is not being used for that purpose.

It was refreshing to be outside the walls again after being trapped for so long. I could see the Norman knights surrounding the castle with their catapults and battering rams. There were banners flying from all their camps which filled every inch outside of the hundred-yard dead zone. The reason for the one-hundred-yard gap is the accurate distance of our longbow. We can shoot much further but without the same accuracy. Being surrounded and unable to get fresh supplies we are not going to waste arrows unless the shot is a certainty. Consequently, the Normans have been free to set up just outside a stone throw from our walls. As we made our way to the coach house the knights, who were camped in front of this building, moved back out of the way. We could have been taken down easily however they were not certain they had me, and they were the ones who wanted the truce. A few of the knights even bowed as I walked past them, their respect gave me great hope.

We were met at the gate house by King Williams steward who introduced himself as Lugos. He invited us in and offered us a drink. John and I accepted as again we were there's anyway so there would be no requirement to poison us if they wanted us dead. Escape would be impossible should we need it. Realizing this I felt regret that I had brought twenty men from the elite guard. Maybe this would be an honorable truce and we would get a chance to consider their offer. I had been wondering what King William was like and was hoping he would be at this parley. It is good to put a face to a name so that I can gauge their character. We waited in the coach house for on an hour before our hosts arrived. I only had the one drink as I wanted to keep my mental capacity for the negotiations.

Four heavily armed guards entered the room which made John and I abruptly stand in preparation for whatever was to come. John had his hand on the hilt of his sword although again this would prove useless if it was required. A heavy-set man strode into the room who would have been a similar age to John. He has an uncut reddish white beard and from the descriptions I had of William I was sure this was him. He came over and bowed to me holding out his hand in welcome. While holding his hand I told him I was eager for him and his army to leave my lands. Fortunately, his steward Lugos could interpret for us although I am not sure all was passed onto William as he seemed to ignore my comment. We were introduced to Bryce who is the commander of his forces in London. King William pointed to our chairs and asked that we be seated. I could see his keen eyes darting between John and me. I expect he was determining where the power was and who to focus his attention on.

To avoid all doubt, I told him that I am the daughter of Alfred the Great and Queen of England. I continued with my initiative and demanded to know what his intentions were from his invasion of my country. All eyes were now on me which is as it should have been. 'These are not your lands and yet you have brought your army here uninvited. War only brings suffering to the people and as leaders it is our responsibility to give them peace, security and opportunity.' The Normans listened as I spoke however, they did not have to listen for long as I had no intention of rabbiting on.

Everyone waited while what I said was interpreted. King William then spoke and after each sentence Lugos relayed what had been said. 'I am King of all Normandy, King of the Normans and will be king of England. We have been spying on your land for years. Your waters are full of fish and your fields are fertile. I believe you are wrong about the responsibilities of a King or leader. The people are here to create wealth and power for their king. The king will give them opportunities. What the people make of these opportunities is up to them. The king owes nothing to his people. England is wealthy and was ripe for the picking once the Vikings were removed. My grandfather was the famous Viking Rollo, who became King of Normandy. Rollo taught me to never stay in one place for too long. Expand your lands and keep your enemies guessing. London castle is a tough nut to crack so we have come to see if an arrangement can be made.' King William then took a drink and invited us to do the same.

King William told us that he had thirty thousand men and had intended to take all of Britannia for the Normans. He said that he wanted to finish what the Romans never did. King William was going to subdue the Picts and beat a submission out of the Welsh. Britannia would be one country under Norman rule. When given a chance to speak I noted that he had not got very far in his conquest, and he would find the north cities much more powerful than he had supposed. 'The Vikings did not just simply leave Britannia. The Vikings were kicked out or at least the remains of them were.

Most of them are buried on Britannia soil. You have thirty thousand men and these plans of conquest and yet you are here negotiating with us. What is it that you now want, besides everything?'

There were angry and frustrated looks coming our way once what I had said was interpreted. King William drank down the tankard and demanded another. He was annoyed but should have expected nothing else when addressing the Queen of England. He continued once he had a new drink in front of him. 'King Andras has conceded London to the Normans, and we expect you and your garrison to put down your weapons and open your gate. The agreement with Andras was to let everyone inside the tower flee. A treaty will be signed with England and hereditary title for all lands south of the Themes between London and Bath will be part of Normandy. England shall have the lands north to York and anything north of York or west of Worchester is free game for the Normans. We intend to bring peace to the land but concede that rather than fill your soil with the lives of our men we would have this treaty.' William said that this had been negotiated with Earl Henry and King Andras. Andras and Henry would abandon Exeter and their people were welcome to stay or relocate. He said that he wished they would stay as he needed them to build his new kingdom.

We needed to know if there were other limitations to the treaty. I asked him whether we would be able to take land back from the Picts and he agreed that this was the case. 'Pictland shall be for whoever gets it first. We will not ally ourselves with the English as one day England will fall however in our pursuit of the large northern regions, we concede that we will be assisting each other to achieve what each other wants. We have the boats so will likely take the north and work south while you can attack by land, as is your only choice.'

John then asked about trade and whether there would be free trade between the regions. When told that there would be, he followed up with land rights of the existing farmers and whether they would be respected. Again, William conceded that the existing rights would be respected where title can be proven. He said that he expected many of the Lords and knights who came on campaign would be granted lands and title and would bring their families over. I looked over at John to see if he had finished and he nodded to me.

'King William, we will need to go back and discuss your terms with our council. Are you open to a counteroffer?' The King nodded and said he was open to ideas and was interested to hear what we proposed. I had to think quickly as although we had discussed different options some of them had been made obsolete from what we had already discussed. 'You and your men leave London and London remains part of England. You can have the southern shore of the Themes, through to Bridgewater on the Parrett River. Everything north of this line will remain with England and we will be open to free trade with the Normans. Powys is allied with England and if attacked the war will recommence. The other Welsh lands are not ours to negotiate.'

There was some laughter from William as he looked at Bryce. 'Please take our offer and consider it wisely. We do not accept your offer as we have put too much into the London campaign to walk away now.' Please remember you are not able to negotiate being trapped like a rat in a cage.

Ignoring the taunt from the King I sent through another query. 'If you will not walk from London will you leave us with Exeter? Everything East and including Winchester will be yours, through to London and Colchester. We will cease our campaigns against you.' William and Bryce laughed again as they rose from the table. They told us we have a week to consider their offer. If they have not given us your answer by then the war will go on until the English are defeated in every corner of Britannia. They both turned and left the room leaving John and I there with Lugos their interpreter. He looked at us both with a pleasant smile and offered us another drink before we left. I considered the offer as I felt like a stiff drink but in the end, I declined, and we rose and went back to the castle.

Back inside the castle we were met by Wulfsige and Hereweald. They took a sigh of relief when they saw us, as they knew we were safe. I suggested we head to the council room as there were many things which needed discussion. On the way up the tower we filled them in on how the meeting had gone. We left out the details for the coming discussion but told them how the meeting was conducted including how we were made to wait for an hour. I was a little lightheaded marching up the stairs and I had only had two mugs of mead. I believe the tension and stress of the occasion was also taking its toll. It was with some relief that we reached the council meeting room, and I was able to take a seat. I asked my steward for some water and fruit to be brought for us all.

John and I filled in the other two on the details we could remember from our parley session. King William has given us a week to agree or decline his offer. Hereweald noted that it was strange that we had a week when surely a day would have been enough. It sounds as though they are trying to keep us pinned down for another week but for what purpose. I had to admit that they did not seem too interested in either of the options we gave them. Either take it or leave it was as good as what King William said and he did not seem to care either way. John agreed as he was happy to agree to our farmers maintaining title on their land and open borders for trade.

London is holding the Normans up and as soon as we fall Northampton will be next. Northampton castle is formidable however it will be more difficult to hold then London. Do we really think the Normans will keep to the treaty? Accepting the treaty will give up all the river land towns between Exeter and Bristol. We need to get these parley details to Emrick. With this information we may be able to get the Welsh countries to ally with us. I asked Dexter for pen and paper as we needed to get this message off before dark. Now that winter had set in night was on us earlier and earlier every day.

We needed to guess what the Normans were planning. How could delaying us help them as if we surrendered, they would have us anyway. They could have conceded Exeter and the west counties if simply to get us out of the castle as they could not be held to any treaty while they were so strong. They were up to something, and it worried me that we did not know what it was. Signing the treaty could well be the death warrant for England and yet waiting out the week, like it seemed William wanted, could also be setting us up for something. Hereweald suggested that it could be a piece of machinery which they could use to get through the walls. If they knew how close they were to breaching our walls they would be emboldened. A piece of machinery such as a new form of catapult with a greater range and strength could see us opened like the belly of a lamb.

All four of us agreed to consider the problem over the week. We finished with the updated message for Emrick and closed the meeting. I was exhausted and decided to go to my room and sleep. I felt like I could sleep for days. I was very worried about King William as he is a man in total control. What I saw outside our walls also scared me as the knights and their Lords looked so well disciplined. Their armor, weapons and banners were all so clean. Their horses were also well decorated and looked strong and clean.

Chapter 21

The King of Norway

We had walked through some of the most breathtaking scenery I have ever seen. Sigvald, Bjorn and I followed the mountain track which was like a highway between the north and the south of this land. The ground was covered by snow and in places it was up to our thighs. Every day there was a hut which gave us shelter from the weather. At each hut we needed to dig out the doors to gain access. Travel on the track had stopped due to winter which meant we travelled in silence and unhindered.

Hunting was difficult and a day into our journey we were getting hungry. The weather had made animals scarce and none of us had a bow. Late on the second day we found a freshly killed dear. Most of the meet was gone, devoured by what looks to have been a pack of wolves who were also likely responsible for the kill. This was my opportunity as there was still intact sinew which I could use for a bow. Working carefully, I was able to remove the sinew from the front leg tendons. There were yew trees around the trail so that night when we reached the hut, I went to work to find a suitable selection of wood for the bow and some arrows. I took additional sinew which I could use to fasten the tips on my arrows. It was practically dark by the time I found the hut and I was lucky I did not get lost as the hut was hidden by many trees and well disguised in the fading light. Inside I worked to the fire light. The warmth had hit me as I entered the hut. I was grateful that Sigvald is competent in the wild and overall, a courteous companion. Within hours I had my bow, and half a dozen arrows. I used the iron from a dagger which I had picked up while leaving Bergen. Using the sharp edge of my sword I was able to separate wedges of metal from the blade. I heated these in the fire and in a crude way I used rocks to shape the heated metal. When completed I had a bow which was probably superior to most I had seen in Bergen. Without the use of familiar tools, I felt proud that I had been able to build this bow. Bjorn and Sigvald also looked pleased with what I had been able to build. I would test it in the morning and then the following night I would work on additional arrows and a quiver to carry them.

The following morning my bow was able to bring down an elk which I quickly skinned for what we needed. Sigvald helped me with the animal, and we ate well that morning. Using the sinew and completed tips from the dagger I was able to complete a further five arrows. I used the skin to create a bagged quiver which would hold the arrows. It felt great to be paying back Sigvald for setting me free. I would have felt uncomfortable relying on Sigvald for the entire journey.

Our time together forced Bjorn to open up to us. Bjorn is twenty which is on the older side of what either Sigvald or I thought. He is small with a slight build, maybe five-foot tall if lucky. Bjorn had a Pict mother and a Viking father. His father raided every summer but instead of returning to Norway he would spend the winter with his mother in Aberdeen. Bjorn learnt many of the customs and language from his father as had his mother. One day his father did not return and a raiding party, the same one which captured me had gone through Aberdeen and taken the opportunity to grab some slaves. Bjorn does not know what had become of his mother. He had had two younger siblings however both had died in their early years from childhood disease. Bjorn longed to get home to Pictland however he was thrilled by the adventure he was on. Bjorn is much like a younger brother and although unlike Tata in appearance or physically, he has a similar desire to learn and a healthy respect for authority. It is pleasant to have Bjorn for company much as Tata or any of my sisters are good company.

All communication during our journey was in old Norse which is assisting my ear to pick up the language and has also greatly improved my conversation. The physical activity including the hiking, hunting, and preparing meals and accommodation had been good for my soul and I felt as well as I did when out hunting with Kenner while at Arrochar.

Coming down from the heights of the ridge we can see out to the horizon. The sea is stretched out before us preventing any further travel south. I could not see Kaupang however that was not surprising as the steep ridges of the fjords were still blocking our view up and down the coast. The journey had taken us ten days instead of seven mostly due to the snow and wintery conditions. After the first two days we had eaten well and really had things go our way. The roads were empty so there was always game for me to hunt. I was not sure what Sigvald's plan was however he said he would present to the King and ask for forgiveness for his people at Bergen. He said that he would offer his service to the King but would hopefully be allowed to return to Bergen to help to rebuild his home. We knew there were many people who escaped the slaughter as we sensed them hiding in the forest as we passed.

I was still unsure of my path and knew to leave myself free of commitments so that I could follow an opportunity, or my instincts should I feel them. The priority should be to get back to England with the nagging voice that I have unfinished business. I needed to get up to Aberdeen to see if Tata still lived and this feeling would be with me until I knew. However, Aethelswith and England needed me, and I longed to be back out on our farm, see my boys and the rest of the family. Thinking about them and home made me homesick and distracted. It took effort for Sigvald to get my attention as he was pointing out Kaupang up in front of us. It is not all that far, and we will be there within the hour. None of us was certain how we are going to be received. I have Jesus and Sigvald has Heimdall to pray to for our protection. My prayers have been working well so far as there are many occasions when I could have perished.

We started walking past farms and cottages with smoke billowing out of their chimneys. How homely these properties and this existence looked? I knew it was perilous due to the warring ways of their people. There was always a risk that a son, brother or father would not return from campaign and just as great a risk that you would be invaded, and your life or property forfeit. This was before the weather became perilous. England really is paradise and for that reason we will be the envy of Europe. We will require a substantial fleet of ships if we are to protect our coastline in the long term.

One of the first things I noticed is that Kaupang has a palisade wall very similar to the one we had seen partly destroyed at Bergen. As we approached the gates the guards stepped across to block our passage. There were few travelers on that day and time, we stood out for this reason alone. 'State your business.' Demanded the two guards in front of us. Sigvald did the talking and told them that we are here to present to Leif Erikson. 'What is your Business?' Sigvald told them that we are here to apologize and seek forgiveness for the transgressions of Bergen. He told them the actions which started and finished off the events of Bergen were nothing to do with us however we can assure the King that all who were involved have perished. The guards studied us and took some time to consider whether to grant us access. 'Have you been to Kaupang before?' Sigvald was able to tell them he has been there on a few occasions, and he had met the king previously. This was enough for the guards to allow us to proceed.

Kaupang is a town which is hunkered down for winter. There is snow almost everywhere and few people moving about. Inside is where the warmth is and building after building, we can see there are fires keeping families warm. Sigvald said that the people of Bergen would be suffering without shelter. 'Many will perish from the extreme cold which we occasionally get in Norway.' Apart from all the snow Kaupang did not look different from what I had seen of Bergen. Timber hunts built along streets with a central tent like structure although this one has sections made of stone.

Sigvald directed us to the leaders building where we were hoping to find the King Leif Erikson. There were two guards at the entrance which glanced our way but let us through. There was no reason for them to suspect a threat so why stop us, I was thinking. There was a massive inside space, and I could see why we were not stopped. There must have been a further twenty guards inside. There was a good chance Leif was here if he had so many men protecting him or at least in council with him. Stepping through the people we could see there was a community meeting. The noise from the crowd and person who had been speaking all stopped as we moved to the front.

With all eyes on us Sigvald stepped forward and kneeled before who I suspected was the king. 'I am Sigvald Arsen, fleet leader of Bergen and I present myself as a representative of my people. I beg your forgiveness for our arrogance to attack you our rightful king. A conflict with Kaupang and King Leif Erikson is not the will of the people however Gunnstein was a brutal man and the people lived in fear. I put myself at your service but hope to one day return to Bergen to help them rebuild for the town has been razed to the ground and the woman and children will perish this winter without support.'

'Gunnstein was always a childish fool. He was full of jealously for his brother and he thought that he needed to be tough to be followed. Unfortunately, tough for Gunnstein turned out to be cruel. People will follow someone out of fear, but they will not die for you unless they believe in you. They will die none the less and Gunnstein killed many of his own men through this fear. The problem for Gunnstein was that they will not give their all and thus he was defeated. Stand up Sigvald Arsen of Bergen for by coming here you have shown yourself to be more of a man then Gunnstein ever could be. I would that you stay a while so that we can catch up on news of your travels however you are free to go when you feel the time is right.' Sigvald stood and thanked the king for his understanding.

Sigvald pointed out Bjorn and I and called us forward. 'These are my companions who made the journey with me from Bergen. Godric and Bjorn, both were captives from Britannia who I have granted freedom.' I could sense King Leif and his commanders looking us over. It almost felt like there was tension in the room. It then dawned on me that I was carrying one of my unique twin blades. These are iconic and associated with me, thus although not named by title they would be wondering why I would have the English leader's blade.

Sensing the moment, I dropped to my knees. 'King Leif Erikson, I also offer my service to you however I do ask for a favor in return. Although bold to request, I would ask that Bjorn here and I are given passage on the next boat which is going back to Britannia. It is our desire to return home to our people.' I could see that there was a man of similar size to Leif on his right who was watching me intently, even more than the others. Leif has long wavey dark hair where this man is possibly twenty years older, and his only hair is his bushy beard. He was possibly another leader from another clan or country. There was so much which I did not know about this world I was in.

Leif turned to the man on his left as he stepped back pulling both he and the bald man on his right with him. Huddled together they were having a whispered conversation, occasionally looking over at me. The sound of chatter was growing around the room and Sigvald looked a little nervous. His nerves made me cautious as I sensed I had been recognized for who I was, number one enemy of the Vikings. In the short time we were there additional armed men had entered the command tent and looking at them I could sense they were ready for trouble.

Leif finished speaking privately and all three of them came back and stood facing me. 'It is with some surprise we have King Godric of England at our disposal. It is King Godric is it not?' I could see that he was not overly pleased, and I figure it was because we were not up front about my identity. I bowed my head and told him that I come in peace and in need. 'I wonder if it is sheer chance which has brought you to us or a sign from Odin. You have caused enormous pain to us Vikings from every clan from all over Norway. King Knut took many of our greatest warriors over to Britannia with an assured victory. I was one of them and I saw our army cut down outside of Worchester. I was one of the lucky ones and we managed to get back to the boats and safety. I now live with the shame that I lived but the knowledge that Odin has given me a second chance. I must follow the guidance of the Gods and repay them for their faith. They have made me King and now I will make the Vikings Strong again. I remember those days as though they were yesterday. The pain is fresh for me and for the people of Kaupang. Even revenge will not erase the pain although I am keen to give it a go, and I am sure the Vikings of Kaupang are also. Sigvald, shame on you for not declaring who your guest was as I know you knew who you have with you. You were forgiven for the transgressions of Bergen and free to go however now I will keep you in my service until the end of winter. The people of Bergen can fend for themselves and perish for all I care. Godric, I can only read the omen that you have been delivered to me as a gift from Odin. Great things are planned for us, and they must be in Britannia. You are the greatest enemy of the Vikings and here you are. From this time forth your life is forfeit at the time of my choosing. Bjorn is a Viking name, are you Viking?' Bjorn shook his head and acknowledged that his farther was Viking. 'Where from', asked Leif? Bjorn did not know and told Leif as much. I could see Leif thinking with his head down before lifting his head and looking around the room. 'Bjorn you are a good omen, and the Gods need a sacrifice as a symbol of our gratitude. You will be killed with honor as a gift to the Gods. If you can take your own life you will be welcomed into Valhalla, if we must do it you will roll the dice on what the gods decide.'

I could not believe I was hearing this barbaric decree from the King of Norway. I put up my hand to speak as until now I had been mostly silent. 'I am Godric the King of England, and I am not your enemy. The war between the Vikings and my people has been going for generations. I have lost both of my parents, two close friends, a wife, and thousands of others who I call friends to the war with your people. The war was on Britannia land, and we were fighting for survival.' My speech was cut off by Leif shouting me down before half a dozen guard made a play for me. With ease I drew my blade and beheaded two of them before taking down a further three who were now dying on the floor. Unfortunately, I did not have any daggers and only the one sword, so I was not able to protect Sigvald or Bjorn. Looking back, I could see that both Bjorn and Sigvald had swords against their necks.

It had only taken seconds and I was thinking that if I went berserk, I could probably break free. It is now dark outside so a burst of strength and I could get to the gates. I have no doubt there will be an alarm and the gates will be closed. I would need to disarm the guards and open it, but I am sure this could be done quickly. These thoughts took seconds but now they have my friends.

Leif Erikson demanded that I drop my weapon or Bjorn and Sigvald would be dead. I had no choice but to comply even though it could most certainly lead to my death. Sigvald has shown himself to be a good and honorable man just as Bjorn has been a good friend. I could not sacrifice them to gain my freedom, I would look for another way. I put my weapon on the ground and was instantly set upon, dropped from behind the knees and bashed across the head. I was punched and kicked for a while until the King said enough. By this time, I was curled up on the floor. Leif told the room that I would die for my crimes against the Vikings. Odin has delivered me to them, and they would do him honor. Bring the boy forward, I looked up in alarm. Leif handed him a blade and told him to slit his own throat. I yelled for them to stop and received a hard kick across the head. I had seen Sigvald struggle against those holding him however the knife was still to his throat so he could not do much.

Bjorn will not be able to slit his own throat he is not Viking. Bjorn is a good man who was innocent of any crime against the Vikings. How can they do this to an innocent. I tried to get up again but found a boot against my back. Looking up I could see the terror in Bjorn's eyes. I saw Leif take the knife back from Bjorn, step forward and slice open his throat. Blood poured from it as his head was being held back by one of the guards. The guard eventually let him go and Bjorn slumped to the floor. I also slumped where I lay, disbelieving of what I had just seen. I cried for my friend, not caring who saw or heard. I was in pain but that did not matter anymore. The guards picked me up and dragged me out of the room and into the freezing cold. I was taken to a pit with a steel grate over the top. The grate was lifted, and I was shoved down the hole, only just large enough that I can touch both sides when standing in the middle. The grate was put back over the top and a lock fitted in place. It was dark in the hole, and I guess it was ten foot deep. I was now cold and miserable as the snow once again began to fall.

That was a long night and although exhausted I found it hard to sleep. My mind was full of demons, and I could not get Bjorn's look of horror out of my head. I also worried about Sigvald and his fate now that he was seen to be an ally of mine. Besides the demons of the mind there was the extreme cold and my aches and pains. Daylight did not bring any respite as without the sun the shadows were like icy tentacles. Around midday some food was thrown down to me, some old roots which were not even cooked and something which looked like silver beet. I ate what I received and did not complain as there was no point in complaining to the solid earth wall. It did give me a thought that a prayer to God would not go astray as I needed a miracle. Over the course of the day, I was never by myself as it seemed that every child in the village took their opportunity to taunt me, most happy with that but the older ones usually added a spit and a piss with their insult.

This was the standard for the following two days until at last the grill was lifted and I was given a rope to pull myself out. It was still before sunrise which was a surprise and as I pulled myself out a man of similar size was pushed into the hole. I wondered what was going on as the man pushed in looked dead.

The guards around me then pushed me down a path which was in the opposite direction to the palace or command tent, whatever it was. I was being led down to the quay and I hoped a boat. At the gates to the quay the guards were questioned however they seemed to know what to say to get me through. I had been given a coat with a hood and was told to put it on before reaching the gate. As soon as this was said I knew that something was up, and I was being rescued. I did not know by who or why but at that time I did not care. This was the miracle I had prayed for and once again God had my back. While at the gate I did not look up as I was led through and down to the docks. I could hear the gentle lol of the sea and sure enough we were on the jetty and making our way to a long boat.

As soon as I had crossed onto the boat the oars were dipped and the boat took off. My hood was pushed back, and I was greeted by Harold the King of Denmark. Harold told me he was doing a favor for a favor. He was freeing me so that I could help him to defeat his German rivals. The Wendish have been raiding our coastal towns while the Saxons are taking our land for Saxon farmers. We have gone to war with both the Wends and Saxons however each time the conflict ends in a stalemate, and we keep losing out.

It felt good to be free although as it was still pre-dawn, I could not see much around me, so it still seemed like I was imprisoned. I could see Harold's face and thought that he was being sincere. He asked me if I thought I could have escaped from the command tent of Leif Erikson if I did not have Bjorn and Sigvald to worry about. I confirmed that I thought I would have been able to get away and this would have been certain if I was fully armed. 'If I help you with your enemies will you help me to get back to England? I need to get home and my best chance is with your support.' Harold agreed that should I help his army to defeat the Saxons and Wends then he would take me home on the first ship of the new season. This sounded like a good offer, so I agreed to help his army through training and strategy.

Our boat was different from the Viking longboats, and I was told it was a clinker. At dawn I saw that this was a royal boat, twice as wide as the Viking boat I had been in. The open sea is rough however It does not bother me anymore as I seem to have overcome sea sickness. Now I feel free and what a joy it is. Harold had a falling out with Leif Erikson as he did not honor their agreement. Harold and the Danes had helped Leif secure the kingdom of Norway. Leif was meant to help the Danes however he said that his people were war weary and would not fight over winter. Harold said that he took me to help train his army but also as revenge against Leif. I did not care about their politics if I lived and could see home and the farm again.

We sailed all day and reached Roskilde on sunset. Harold's son, Crom, said that we had made good time with strong northerly winds. We had five boats in our flotilla. I hoped Sigvald is set free so that he can go home to help his people. I feared he would be punished for my escape after seeing what they did to Bjorn.

Roskilde is a fortified seaside town with round circular stone walls. They look strong and I suspect would take some effort to breach. Inside the buildings are also made of stone and look comfortable and homely, especially given the bleak conditions we were enduring.

That night I ate with the king and his family. His wife Dorette was sick so did not join us however Harold's four children ate with us. The palace did not want for anything as the quarters we dined in were as good as any I had seen. It reminded me a little of the palace in Winchester. There were two fireplaces which the servants had burning nicely. The room was so warm that I was able to take my coat off as soon as I entered. Crom is the eldest and then comes Amalie, Sven, and Joan. Joan is the youngest and was a similar age to what my Egbert and Rick would be. Egbert and Rick would be eight and nine respectively. Joan has blonde hair whereas the older three have the kings thick red hair.

While sitting around the dinner table the discussion went to how poorly things were going for the English. I asked for an update as I had not heard anything since when York was under siege from the Picts. There were obviously more events since then and the way Harold had said it, I was now concerned to find out. Harold told me that King William of Normandy had conquered the south of England. I had not heard of the Normans and needed to know more. The rest of that night's conversation centered around the Normans and what Harold knew of not just the Normans but the other peoples of mainland Europe. I had a lot to learn and as I listened my mind kept going back to England and my people under siege from both the north and the south. I longed to get back to my family, to do what I could to assist them and my people. It was not possible as I now had an agreement with the King of Denmark, and it was winter when no boats crossed the channel. Instead, I needed to get on with business here, do my best to honor my agreement and then get home to try and make things right once the weather improved. 'I need a forge to build my weapons.' My mind was clear now and I wanted to get started first thing in the morning.

The following day I was given access to the royal forge. It was not as hot as I would have liked so I took some time rebuilding the stove so that I could increase the heat and control the carbon levels. With my newly adapted forge I set about constructing my weapons. First, I wanted to build my twin bladed swords so that I would be properly armed. I would follow them up with six throwing daggers and lastly a quiver full of iron tipped arrows and a bow. Once I was fully armed, I was content, for the time being. With weapons in hand, I should be able to recommence weapons practice to get my skill level back up. I was aware that it had dropped over the last few months since leaving Glasgow. Continual practice is the only way to stay on top of your skill with weapons.

Crom trained with me and had a lot of promise as a warrior. Crom is only twenty but already heavy across the shoulders with good strength with the sword. He is a good-looking lad who keeps his red hair short. He resents his hair and hates it getting in his eyes. A sentiment which I agree with, the hair in the eyes bit, and I appreciated his open honesty. Crom introduced me to the commander of the guard who is physically like many Danes I have met, tall with large chest and shoulders. Gorm would be my father's age and looks to live and breathe the army. He seemed to have heard of me and was interested to know if the stories he had heard were true. He knew of the battle of Hastings, Worcester and Winchester and wanted to know about all three. I was surprised he was so patient as he listened to my account of these battles. I told him about the taking of York and Bamborough castles and how our intent was to bring peace and security to the lands. All that seems to have happened since has been war and destruction with the Picts and Normans squeezing England and its people. I told him that I longed to return to help my people.

Gorm said that Denmark was also in a precarious position with the Vikings to the north and the Saxons and Wends to the south. 'There are also other German tribes and a new force of Russians to the East. The stronger Denmark becomes to more these foreign powers look to us for profit. It is a balance between staying under the radar by not growing too strong and being strong enough to defend oneself should an attack come. We have lost the balance and have become strong enough to draw the attention of the German kingdoms and now we are facing constant attacks. I hope that you can help us to defend ourselves and our borders.' I told Gorm that I would do what I could as defense was where my focus had always been. I said that with a strong and secure people it was easier to mount an attack. If your people are not safe, then the minds and hearts of your army will still be on home when they are on campaign. This is a recipe for failure and too often it is the case.

I was shown the armory and introduced to many in the guard. I commenced joining in on their training sessions and was given daily tours of the countryside and defensive buildings. I was taken south to the defensive wall between Denmark and the Saxons. There is a stone wall six-foot-high which stretches forty miles from Husum to Schleswig, two defensive towns at the south of Demark. The lands of the Danes used to extend another fifty miles south however the Saxons have continued to nibble at their lands resulting in the construction of this defensive wall. It was easy to see how vulnerable Denmark was and how it was going to rely on military strength to protect from both sea and land attacks. England needed to secure its own land and build its own sea strength. Without a navy England, like Demark, would always be vulnerable. I set to work meeting and getting to know the men. The Danes speak mostly old Norse although there are some words which I did not recognize. I am a military man from the land like most of the men in the guard. It was easy to like these men and before long I was buried in my task of helping them against their enemies.

Chapter 22

Deception

The English guard arrived and commenced the major battle to clear the Normans from outside our walls and reclaim London. Dexter came running in with a message from Wulfsige telling me of the battle. It was a surprise as we were not aware that our army at Worchester were coming to our aid. We were expecting something however we did not know what. I made my way to the castle walls so that I could see what was happening outside. On the walls I saw Hereweald and Wulfsige pointing and discussing what was happening outside. Looking out I could see what looked like the Worchester cavalry and infantry engaged with a smaller number of the Normans. Wulfsige said that he thought we had maybe five thousand men in the field.

King William seemed absent from this battle, and it was surprising that the Normans did not have more men involved. I wondered if we had caught them out although I was worried that we had fallen into a trap. From the parley session a week earlier, we were sure that William was planning something, the way he had laughed and conducted himself throughout. Now Worchester had arrived in force to liberate London. Something was up and Hereweald confirmed that he had the same suspicions.

The battle lasted all day with the Normans fighting until the last man was dead. They should have surrendered or at least fled earlier in the fight when they had a chance. Their warriors were fanatical and did their king proud, but the waste of life was a disgrace. From the start they did not have a chance as Worchester had the larger and I think a better trained force.

Once it was clear that the day was ours, we opened the gates and allowed our garrison of close to fifteen hundred men to join the rout. This was the first time the men had exited the castle in months and their enthusiasm matched. I stayed on the walls all day taking in the ebb and flow although the outcome was never in doubt. There were many knights which were taken down with the Norman army. The Normans loved their banners depicting their family lines and connections. The battle was still a mystery, and I was still fearful that it was a trap although this seemed less and less likely as the day wore on.

At last, the battle was won, and I joined John, Wulfsige and Hereweald to ride out to meet our victorious commanders. We were met by Swidhun and Gerome the leaders of the English forces. The usual greetings were made including an emotional reunion between Hereweald and his son. Swidhun was thought dead years earlier from the first battle of Jarrow. Months back we found out that Swidhun had survived when he showed up in Worcester. This had been fantastic news, but it was nothing like seeing each other alive and well. The entire scene was emotional for all of us, and I too was overwhelmed to see Swidhun whom I had known since I was a young girl growing up at Winchester. We had played together in the palace grounds as Hereweald was already a recognized commander in my father's guard. Swidhun was almost a replica of his father with a serious and reliable disposition.

Before heading back to the Castle, we sent men through London to uncover any Normans who might be hiding and waiting on ambush. The Norman ships which had not left the ports were also possessed although it is clear most of their boats had already left the docks. Once London was secured accommodation was found for many of the men while the others set up camp outside of the city. Moral was high as the win was comprehensive. London was back in English hands which is a strategic win. Back in the castle we organized some food and drink for the council room and invited Swidhun and Gerome up for a meeting.

Over some mead and bread, we chatted about life in London and what was happening in Worcester. Swidhun mentioned that they had ridden at short notice in response to our message. 'Looking at the walls it seems as though we got here just in time.' John questioned the message as something sounded odd to me and John must have been thinking the same thing. Swidhun said the message spoke of the Parley and that we needed rescuing immediately as the walls were breached. Send everyone was the message.

John looked at me and said that we have been played. 'Our pigeon has been intercepted and our message has been changed. The parley must have happened the way it did so that we would send a communication to

Worcester. Norman numbers were low which means their entire army is probably falling on Worcester as we speak.' John looked at us in horror. London is a strategic victory however the loss of Worcester and its surrounds would mean the defeat of England. English strength comes from the west country, its castle, resources, and people. King William was smart to sacrifice London for Worcester. It looks as though we have been fools.

Sensing our position Swidhun said that the men would rest the night and then ride back for Worcester. He did not look too worried which made me think he was way too casual. 'We did not trust the message as it did not follow the code which we were using. We only sent half of the entire guard and sent riders for Exeter and Powys to send all the men they could. We did not know if it was a trick but suspected that it could be. We brought five thousand men here and were prepared not to engage if we were outnumbered. When we saw that we outnumbered our foe we decided to engage and free London. Worcester will be under attack, but there are enough numbers to slow the Normans down.' I liked their confidence however I hated the uncertainty. We agreed to send the cavalry back to Worcester at first light. Gerome took a message to them to ensure they did not stay up late celebrating. Telling them that Worcester would be under attack would be enough motivation. They will want to get back knowing their families are in the firing line.

Although we had been victorious it was a somber night as we contemplated what was happening in Worcester. John and I will go back to Worcester along with the cavalry. Our main command should be in our most important and strongest city. It will be nice to have different surroundings on the journey and once there. I only hoped that it would not be another siege although if it is then Worcester Castle will be more comfortable.

Emrick had been wise to keep half the guard and reinforce the guard with Welsh from Powys. They were still in trouble as William could have over ten thousand men for this attack given the small number which were left to defend London. The men he left were always going to be slaughtered which shows the type of man William is. He would happily sacrifice two thousand men to achieve his goal. That these men would agree to this sacrifice was also disturbing. There must be a fanatical cult or fervor which is dictating the actions of these people.

I was up the following morning and down in the yard ready for departure with the men. It was going to be a full day's ride and we would be arriving after dark. We could stop at Northampton although we will not make this decision until we get there. The decision will be based on intelligence we may or may not receive while we are there.

We left while it was still dark and slowly the sun rose at our backs. It was a still and chilly morning with a crunchy frost under the hooves of our horse. The windless morning soon became a picture-perfect setting, one which made me grateful to be alive. The white frosts sheeted the rolling farmland between London and Northampton. With the sun high in the sky we reached Northampton where we stopped to see Ethan and catch up on their situation. The roads had been mostly empty of travelers which is not uncommon for this time of year.

Ethan had received confirmation that the Normans were attacking Worchester however the battle was in the fields to the south of the city. Although outnumbered the message said that the defensive positions were still holding as King William seemed intent on sacrificing his men on our lines. We were expecting more from the message however Earl Ethan stopped short and instead invited me into his chambers for a private word and a hot tea. I looked across at John who nodded and showed that he did not think this unusual. It was concerning to me that there was a message for my ears only. Ethan told me that Earl Henry and King Andras were fighting with King William against Worchester. The message was clear on this however difficult it is to believe. I was angry with this news but not surprised. I had thought little for Andras since hearing that Godric might have survived. Everything I had been hearing from Exeter and Andras had been unflattering and he was already showing himself to be an unsatisfactory leader. This treachery hurts as it joins a third of southern England with King William and will result in many additional English lives being lost. I thanked Ethan for the news and told him that it changes nothing. 'London is secure, and Worchester must also now be saved. With the three northern cities and the lands up to York we can hold out for Winter and prepare to hold out against the summer press. We have allies and although things look grim, together we will make England strong. Keep sentries on your southern border and call for support from either London or Worchester, should you be attacked. London will reinforce its numbers from Colchester and as far east as Tretford. The entire East Anglia and old Mercia is now in English control including the important port of London. Wulfsige will be reinforcing the old Roman walls around the city and commence building fortifications along the Themes River. The Normans were bringing in a lot of ships loaded with men and supplies through the London docks. King William was being cunning and may have been expecting a quick victory at Worcester but if we can hold Worcester and then London this move of his will be a costly mistake. Stay strong Ethan as you are surrounded by friends. We will not let Worcester fall and if it goes into a siege, we will send you a message to rally a force of men from the northern towns. The Picts will not attack in winter so we can afford to use these men to free Worcester. I will send you an update as soon as I have decerned the situation in Worcester.' Earl Ethan nodded and thanked me for the private council.

The men and horse had rested and eaten. On my returned they told me they were ready to head off. I agreed that we should make for Worcester and was given my horse which I swiftly mounted and kicked forward. John and Gerome were with me as we lead the three thousand horsemen out of Northampton. The castle walls at Northampton were always impressive to look upon and It reminded me about something I had often wondered about when I was younger. I thought it strange that the King of Mercia had their capital in Repton when Northampton was a bigger and more secure location. Northampton castle was the third castle to be built in Britannia after Bamborough and London. Repton was central for Mercia however it was only defended by a palisade wall. Maybe this explains Mercia's struggle against the Vikings and Wessex. Mercia has vast lands however it was squished between two opposing forces. A familiar scenario to what we are now facing with England.

It has been dark for two or more hours and we have been progressing carefully since. There is always a risk of ambush although due to the speed of our journey there is little chance that King William will know that we have left London. We want to take all precaution and it will be better to reach Worcester undetected. With luck we reached the northern gate of Worcester without being harassed and maybe even without being noticed. Worcester is now a large city and can accommodate all the men and horse. The first thing John did was visit home and his beloved wife Leofflaed.

They had been apart for months since we had fled Winchester and been trapped in London. John invited me to stay with them and I accepted as I was not sure how safe the farm would be.

Leofflaed greeted us with open arms, and I could see that she was already inundated with guests. Emrick and Hilda were there with the children. Hilda and I embraced, and she told me as means to explain, that the farm was too exposed with the large Norman force to the south. I understood but did note that I longed to visit the farm again. Swidhun was also to stay with us at John and Leofflaed's which probably brought this central house to capacity. John asked Gerome to organize a council meeting in the town hall so that we could be brought up to speed with the state of the war. We refreshed before walking across to the town hall for the meeting.

The hall was full of commanders, councilors and leaders of England and Worcester. There was obvious concern amongst the throng for news from the east. Fortunately, John was able to confirm a positive account of events in the East with London and Northampton. I wanted the latest update of the fighting in the south with King William. Emrick was able to give a thorough account of the existing situation and the way which he thought it might play out. He noted that the additional three thousand horse would be a much-needed boost to their defense which was at risk of collapse. It is thought that King William has twelve thousand Normans and three thousand English from Exeter who are fighting with him. Fifteen thousand strong of which up to eight thousand are armored knights. We are simply defending as we believe that to attack would be too costly. They have thrown men at our defensive positions and with our superior archers we have been able to force back their advances. Our arrows travel beyond the shield walls and take out their knights when we can get past their armor. We have eight thousand in the field with three thousand from Powys. Together we are a formidable force which has kept the Normans from advancing on Worcester. A request has been sent to some of the other Welsh states and with luck we may receive reinforcements. They should see that their future is tied up with ours and that King William and the Normans will not stop with England. This is how our message was pitched.

I thanked Emrick for the update and said that once again Worcester was truly the spine which is holding England together. I asked if there was word on Godric, the Vikings or the Picts. Emrick said that the Picts had retreated to Bamborough for the winter. There was no Viking activity and no further news on Godric since the news brought back by Swidhun which said he had been captured and taken across the sea by a Viking raiding party. I expressed my thoughts that the current assault on Worcester will cease when the bleak weather and lack of progress takes its toll on King William's army, which is exposed to the elements. 'We must use every opportunity to rotate our men so that they can remain fresh. The cavalry can be used to harass their supply lines. This is our country, and we know it better than the Normans. The roads south to Winchester and Exeter should be targeted. Gerome can you please take responsibility of this critical task?' There needs to be little risk as we do not want to waste lives.

There was no mead or celebration after this meeting as we all knew we were still fighting for our lives. The old Wessex was now occupied by a foreign force. England needed these lands as they are rich agriculturally and they are strategically important for access to Europe and key fishing grounds.

I now longed to return to John and Leofflaed's house to see my children Godric, Albert and my stepson Egbert. I have been away far too long as a mother and hoped that they still remembered who I was. Egbert and Godric Junior would know me, but Albert is still very young. I did not see them when I dropped home before which was deliberate as I knew that it would be hard to leave them so soon after to attend the council meeting.

The battle lasted another three weeks and ended with King William offering Parley. John and Emrick agreed with my sentiment that we refuse to Parley. We wanted to keep the pressure on them through the harassment of their supply lines. The weather had only become colder and more miserable and without fresh reliable supplies the Norman army were starting to suffer. With the harsher conditions the Norman leaders were losing their cool and sending their men on suicide missions. Each time their men were offered our commanders obliged and shot down the sacrifice. It was sad to hear what was happening and worse to know that most of those being sacrificed were English from Devon and Cornwall.

Eventually our tactics worked, and the Normans were forced to withdraw back to their towns and cities and the warmth of their fires. We decided not to pursue them and use the time to give our men time to rest and recuperate. Powys guard was able to return home led by their King David and his eldest son Cadfael. They promised to return in the summer if required. I thanked them and once again offered our services in return if needed. We did send an additional one thousand men to Northampton and London to reinforce them should there be an attack. It was now time to build our stores of weapons and preserve our food stores.

Chapter 23

Unexpected News

The winter had been harsher than anything I can remember, and we have been eating bark soup with herbs which can still be found in the surrounding forests. The women tell me that it has been this bad before and the bark soup had got them through. We had meat and fish when the men caught it however, this was very infrequent due to the conditions. The snow was now thawing which was a good sign that the change in season was getting closer.

Winter had not been a time of rest as Bergen had been burnt to the ground by King Leif Erikson and his men just prior to winter setting in. Very few men had survived apart from those too old to fight and the boys who are too young. Tata is a natural leader as was his older brother and took charge of the work to rebuild Bergen. The walls were completed within days and makeshift accommodation was completed within a week. Once there was enough shelter for the survivors Tata split the crews into those who would build boats, those who would continue with the shelters and those who would hunt for food. Bran oversaw the crew building the shelters, Ivan was commander of the boat building crew and fishing while Tata took charge of the hunting group and the Forge once it was constructed.

Tata is as powerful as any Viking and has the presence to back his words. Tata told us that we were fortunate that it was winter as it would give us a chance to rebuild before the rest of the world can come and take advantage. 'Bergen is a strategic location with direct access to the northern Fjords and the Pict coast and islands. I have been speaking to those from these parts and these are very rich fishing grounds. Other resources such as Iron, Copper and Gold are also plentiful and will be sort after with news of the sacking of Bergen. There are also many women and children here which is what you need to build an army. We will be targeted once the weather improves so we need to rebuild and train a guard to defend the walls. Age and sex should not be a barrier as I have seen women here who are stronger than most men that I have met.' I agreed with him as some of the women here are obviously warriors and can handle weapons as well as any man.

Helga who was the wife of the late leader Gunnstein had been happy to allocate power to Tata. She soon began courting with Ivan and shared in the command of Bergen. At some point Tata and Elgar became a couple and I could not blame them given our situation and isolation. Given what was taking place around me it felt only natural for me to fall in with Bran, one of my closest companions whom I have known since I was a little girl growing up in Carlisle. Bran is intelligent and compassionate to people and animals. Bran was always too low a station for my father to allow us to become lovers. My relationship with my father is never going to be the same again since running away with Godric and disappearing without word. He would have worried for a while and then moved on. Father is pragmatic and will be saddened by my disappearance. He has my son Rick and my brother Munro and his family so the family line is secure. Bran worships me which I believe is a great quality to look for in a partner.

My child was born in amongst the darkest days of winter in the Viking town of Bergen. Does this make him Viking, I joked with Bran and Tata? They both laughed at my quip and said he could always claim it but only if it was to his favor. I named him Ramsay after my old friend who had been killed when defending me when camped outside Arbroath. My relationship with Ramsay had been like that which I had with Bran. I don't think I could have courted Bran if Ramsay were still alive and vice versa. Either one on their own and I could easily picture us being together. My son Ramsay is a strong healthy lad who has taken well to the breast. I am eating whatever meat I can get to make sure he gets what he needs to grow big and strong.

Elgar is a powerful shield maiden with the Bergen Vikings who had managed to survive the loss at Kaupang and the sacking of Bergen. Elgar is now pregnant with Tata's child. I can see Tata and Elgar comforting each other after the day's workload. Elgar is maybe ten years younger than me but besides this she is not too dissimilar with braided blonde hair and a muscular firm figure. I am not as muscular which does not need mentioning but makes sense as I have never been a warrior. I am not shy of hard work and besides looking after baby Ramsay I have been assisting the women rebuild the interior of our buildings, from clothing and blankets to pottery items and decorations. Everyone in Bergen has worked diligently over winter and I feel pride in what we have been able to achieve. This is all on top of simply surviving the winter. Bergen is now presentable to the outside world.

Tata has begun training up a guard and any one between the age of thirteen and seventy has been welcome to come to lessons. Tata has made many weapons including swords, spear tips and spears, arrow tips, arrows, and bows. It seems that Tata is proficient in all manner of things which isn't really a surprise knowing the family he comes from. Training is going well and although I have not taken part, I often watch them train while on my break or when feeding Ramsay. Bran often takes a group and assists with sword practice as this is his usual weapon of choice.

With regards to numbers Bergen has roughly two thousand people. This is still a good-sized settlement and with time should once again be self-sufficient. I could not worry about the distant future and whether Bergen would be a threat to the Picts or indeed England. These people needed our help and we had given them all the strength and knowledge we could. We helped them survive winter and rebuild.

One day after all the snow had melted, we had a visitor come down out of the hills. He was known by everyone and seemed to be well received. I was told his name was Sigvald and he was one of the commanders of the old Bergen. We gathered in the command shelter to eat and share information with Sigvald. It turns out that he was the commander who had captured Godric way back last season in Stonehaven. Sigvald had managed to flee during the sacking of Bergen. He told us that he had more to tell however he wanted to know how Bergen had faired so well over Winter. I could see that he was genuinely impressed as he looked across the table at us.

Sigvald lingered on Tata before asking if Tata was brother to Godric Amity. Tata was also looking directly at Sigvald, and his face dropped as he admitted that he was. 'Do not be upset my friend as I believe that your brother still lives. I helped Godric escape during the sacking, and we made for the forest and safety.' From there Sigvald recalled their adventure and how Godric was again locked up to be sacrificed to the gods before his eventual rescue by Harold the King of Denmark. 'Godric may be dead however I believe Harold would not have risked what he risked if he intended to kill Godric. I believe Godric is alive and may well be fighting with and for the Danish as repayment for his rescue. I was imprisoned for assisting Godric and then forced to train the Kaupang guard over winter. Once winter finished my punishment was complete and I could return home. In my heart I know that your brother lives.'

I was stunned again with the unexpected news about Godric. It seems that he is difficult to kill even against impossible odds. I could see that Tata was thrilled as he thanked Sigvald for the news. Sigvald told Tata that he and Godric had become friends before their imprisonment at the hands of King Leif Erikson. He apologized for raiding the Pict coast and for taking the slaves and valuables they had taken over the years. He said he was never comfortable with the job however he felt it was his duty as a Viking. Tata said that he accepted Sigvald's apology and told him a little about how they had rebuilt Bergen so that it could not only survive winter but survive the coming threats once the weather clears up. That council meeting became a celebration, and the wider community was able to share in the celebration, as meager as food and drink supplies were.

Over the coming week we planned how we were going to get down to Denmark while avoiding all other Vikings. We were going to need to land in Denmark and find Godric without the alarm being raised with the Danish. It sounded like another impossible mission. We continued our work in the town and I felt sad that we were going to be leaving these good people. Inside I was now one of them and I wanted to help them to survive and be successful. They had treated us like their own even though we are strangers from a land far away. There was a bond which I knew the others from Britannia felt. The rescue of Godric is important and the reason we were here in the first place. We could not stop now so had to plan to leave. Sigvald would stay and continue to train the guard and fill the leadership vacuum once Tata and Bran left. Ivan had said that he wanted to stay with Helga as Helga was expecting a child even though they had thought she was beyond the age of giving birth.

Elgar said that she would travel with us and show us the way as she had been to Denmark and Kaupang before. She was also carrying Tata's baby and did not want to be separated from him. Some of the older men and widowed women offered to come and help row the longboat for us. In the end we had a boat of twenty-four which included ten men and fourteen women. I was impressed with the courage of the women and would not have wanted to have a disagreement with any of them. Baby Ramsay was going on his first sea voyage, and I hoped that he would take to the sea as well as he had taken to feeding and life.

In was evident that Bergen was in good hands being left with Sigvald. He was well liked by the people and extremely competent at everything he put his hand to. Leaving Bergen was a sad day for us and the people. It seemed like the whole town was out to see us off. We boarded the boat with plenty of food and water with the food being mostly dried and salted meats. Elgar wished her mother well and promised to return someday. This sounded ominous although I feel it is an honest appraisal given the unknowns which were ahead of us. Survival is never guaranteed when heading out into the sea.

We rowed out of Bergen to great fanfare with a promise to return sometime in the future. I had forgotten how much I dreaded being at sea, but I knew this was my only chance of reaching home again. Although I was with Bran, I still longed for Godric and knew it was my destiny to help him. I hoped that he would understand that I had thought he was dead. I was not going to betray Bran and hoped I would be strong enough to resist my attraction for Godric. I could deal with these thoughts later however for now I was with Bran, and he was like a father to baby Ramsay.

The water of the fjord was gentle however this ended abruptly once we cleared the head of the fjord. The sea was churning, and I immediately took fright. The storm was fresh in my mind although it was last season. The sea was nothing like it was then however the power of the sea scared me. The wind was from the west, so we needed to work hard to tac south and keep off the coast. Tata had also wanted us to be just within sight of the land so that any other Viking boats travelling up the coast would hopefully not see us. It was a good plan as we were equipped for a rescue mission but would be sitting ducks to a well-armed Viking long boat. Eventually, we made good time down the coast as the wind direction changed to our advantage, coming out of the north. Once more I did not row as I needed to nurse and hold my baby. The women warriors kept up with the men and we would not have noticed the difference if looking at the boat cut through the water instead of who was rowing. I was impressed and vowed to be a better example to the girls of our kingdom.

It was late in the afternoon, and we were rounding the southern tip of western Norway. I started sighting boats in closer to shore and knew that if I could see them then we could also be spotted. Elgar said that we could leave the coast at this point as we were required to cross the Skagerrak to Denmark. Given all the boats I could now see this suited us as we shifted the sail and began rowing away from the land. The sea was still choppy, but the sky was clear. Elgar said that once we sighted the land to the south, we were to head west and make for the fishing town of Esbjerg. Esbjerg is central to Denmark and will be a good safe place to land. If we went east, we would hit all the high population areas of Denmark and would surely be captured. Demark is a sea faring nation which patrols its waters well. This makes sense given its Viking neighbors to the north.

'We will be safer travelling by land, and we will be less of a threat. Esbjerg is a fishing town on the west coast. They are used to trading with us Vikings and with the Francs and Normans. We will not stand out which will allow us to dock our boat and either walk or buy horses to travel to the capital. Meanwhile we speak their language and listen to the events of the nation. We want to listen for Godric's name or the location of the battles. Godric will be where the action is, you can count on it.'

Chapter 24

Time to Go Home

Raids had continued through the winter, and I was told they were more frequent than usual for this time of year. Raids are annoying and can affect moral and vital stores however I saw them as training opportunities. I had the army divided into different regiments for archers, cavalry, and infantry. The idea is to anticipate raids so we can practice our training drills in real life situations. It basically means positioning our men in positions where we think they are most likely to see action. This has been an enormously successful training enhancement with both the Viking and Wendish raiders providing this opportunity.

King Leif Erikson of the Vikings did not take my abduction well and despite the bitter winter conditions he has been sending his crews into Danish waters to show his displeasure. I think it fascinating how two powers can be fighting on the same side one minute and at war the next. All on the whim of one individual. I am also certain that his campaigns against the Danish have been costly. There have been heavy losses inflicted on them from the Danish warriors and the weather would have also finished off a few with the water crossing and exposure. There are good reasons why these boating warriors stay at home over winter. The seas can turn against you in a matter of hours and even if it doesn't the bitter cold can suck the moral out of even the hardiest of warriors.

King Lothar of the Wends was raiding for different reasons. I gathered that Lothar wanted to keep his army engaged over winter to keep them together. There was some desperation in their raids, and they were mainly searching for stores of food. They must have had a bad harvest or at least one interrupted by something like war. The Wends did not have as far to come as they could raid up the coast across the Baltic sea. Either way the Wends were also proving a good training ground for our army.

I have instilled in King Harold and his son the importance of preservation. Resources are limited and thus we must preserve ours while our enemy throws theirs away. Skilled warriors are also a resource which needs risk free or at least risk reduced practice. We have used the winter to reinforce the wall between Husum and Schleswig, adding an additional meter along most of its length. The Danes have defended and built while our enemies have attacked, and many have died. The Danish fleet has stayed in its well defended harbors of Roskilde, Jelling and Lindholm. These harbors are deep and protected by rock walls and barracks overlooking the harbors. Each barrack has catapults which can sink boats with stones travelling over two hundred yards, if needed.

My acceptance with the Danes did not come easy. King Harold had insisted that his commanders work with me and listen to my direction. These men did not take other people's instructions easily let alone an enemy leader. I tried to explain to them that I was not their enemy and that I owed their King for my rescue although this had little effect. There was open conflict on one occasion where I had to pin Gorm to the ground until he surrendered. He was arguing for the archers to be on foot for accuracy however I was saying that from experience they get greater distance from horseback and the accuracy does not make a difference when shooting a hundred yards or more. Further to this the additional elevation means they can keep shooting arrows at the back ranks of the enemy even when the forces are fully engaged. Being on the horse will also enable them to carry their sword more easily and to store their bow when they engage with the sword as a last resort. The argument made sense to me, but I was trying to see things from Gorm's side to make sure I wasn't being pig headed. Gorm would be fifteen years older than me and even with his strength and experience I had no trouble besting him in hand combat. With my knee on the back of his neck and an arm pinned behind his back I had him in pain and completely disarmed. I kept the pressure on both the arm and neck until he at last said that he gave up. There were over a thousand on the training ground that day and our physical conflict would not be forgotten in a hurry.

Gorm was not the only one I had to win over as the King's sons resented the favor their father was giving me. They questioned his wisdom and what I could know that they did not. There is no doubt that the Danes are brave and fearsome warriors, very similar to the Vikings in that way. I still have plenty to learn and was learning from all the peoples I have been able to meet. There are the personal aspects of self-control and will power as well as the tiny nuances of battle. A good example is my understanding of boats, sea travel and sea warfare. With regards the sea there is the reading of the seasons and daily weather predictions. My ignorance could not have been greater before being captured by the Bergen Vikings. I tried to explain this to Crom and Sven but neither wanted to hear it. We agreed to disagree, and I simply told them I had honor and would do my best to repay their father for saving my life. They were content with this but told me they would be watching my every step to ensure there was no treachery.

Besides the King I did have friends within the court. The king's wife Dorette and his daughter Amalie were always kind and would often snap at Crom and Sven when they were trying to belittle me. The boys did not like this, and it only seemed to drive the divide further. Harold would have the last say and only then would they follow. This was a very masculine world and as such the women seemed to be almost invisible. I explained to the King, his wife and daughter the importance of utilizing his entire resource which includes the women. I gave examples of how the Viking women often fought alongside their men and for us the women would work the land as often as the men which enabled the men to go to war. Women did not work the forges however they worked the leather and created the art which adorned our places of worship and homes. They made the clothing, rugs and blankets which kept the people warm over winter. With regards their contribution to the guard they made the armor and saddles for the horses. Men could also do these things but as the men were constantly building and training there are many important tasks which would not get done if the women were not given the training and the freedom to help. I could see that Harold understood the wisdom of my words and Dorette and Amalie set about recruiting women for the very tasks I spoke about.

My time was split between working with the women and training with the men. The men resented me because of this, and I know they did not trust me. Amalie was only eighteen and not promised to anyone and Dorette is the king's wife. The other women were typically married and if it were not for the King their husbands would not have let them partake in these projects. The king demanded that they be allowed to help build the Kingdom and the open resistance melted away. This is part of the reason why I had the men working on lifting the southern defensive wall. Physical work is a great way of distracting someone while at the same time lifting their confidence so that they are not feeling insecure. These women had a real thirst for knowledge and learning new skills. They are easy to work with and seem to have endless energy, even with their babies hanging off them. I became close with Dorette and Amalie as they became the natural leaders of these women's groups. Similar work teams were established in the major towns of Denmark and before long they were producing leather and shaping this into light armor, saddles, and reigns. They were producing strings for the bows and producing arrows by the hundreds and thousands. With Denmark being a sea faring country many of the work groups concentrated on making baskets and nets, and sails and rigging for the boats. By the time the weather had turned Denmark had become as productive as any country I had known. They had strength and determination in abundance, and this now had direction. I was so engrossed in the progress of the Danes I had almost forgotten that I was English, and I needed to get home to my people.

I did get myself into some hot water when I started courting Amalie. Amalie is a busty redhead who I instantly found attractive. She is sensual and engaging in almost everything she became a part of. It was like I was being seduced from the moment I was brought into the Kings Court. Harold warned me about his daughter as he told me that even the most experienced men could fall for the charms of his daughter. Given the early warning I had made it my mission not to be drawn in by the sway of her hips or the occasional glimpse of her bosom. We worked closely together as we pushed to get the women working on the various projects. Amalie would sit within my body space and always seemed to take the opportunity to brush past me bumping me with her breasts. Within weeks I was beside myself with lust and only the strongest of will power was stopping me from making a move. Amalie always seemed so innocent of the affect she was having on me. Making things worse was seeing the affect she was having on other men of the court.

There were two other men who are trying to win Amalie's favor. Gerard is the chief steward of the King's court while Frans is the head guard of the palace. Both men seemed to be competing for her affection and not always cordially. Within weeks they seemed to identify that I was a threat to their situation, and both joined the king's sons in their dislike for me. Apart from the support of the women and my physical attraction to Amalie my time in Denmark over the winter would have been lonely and miserable. As it was, I had the King's support and his daughter to warm my bed. Amalie was everything that she promised, and I soon found out that her sensuality was not all for show but delivered everything a man could want. There was a period over the shortest days when we never left the bedroom. It was now obvious to the others at court, and I knew I had put a target on my back.

It was the King who warned me that there were some who wished me harm. I had now been in Roskilde for over six weeks and began to wonder if I was being set up. The king already had my thoughts and strategy on war and everything about the Danes was a country on the move, even though it is a bitterly cold winter. I did not need the warning from the king to be watching my back as I could rely on my sixth sense. I was free to roam in Denmark but was in a sense a captive as I had a debt to be honored. Apart from during my most intimate moments with Amalie I always had my guard up.

One day I was walking between the stables and the main house when I was set upon by half a dozen armed men. I was unarmed apart from a dagger I used for cutting fruit. There was no talk just simply an attack. I slipped into the dance of life and although dark I moved through their attack and one by one disarmed them. The men started dying as the attack continued. Just when I thought I was finished with the men another four or five joined the ones still standing. I was tiring as the melee continued and was thinking it might be time to try and flee. Just as I had this thought Crom, and a couple of his guards came around the corner and saw what was happening. I know this as he and his guard joined the melee on my side and with their support, we had soon destroyed the attackers. From this point on the animosity between Crom and I disappeared, and we began working closely together. Unfortunately, ten good men lost their life in that melee. As I explained to Crom and Sven, men are a resource we cannot afford to lose. The winner will be the nation who can preserve its resources better than their enemy. I could see that they now understood what I was saying and were now willing to listen to me.

I attempted to distance myself from Amalie however she was just too good at what she did that I was like a fish on a hook. Gerard was arrested as the organizer of the attack, and he was hung in the town square for his troubles. Gerard was old enough to be Amalie's father so from where I stood, I thought he received his justice.

With the end of winter, we had extra time to increase training times and work on our projects. Raids continued however did not increase in frequency even with the improved conditions. I know we had been doing significant harm to the Wends and Vikings and this was probably what was holding them back now. News came through that the Saxon King Henry was building for an attack on Denmark. This intelligence came through travelling minstrels who were coming north with the new season. Price Otto had pushed east over winter and had taken all the land up to the Oder river, just short of the Wendish city of Szczecin. Word is being spread that the Saxon's are encouraged by this success and are set to expand north and bring Denmark into a Saxon empire. The council was called to make decisions on how to respond to this intelligence.

Gorm led the chorus with the push to meet Otto in the field. Both Crom and Sven agreed, and Frans also put in with this plan. I had remained mostly silent as the virtues of an attack south were discussed. There was even the option to come in and take easy land off the Wends now that they were getting squeezed by the Saxon's. There were two armies which were a threat, Henry's main force at Bremen and Otto at Hamburg. It was not known if they would unite however the thought was that an early advance and attack on Otto would be better than waiting for the two armies to combine. A second debate started over the benefits of these options. I continued to remain silent and listened to the arguments and counter arguments.

King Harold had also been mostly silent, and I noted him watching me. I had felt his eyes on me earlier but allowed him to watch my features as the discussion flowed. Some mead and snacks were brought in and put on our table. We had been discussing the battle options for an hour and even though I had contributed little I was still hungry and thirsty from my deep thoughts. The king, Hans, Johan, Lauge and I were still undecided while the others had made up their minds. They wanted a swift attack on Otto. Hans is the commander of the Archers, Johan the commander of the cavalry and Lauge the commander of the Infantry. These were new positions which I had created, and I had spent the most time with these men. I don't think they were holding back because of me although I think they probably had the same reservations.

While eating the King asked me what I had thought. We were all sitting around the table, and I sensed the others end their conversations when the king spoke. 'I think that you should take all your men and ships north to Kaupang and attack Leif Erikson when he least expects it. Shortly Leif will be receiving the same intelligence about the Saxons. He will be battered and bruised from the campaigns last year and the long winter campaign he has waged against you. He will be relieved for a break and will release many of his warriors back to their fields for the coming summer. Quietly he will hope that you engage in a long and protracted war with the Saxons. Then in late summer, after harvest he will once again form his army and he will sail for Roskilde. There is the greater opportunity of surprise if you go north and defeat Kaupang. Norway can easily be added to the Danish empire. Culturally you are very similar, and you both speak the same language of old Norse.

I looked around the table and I could see everyone thinking. This brief pause was enough for Gorm to criticize my plan stating that we would be vulnerable to the Saxons and could lose everything while we are away to the north. I nodded agreement as Gorm told us all his concerns with my plan. Once he took a break I jumped back in before anyone else took the chance to speak. Our wall from Husum to Schleswig is defendable and will not allow them swift and easy movement into Denmark. We must keep a small fleet of defensive boats and a fifth of the Infantry and Archers to defend the walls. The neck of Denmark is narrow and will not be easily traversed. Their cavalry will be useless against our wall. The Saxon's will be greatly slowed in any case, and they will be cautious as they will be unaware that we have gone north. Roskilde and Vilborg both have formidable castles and Jelling and Lindholm have defendable fortifications. Denmark is stronger defensively then offensively. I would go for our weaker opponent and allow the stronger opponent to destroy itself on our defenses. If we can defeat Norway, then we will not have an enemy on both sides. We can raise a greater army and from this position of strength we can expand south and east. The Wends will not stand a chance against us and the Saxon's will be required to negotiate an embarrassing surrender and loss of land. This will not all happen this year however I see this playing out over the coming two years.

Gorm was still staring at me, and I expected some form of rebuttal. Gorm is a smart commander, not that much older than me. People like Gorm rise to their position due to their intelligence or because of their connections. Gorm may have both however I suspected he was smarter than anyone else. Gorm held up his hand as others had started to speak. 'This is a solid plan and one which I can endorse. Please raise your hand if you agree with the option to push north and defend our southern border.' The hands of Hans, Johan and Lauge shot up to join Gorm's. Crom and Sven followed with their hands seeing that they were now outnumbered. After I added my hand to the uniform agreement the King at last put his hand up. The king then spoke and said that he liked the plan as attacking Kaupang was unexpected and had not been considered by them so it would not have been considered by their enemies. It is brave to leave your belly exposed but we know that our belly although exposed it is not unprotected. Like Godric has said, our defensive strength is our advantage.

The following week all preparations went into going north. The men who were chosen to guard the wall were sent to the wall to give the impression that we were still going to meet the Saxon's in the field. These men were also given instructions to ensure that nobody travelled south. Anyone who came north was to be told that they would not be allowed south again until the end of the summer. The explanation was to be that war was coming. Everyone would know that war was coming so would not question these instructions. We wanted our planned attack north to remain a secret for as long as it could be maintained. All preparations were done with haste as we wanted to be off and ready to hit King Leif Erikson with surprise, all within a week of our council decision.

As planned, we were off within six days and with a fleet of seventy boats and six thousand men, we landed to the north of Kaupang. The north was a much better staging post as there was no river to cross. Coming in from the north meant that we could be spotted however at this stage it did not matter. I believe we have the force to beat Kaupang and Harold had wanted to get on with it. I felt the emotion as I thought of the coming battle, and I hoped that this emotion had not clouded my judgement. I had not realized how I was still angered by the killing of Bjorn. Bjorn was an innocent with a good heart. Leif had cut his throat just to upset me and by the way which I felt it was obvious that he had succeeded. I was looking forward to this opportunity of revenge and had thus come prepared for war. The excitement was running through my body like a wild animal waiting to be let out. I was in the command boat with King Harold, and I knew that he was aware of my hunger. The smile on his face said it all as he told me I would get my chance at revenge. This made me laugh as I became aware of how obvious my emotions must have been.

We landed and commenced our march to Kaupang. The landing location was only a mile north and although after noon we were not going to wait. Our opportunity was now so we broke into our regiments and went straight for Kaupang. Each regiment knew the other's role and plans. This was it, our moment of revenge.

The guard of Kaupang came out to meet us as we approached their palisade wall. Once they saw our numbers and obvious intent they soon fled back into the town. They would have seen how large we are and that there was no point meeting us in the field. We are six thousand men which will be more than all the men, women, and children in Kaupang. King Leif Erikson will know that he is doomed unless he flees for his life. To flee would be a disgrace and to forfeit his spot in Valhalla so I thought he would stay and fight. Speaking to the King I asked if he could send a message to spare the women and children who do not fight but surrender. 'These would be your people so you must show mercy to as many as you can, including the fighting men.' Harold nodded that he understood, and he gave the command to his commanders.

The ferocity of the next half an hour was as intense as anything I had been a part of. I copped a spear graze to my shoulder and was lucky not to lose my head. We attacked the walls and gates relentlessly until we were over in numbers large enough that we had the gates open, and we were into the city. There was panic on the inside as we struck in groups and ran the streets looking for opposition. There were attackers on every corner and care was needed not to waste our lives being hasty. I knew where to find the palace and that is where I headed. King Harold stuck close to me along with Crom and several of the guard. I knew that Harold was putting his faith in me from what he had seen in the Palace months ago. He had seen me train his men many times since then and heard about me fighting off some attacks such as the one because I was with Amalie. We both knew that I had revenge in my mind, and it would take an army to stop me. Harold wanted to be there the moment that King Leif Erikson was cut down.

There were over twenty burley men guarding the entrance to the palace. As we went to attack the palace doors swung open and another fifty or so men poured out. This was their last gasp of survival and a smart move. I was impressed however nothing was going to slow my determination. Leif Erikson was among the men and my berserker mindset engaged as I danced through the guard with all eyes on Leif. We were fortunate as more of our men joined the melee from the adjoining streets. King Harold was close by and twice I had to throw a dagger at an attacker to stop him being cut down. I was in the zone however this included Harold as I needed him to live to bring stability to this region.

The melee felt like it went for longer than it probably did. I cut, stabbed, and sliced my way to Leif. Face to face we both paused for perhaps a microsecond to at least recognize each other. He let out the word Godric, as I engaged him. Three moves and I had taken his head. I grabbed the head by the hair and lifted it above my own head and roared as loud as I could. Lower your weapons I shouted. Nothing happened straight away as the fighting was frantic however slowly I notice a slowing of the motion around me. Harold and some of the guard stood around me and helped me keep the head of Leif Erikson aloft. Then it was over, the fight for Kaupang and Norway was over. I knew there would be new battles as Norway would not lie down and surrender so easily. However, this is a significant victory which would be sung about for generations. This is the furthest north the Danish have ever been and for now the southern half of Norway could be included in the Danish Empire.

The news was not all good for us as Crom had taken what looked like a fatal blow across the head and had been run through the belly. Harold looked at his son and asked for him to be cared for. He looked to me to help prepare the city for the transfer of power. I told him we needed to find the biggest open space and talk to the people. We need to let them know that they are now part of something greater and together the world was going to be a better and more secure place. With security they will have wealth and a long life. King Harold was looking at me as I shared this with him. With emotion he took a step and embraced me. 'You are a King I could follow, young Godric.'

Kaupang has a massive market square just up from the docks. This is the square with the pits, one of which I spent two miserable days in. All Kaupang were invited to hear the demands of the new king. It was phrased this way however what they were given was far from demands. The people were welcomed to the Danish empire as kindred spirits. The King spoke their language and the Vikings and Danes have fought together on many occasions. Norway can rely on Denmark and Denmark would see that Norway was strong again. 'We have been getting attacked by Leif Erikson all winter even though we are supposed to be allies. Leif was an impulsive and arrogant leader who did not look out for the welfare of his people. This had to end, and I promise you that you will be an important port and city in the Danish Empire. Celebrate as you are now free from the tyrant who would as easily slit your throat as feed you. We will build Kaupang from a town into a city with jobs for all its people. You will travel the oceans and bring back enormous wealth as your ancestors before you.' I did not like the sound of this as the last thing I wanted was to have these warriors landing on English shores and killing innocent people. I had a sinking feeling that I had started something again much as I did with the Picts. I have heard that to make a mistake was human but to make the same mistake twice was stupidity. I hoped I was wrong about my feeling.

We stayed in Kaupang for two further weeks, moving out through the community to spread the word about the Danish and how the southern part of Norway was now part of the empire. Most seemed to take it onboard and accepted us with open arms. Harold told them that there were spots in the army however they were better off looking after their farms and building a decent store for the following winter. Everyone was war weary, and it was smart not to call them into another battle which was not really theirs.

Crom died the night we took Kaupang. Crom was difficult and grumpy at the best of times however after a rocky beginning we had become friends. I was sad for the King however he seemed resilient enough to not show much grief. There was a certain level of exhaustion from the preparations, battle and tidying up which we were doing. I put this resilience or aloofness down to the exhaustion. His mother Dorette will be devastated as Crom was her golden child. Sven had taken a few knocks however had recovered quickly and was already taking the role of the heir to the throne which was mostly supporting his father. Sven was only sixteen but had fought well from what I saw.

I felt like I had achieved all that I needed to achieve with King Harold and knew it was time to try and leave. King Harold wanted to get back home to take on the Saxon's and I know he wanted me by his side. The year was already getting on and I needed to make the most of the weather to get across the sea. I had my revenge on Leif Erikson for his mindless killing of Bjorn from Aberdeen. This made me happy but not content. I was unsettled and I put this down to being homesick. Amalie may not let me leave either, so I started thinking about a secret escape such as how I left Kenner of Strath Clyde all those years ago. This was no good on this occasion as I needed their boat and rowers to get across the sea. I was still in the middle of a fix and was yet to come up with a solution.

Chapter 25

Unexpected Threat

The boat is securely docked at Esbjerg, and we were assured by the guard that all boats are well protected for their owners. We were able to give the guard a piece of silver which had been given to us when we left Bergen. Although armed and a good-sized group it was not unusual for groups like ours to move around the countryside. However, we thought it prudent to not test this theory and so six of us set off from Esbjerg, seven if you count baby Ramsay. There were many women with the group however I could not bear to leave him behind. Travelling as a group of six meant that we were hardly even noticed. The remaining eighteen were to stay in Esbjerg or the surrounding district. We could not be sure how long our mission will take and how quickly we will have to flee.

Besides Elgar and Tata, Stuart and Ronnie joined us for what we hoped would be a short and quick journey. Stuart is a Pict from Strath Clyde and Ronnie is Viking from Bergen. All the men from the boat which left Britannia found love over winter. The men were outnumbered five to one so even a blind one-legged cripple would have been kept warm. Stuart is hardly this as he is only a little older than me and an extremely resourceful man. He was a farmer back home before he was captured by King Oengus's men. Stuart had helped Tata with the hunting and provision of food for Bergen. Quiet and resourceful is how I would describe him. Ronnie is a widow and a shield maiden. I have not seen her fight however I have no doubt that she could. She has braided mid length blonde hair and upper arms as big as most men I know. Her arms are nothing like Godric's or Tata's however they make my arms look puny.

The countryside is very flat unlike what I am used to in Strath Clyde or what I know of Norway. There is water everywhere in every direction which I suspect is a result of the land being so flat. It is all beautiful and green as the warmer days are already helping everything to grow. Although the days are warmer it is still cold as it is extremely windy, and the wind is carrying a cold chill. Baby Ramsay is rugged up tight and with luck a good sleeper. Rick was a terrible sleeper however we had a wet nurse which may explain why he did not settle. We have no such luxury here, so I was forced to feed Ramsay. It took a bit of getting used to but now I regret not feeding Rick myself. I feel much closer to Ramsay then I ever did Rick.

We were making our way across the country from west to east to get across to the capital. Elgar's knowledge of Denmark was all we really had to go on. Some of the other shield maidens had been around Denmark on a boat but Elgar was the only one to have been to the Capital. I felt like we were getting so close to Godric and our original mission when we left Britannia. As we had the baby we travelled slowly and on foot. We found an inn in Kolding with two spare rooms. Bran, baby Ramsay and I shared a room while the others shared the other room. It was great to be on dry land again however I was not used to walking for so long and with the baby. My back ached and my bosoms were sore. After eating we went our separate ways to get an early night.

The following day we continued eastward making our way around beautiful lakes and over countless bridges. I thought it was wet in the west but that was nothing to what we were seeing now. The walk was more difficult this day as my legs and back ached from the first day. With all the bridges there was also much more climbing up and down. Although we intended to go further, we stopped in Nyborg. Baby Ramsay was crying a lot so was obviously sick of being carried around and unable to feed whenever he wanted. Nyborg has a small fortification with a small garrison of guards. Elgar was jobbed off to do the talking if they stopped us for questioning. Fortunately, we were allowed straight through which reduced the chance of something going wrong. We are all armed however we are not carrying our weapons openly. We found an inn with three spare rooms, so we booked them all. As we are three travelling couples this gave us our first chance of privacy since leaving Bergen. Consequently, we ate quickly, and all disappeared to our rooms. I was grateful for the coins we were able to bring although a thought in the back of my head said that it was probably stolen from Britannia anyway. Before leaving it was agreed that we could sleep to mid-morning. I would have been happy to head off early as I knew baby Ramsay would be up which meant that Bran and I would be up however majority rules.

As it turned out baby Ramsay slept in which was probably a result of all the crying, he did the day before. Bran and I were still awake however the time was not wasted. After some breakfast we exited the town gate and continued our journey east. We had been speaking with people, when we had the chance, to find out any news. Most people were excited to tell us what was going on as the talk of war was in the air. It seems that king Harold had taken the fleet north to attack King Leif Erikson of Norway. There was no news on how this campaign had gone but everyone seemed optimistic. Godric was spoken about with the highest regard. They say he has transformed the Danish army so that they could not be beaten. Some had friends or family in the army who had trained under Godric and not one had a bad word to say.

There were some concerns about a massive Saxon army building in the south however everyone believed King Harold would be back in time to deal with them. Godric was obviously alive at the time when people heard these tales. If Godric had survived this far then he was still alive. I am here with his baby but sleeping with one of my lifelong friends. This news had a funny effect on me and then my relationship with Bran. I could see that Bran was concerned as I sensed that he was all in with me, and he was hurt to see that I still had such strong feelings for Godric. Bran is astute and would have known this was possible and that his relationship with me was probably temporary however it is human nature to be optimistic. I loved Godric and hoped that he would be back in Roskilde soon.

Today we were going to walk all the way to Roskilde. The path is wider and there is more traffic however the path is also straighter and less waterlogged. I could feel the excitement and knew that if we could only see Godric that everything would work out and we could at last be heading home. With Godric's favor with the King, we could get provisions and an escort back to Esbjerg and our boat. There were bound to be fortifications and guards at Roskilde however so far everything had been going better than could be hoped.

We reached Roskilde on dark as the walk had taken longer than I had hoped. Baby Ramsay had been great up until midday however since then he had cried himself to sleep on two occasions. We were all adapt at tuning out, so we did not hear the cries. Passersby would stop and stare and probably thought we were being cruel. Babies must learn that they do not get their own way by crying. We did not have time to stop, and I reasoned that I was doing Ramsay a favor, in the long run.

At Roskilde we were questioned however Elgar was able to explain that we are travelers, and that Bran, Tata and Stuart were here to join the army. The guard looked the men up and down and looked pleased with what he saw. We were ushered through and told of a good affordable inn for families of the army. Elgar thanked the man, and we entered Roskilde which is a very busy seaside port. It reminds me of Arbroath only three times the size. The harbor is extensive however mainly filled with fishing boats as the fleet is away at war. We had a great choice of Inn's however we thought that it was best to accept the advice of the guards.

The Inn is large and has two busy bars. However large the inn was, the innkeeper told us that they were full. It was now dark, and we needed a bed for the night. We ended up jumping from inn to inn looking for a bed, but it seemed that the city was full of all those preparing for the war. Tata thought that we may have success at the barracks as most of the army are away and they might have six beds for us. Bran and Stuart agreed that it might be worth a go however Elgar and Ronnie did not like it as they thought that it was too risky. I had the deciding vote, so I cast it in favor of the men as I did not have a better idea and I was cold, wet and exhausted. Baby Ramsay needed feeding and I needed somewhere to sleep.

The guards at the gate to the barrack told us to go away, that they were not a charity. At this Tata decided to play his trump card which was a massive risk. Tata told them that he was Godric's younger brother and that we were here to see Godric and could assist in a similar way as Godric. At mention of his name the men stood taller and straighter. Looking directly at Tata they questioned if it was true. 'As true as you have two ears and a nose,' Tata told them. This changed everything and we were shown into the nearest barracks and given a room with six beds. We were told that the mess was still serving food and would be for another hour. Tata thanked the man who had shown us to our rooms and then asked if he could show us to the mess. I thought Tata was a genius as we all sat down to some warm beef and soup. The feed was much better than anything we had had since leaving Bergen.

In the morning we were woken by the royal guard. They had come to escort us to the palace. It seems that word had spread, and I hoped this was for the better and we could have our own rooms in the palace. I did not wish to be ungrateful to the men at the barrack however I would much rather be in a palace with the comforts which come with that. There was an air of excitement among us as we followed the royal guards. The palace was unexpectedly large for what I had thought was a small country. I guess that they required something which was defendable from a naval attack as they were exposed to the sea. They also must have had wealth from trading and raiding.

Inside the palace we were taken into the throne room and there we met Jake the steward. He got us something to drink and said that the queen would see us shortly. Queen Dorette met us after a few minutes along with her daughter Amalie. Both women are stunning in their appearance, the queen with thick shiny black hair and the daughter with thick auburn hair. Tata stepped forward and spoke for us. 'Thank you for seeing us. We have travelled a long way to see Godric. I am Tata, Godric's brother and these are my companions. Kenner, Bran, Stuart, Elgar and Ronnie. Those in the room seemed to be listening intently, taking in every word. Tata spoke in Old Norse which is the language of the Danish.

The queen welcomed us and said that we must dine with them this evening. She said that Godric was away with King Harold although he was expected any day now. Amalie asked Tata if he had the same skills as his brother. 'Godric is surely one of the most resourceful and gifted men we have known' Tata said that there were some family traits however he would be happy if he had half the talents that his brother has. The queen beckoned Jake over and asked him to find us suitable accommodation. Given his instructions Jake ushered us from the throne room and down a long corridor. We walked past a couple of small courtyards and then through a larger open courtyard. Here we were shown to our wing of the building where we were given three adjacent rooms. Jake had rightly assumed that we were three couples.

We asked Jake if he had time to show us around the city of Roskilde. Our things will only take a few seconds to drop off and then we will have the entire day ahead of us. Jake flashed annoyance but soon covered this up with a smile. 'I can give you an hour which should give you enough of an idea so that you will not get lost.' I thanked him and quickly checked my room, and we all dumped our possessions, except for our coats and concealed weapons. Jake showed us the rest of the palace including where we could access the grounds. These grounds look well cared for and I longed to explore them further. We were shown the armory and the practice yard where there were a couple of dozen apprentices practicing. The forge was not far from the armory, and I could see this excited Tata. To amuse him we all followed him into the heated but open building. Tata was looking around and noted that he could see Godric's hand in its layout and even construction. There was a blacksmith hard at work who downed his tools when he noticed us. Coming our way, he pointed at Jake and yelled that he should not be bringing visitors into his place of work. The blacksmith seemed quite put off by our presence, so we turned and left in a hurry. Jake seemed annoyed again and was shouting back before we had left the forge. Outside he huffed and said that Gudbrand had always been a hot head and we should not take him as a representative of the Danish. Tata noted that it is Gudbrand's place of work, and he is obviously very passionate about it and what he does. Tata said that he understood the frustration even if this was just to back up the poor blacksmith because he himself was a blacksmith.

True to his word Jake gave us only an hour before he told us that he needed to be somewhere else. It looked like we were now free to roam. Tata told us to be careful as we are still foreigners in the grip of a potential enemy. We do not know the terms of Godric's work here, whether he is here as a servant or prisoner or even as part of a debt. I agreed that caution is required and asked that we meet back at our rooms on dark. This should be in time for our dinner invitation. The others agreed and walked off in couples. Bran stayed with me, and I wondered what was going through his head. Knowing that my beloved was alive must have been eating him as we had been close for decades and were now lovers. I worried what Godric would think when he found out but hoped that baby Ramsay would be enough to overcome this surprise. I had empathy for Bran and thought I would show him a good time this evening before Godric returns.

Bran and I spent the afternoon in the grounds where I saw lots of plants and trees that I had never seen before. The ground was damp, and all the plants are shooting as though they are reaching for heaven. The new life of spring always brought me alive with wonder and hope. Bran was quiet generally and that afternoon was no different. We spoke sporadically and Bran took baby Ramsay most of afternoon, giving my arms a rest. While in the garden Amalie came out and joined us. She commented on Ramsay and how lovely a baby he was. Ramsay has blue eyes like Godric and Tata which Amalie seemed to pick up. 'The baby has the look of Godric. Could it be that this is Godric's son and not yours,' as she pointed at Bran? Bran blushed and agreed that this was Godric's son and not his. There was a look to Amalie which I did not like but could not put a finger on it. Amalie then turned to me and wanted to know if Godric and I were still lovers. I told her what I knew which was that we had been lovers in the past however Bran and I were currently lovers. Out of the corner of my eye I could see that this put a smile on Bran's face. Something was wrong with the questioning from Amalie and my female instincts told me to be careful. It was almost like Amalie was jealous and she would only be this way if she were herself a lover of Godric's. She left shortly after and by that time I thought I had it worked out.

I had to distance myself from Godric at least until we were away from this place. Amalie was a threat to me and baby Ramsay as we were potential rivals. The others in our group knew me as Bran's partner so this was knowledge I alone had to deal with. That evening we met up at the agreed time and were met by Jake who showed us the way to the dining hall. Dorette and Amalie were already there with a red wine in hand. I felt like I needed a drink to smooth my nerves. Baby Ramsay was not with us as Jake had a maid with him when he came to get us. Jake told us that the maid would look after the baby until we returned. We could not refuse however this did make me slightly nervous.

We were offered either mead or wine when we entered the room. I had tasted wine before however the chance to drink wine in Strath Clyde was rare indeed. Consequently, I accepted the wine as did Bran and Stuart who were probably thinking the same thing as me. Tata, Ronnie and Elgar took mead which seemed only right as it was an even split. There was a beautiful warm fire going and Dorette invited us to go over and have a seat by it. We obliged and before long we were all perched around the fire which was in a hearth in the center of the inner wall.

The food did not come for some time which gave us a good opportunity to swap stories and be affected by the drinks which seemed to keep coming. Dorette was very interested in England and the different countries on the island. They had heard how the Vikings had been defeated by the English and the famed Halfdan had lost his life. During these stories we heard how the Picts had squeezed England from the north and the Normans had invaded from the south and now controlled half of all England. I could see that this upset Tata as he asked questions to find out more. There was not much more other than the Queen was being held in the tower of London.

They told us about the Saxon's and Wends in the south and about how they were massing for an invasion. They are beyond a defensive wall so when they come it will be slow going for them and costly for their army. Dorette was direct and asked me what my relationship with Godric was. She said that she thought he was husband to Aethelswith, queen of England. Here I am carrying a child which I have had with Godric. 'This is a strange situation indeed. It seems that Godric is a bit of a player which is a man's way, I guess. You are a beautiful woman and hard for one such as him to resist, I should think.' This talk about Godric and me made me blush again and I am sure it was made worse due to the heat in my face from the wine. I agreed that we had been lovers however that was when he was in Strath Clyde and a prisoner of my Father. These things have a life of their own and we are often moved along by events. Before I knew it, we were lovers even though it was against my father's wish. I am now with Bran here, my lifelong friend. I reached over and squeezed Bran's hand. Tata spoke up to come to my rescue. He said that these things have a way of working themselves out.

Tata started enquiring about the current campaign and how likely success was. He asked how many boats had set off and how many men this equaled. When told the rough numbers I could see that Tata was impressed, as were Elgar and Ronnie. Elgar said that with those numbers Kaupang will fall. She told Dorette that she had fought for Kaupang the previous year and knew that it was now weakened. 'This is a good time to attack Kaupang. With the army you have sent you will be victorious.' She smiled and nodded at what Elgar had said. I could see that this pleased her and Amalie.

Dinner arrived at last, and we all left the warmth of the fire to join the table. There was boar and vegetables which was an awesome feast, much more food than we would be able to eat. My mug was refilled, and it seemed destined that I was going to be drunk and wake with head pains. As we all got more intoxicated the conversations flowed to dangerous topics such as what we were doing here and the demise of England. Dorette said that she did not think that Godric would be leaving as he has a new lover and has made a life with Denmark. I could see the danger in these discussions however I was too drunk to direct the conversation away from them. By the time I woke the following morning besides the pain in my head I feared that I had said too much. I hoped that I did not dig graves for us or for Godric. Oh, how my head was hurting. I rolled over and saw that Bran was also holding his head in pain. It was like we had been poisoned. In a way we had been poisoned only it was of our own doing. Next, baby Ramsay started crying and I suddenly wished I were dead.

There was no other option but to get up and get out into the fresh air. It was drizzling outside so once we had coats, we headed for the gardens. The rain, damp, fresh air, and exercise seemed to do the trick as my head pains started to disappear. I do not think it was working so well on Bran as he was stumbling around with one eye still closed. It is funny how seeing someone in more discomfort than you can make you feel better.

Chapter 26

The Squeeze

There was nothing which could be done for him. Albert was still hanging onto life however he was not expected to last long. He has caught a disease and has been limp and dying for two days now. Rupert the medicine man said there was nothing we could do. 'Albert is in God's hands now.' This cuts to my heart as we have just spent a wonderful winter together. Albert was growing up quickly and for his age he already looked to have taken after his father. He is disobedient and cheeky, but I love him for that. Even Godric junior has enjoyed having him around. Finally, his younger brother could walk and talk and join in with mischief.

I have hardly left his side since he had fallen sick however I was now needed at the council meeting. William has launched a massive attack on Northampton, and we needed to agree on our next move. The thinking is that the Normans are trying to cut our country in two and although formidable Northampton has a smaller garrison then both London and Worchester. We are confident that Ethan can repel one or two thrusts however we are not sure about a prolonged attack. The runner told us that there were over ten thousand men around the castle. I do not want to leave my Albert as I am his mother and even holding his little hand gives me hope. Yesterday his eyes flickered open, and he looked at me. I find myself crying when I think of that moment. He knows I am here, and I am not going to leave him. I am a mother first and a queen second. I sent the runner back and abdicated my responsibility to John. John is as reliable and wise as any of my commanders and I would trust him with my life like no other than Godric. How I wished Godric was here to see his son.

There have been no further messages about Godric or Tata. Both are over the sea in Norway with few friends and an angry sea between them and their home. Godric has not even met Albert as Godric was captured on campaign at Jarrow shortly before Albert was born. I have thought of sending two boats over to Norway or Denmark to try and find out if they are still alive. We have commenced building a fleet of boats over at London and have spent most of winter fortifying the docks. The going was tough due to the miserable conditions however with determination the men have completed several boats which I have been told are seaworthy. We have not travelled back to London since breaking the siege. Wulfsige and Hereweald are still communicating with us through our pigeons even though we know that this communication method had been compromised in the past. At least now we control the land between London and Northampton. It would be fool hardy to send men and boats across the sea when we have no idea how to sail the sea or where we are going. Most of the countries across the sea are likely to be hostile to us and we cannot afford to lose any men.

Egbert and Godric junior miss their father and have also spent most of the last two days with me. Egbert is eleven and Godric junior is now eight. Both have started working as apprentices in the Forge. Bevan and Bert are taking good care of them, and the extra help has been welcomed as war tends to make blacksmiths very busy.

The war has galvanized the entire community from the mines and processing plants to the millers, farmers, and army. Everyone seems to be busy and like me I am sure they long for quieter times again.

John came home late and found the household were all still up. 'We are to ride to the aid of Northampton the day after tomorrow. We cannot afford to lose one of our northern cities so we must keep them off their walls.' I asked him about the threat to Worcester and what this risk is. He confirmed that they would once again rely on their alliance with Powys. 'We will leave two thousand men at home which should be enough should an attack come. Our army has swelled over winter with all the refugees making their way here. We can send close to ten thousand to meet William on equal terms or close enough.' John confirmed that no risks would be taken. This would be a stealthy campaign and the Normans would not be engaged in an open battle. The boys went to bed and John, Leofflaed and I sat around talking for another hour.

It was then that I noticed Albert had left me and left this world. I lifted my baby boy and cried into the nape of his neck. My little prince died with me holding his hand. John and Leofflaed comforted me. I was honored by them as I was fully aware of their own losses. All three of their children had been killed in the Viking wars and yet they had the strength to show me so much comfort. That night I slept with Albert in my bed. I wanted to hold him to make sure he felt safe until he was welcomed into heaven. Jesus spoke about the beauty and innocence of children. Surely god would welcome Albert's soul and grant him eternal life. 'I will see you one day my little star, be at peace and know that you will always be in my heart.'

The following morning, we took Albert out to the farm, and he was buried in the family plot. Everyone on the property stopped what they were doing to witness Albert's burial and to share my grief. The support I received humbled me and confirmed what a great community the farm was. I was thankful that Egbert and Godric junior were growing up as brothers in this community. Emrick said some kind words and we all feasted to Albert.

Emrick left with the army the following day. They were an impressive site riding out of Worchester valley on the eastern road. John stayed to administer Worchester and I should have moved into town to assist John and make decisions however I felt burnt out and needed time alone on the farm. Instead, I took some provisions and took the boys into the hills to visit their fathers' caves. The boys loved hiking in the hills much as their father had. Both boys were armed as was I. Along the way the boys took opportunities to practice with their bows on targets and the odd hare. The boys do not seem to have the patience to hit anything and given how bold the animals look I think the animals know it. Coming back that afternoon we were later than we had planned. It was just on dark and the trees around our path suddenly became filled with pheasants roosting for the evening. This thrilled the boys and me also. We all pointed and laughed, and I knew I was already feeling much better.

There was no news from the front for the first two days which did not mean anything either way. I had moved back into John and Leofflaed's house by the third day which is when we finally received a runner. The news was not welcomed as it said that there was a force of Picts from the north and William and the Normans from the south. It seems that our army is trapped by the Picts and the river to the north and King William from the south. There are skirmishes around the edges of the army and our retreat is now blocked to the west. Emrick has dug in and is constructing as many defensive fortifications as possible. John gave the runner a drink and sent for a council meeting. These were difficult circumstances and we needed to think of the implications.

For some reason, the Normans and the Picts seem to have aligned with the plan to wipe out England. The Picts have both Strath Clyde and Pictland banners, and their numbers would be close to ours. Without the river our army could be smashed from both sides. The runner said that the Normans were demanding our surrender for the sake of our men. John said that this was a good sign. 'If they are demanding our surrender, they are not so sure of victory or the cost of victory. We must have a plan, something to give our men hope.' I asked John what could be done, and he just shook his head and said that he wished he knew where the Welsh were.

Options were discussed all evening and we were still up when the sun began to rise. We had sat by candlelight all through the night with a small fire for warmth. It was only John, Leofflaed, Bevan, Bledri and me. Leofflaed was a bystander however her presence was important as it supported John and the rest of us. It also gave us the outlook from a non-military background. I felt exhausted and from looking at the others I knew that they were the same way. The option which was given the most consideration was having Ethan open the gates and having all ten thousand men squeeze into Northampton. The positive was the avoidance of a battle we were unlikely to win and thus we preserve our men for a better situation. However, negatives were too many and too easy to think of. We kept coming back to this option as it gave our minds immediate relief. The negatives included the castle being too small for so many men and animals. The horses would need to be abandoned and even then, the castle was too small so although they could squeeze in, they will be crammed like hay in a bale. With this many men the Northampton stores would soon be empty, and starvation and disease would take over.

Another popular option which was put forward by Bledri was an arrow assault back to the west. It would be a push deep into the enemy forces with the aim of breaking through and making for the safety of Worchester's walls. This was also very risky as it depended on where the enemy were set up. It is likely that the large force was now positioned between Emrick and Worchester so this arrow assault would only end up in the death of many or most of our men. With this assessment Bledri suggested they may break out toward the southeast and London. This appealed to me more however it would then leave approximately twenty thousand of the enemy a shot at either Northampton or Worchester and we still do not have the Welsh. Although London does not have such great defenses, besides the castle, London is a large city which could accommodate the men and animals. Food can be supplied from Colchester and the rest of East Angles. With the boats we might even be able to get some of the men home by sailing them around and up the River Seven. The problems of this plan were pointed out as being these boats would have to make it past the Norman fleet which will be sitting off the south coast. At least the men would be alive with this option although possibly only temporarily. The army are key as without these men we will struggle to make it through to the following winter.

John noted that we had no word from York, Repton or Nottingham. These northern towns must either have fallen or the Pict army has taken a wide berth and cut off attempts to warn us. If they had been attacked, I am sure we would have been warned and I said as much to the group. John said that he agreed and said that the implications are that we have men who could harass the Picts and at least keep them uncomfortable and on their toes.

The final option was to throw together a force of the remaining men and women who were trained to fight. This force could attack the outside ranks of the Normans and assist our army to break out. Such a move would risk much as Worchester would be mostly undefended and there are still unknown forces around such as Andras and Henry from Devon.

At last, I put up my hands and said this is enough. 'Thank you everyone for the suggestions however now we must go away and sleep. When we wake, we can consider the options and with the rest some wisdom may fall on our situation. John stood and said that he agreed. We will break and meet in the midafternoon. I will invite the council members who are still here, and we will meet in the town hall. We all wished each other a successful sleep and went our own way. Bledri and Bevan both went back to the farm however I stayed in the room I had at John and Leofflaed's. The thought of my own bed out on the farm was appealing however I was just too tied.

That afternoon I was sitting around the council table still feeling groggy from the all-night meeting we had just pulled. It did not matter as my head was still clearer than it had been in the morning. Just as we were about to start a rider came up to the town hall. We had all heard the hooves on the stone streets and had stopped to listen. A rider could have good or bad tidings, so I prayed that they were good on this occasion. There were twelve of us in the room which included some who were not councilors.

The rider was a little out of breath, so he was given some water and a seat at the table. The rider was Gethin, steward to Kind David. He told us that the tidings were bad as King David has been killed and Cadfael is now King of Powys. This was ill news as all of us in the room knew King David and had been fond of him. Powys and England had forged an unbreakable bond. The commotion died down so that we could give Gethin a chance to continue. We request aid as Deheubarth have sided with Morganniog and they are taking Powys town by town. They out number us and although we fight with courage, we do not know how long we will be able to hold out. King David died at the battle of Builth Wells which we still hold but are at risk of losing as we are mostly surrounded. I have ridden as hard as I could, but I fear it might already be too late. John spoke up now and asked Gethin if he had received our call for aid. Gethin looked surprised and said that there had been no message arrive from England. This news was also tragic as it meant that our runner had been cut off and was likely dead in a ditch. It also meant that no help was coming.

Deheubarth is a major country of Wales on the southwest coast with St David as its capital. I knew St David's and the thought of that place and Deheubarth shot fear through me. Wales had been peaceful for so long that I wondered what had stirred it up. Bledri, who was Welsh said that there was something fishy going on as Deheubarth and Morganniog were traditional allies of Powys. Gethin spoke up again and said that Morganniog were being led by a King Andras of Devon. 'The Morganniog and Deheubarth armies have joined, and King Andras has joint command along with King Morgan of Deheubarth.' Hearing this news almost made me vomit. How could I have made such poor judgement to have married such an animal. We are his people, and he is doing everything to bring us down. I had many emotions run through me at the same time including shame, hatred, fear and despair. I wanted Godric more than I have ever wanted him before. I wanted to bury my head into his shoulder and cry, but I could do neither. We were now alone, and we needed to act.

With the ill tidings there were many discussions going on around the room. John called the room to order and acknowledged the news from Powys. He proceeded to ask Gethin some logistics questions to gauge the situation in Powys. Gethin told us that they had three thousand men in the field and could draw on another three thousand from the northern towns. He told us that Builth Wells was difficult to defend and they were at risk of being overrun. Bledri then joined the discussion and suggested they retreat to Newtown which has a small keep and walls which can be more easily defended. There is a wide river on the east which limits the opportunity of the enemy. 'It might already be too late for that,' spoke Gethin also with despair. John then told Bledri to call the men from the north and have them assemble and prepare at Newtown. Gethin looked at him and questioned that the north would then be undefended. John told him that the Picts are all down here in England, your north should be safe, and the threat is in the south.

'We will look to send you some aid. We will send some riders back with you to make sure you get back and are not cut off. We will be engaging the Picts and the Normans but make no mistake, the news you bring are ill tidings and give us heavy hearts. Our army is currently engaged in a two to one battle over at Northampton. Please stay and have refreshments and a rest and let us know when you are ready to return. We will give you a fresh horse and an escort.' With that Gethin was shown from the room and I expect and hope he was taken to a room to eat and sleep. I looked around and John was looking right at me. Our situation seems to be getting worse as we wait.

John spoke again and this time it was with the authority of the Council leader and elder which he was. 'A wise man once told me that only a fool acts with haste in the face of a threat' Haste is what the attacker expects and usually gets which gives it an additional advantage to that of the threat itself and the surprise. At times like this we need to take a deep breath and assess our options. Firstly, Powys will need our support however they can call on their north which should give them time. Secondly, our army of ten thousand will have to set up defenses and defend their position ferociously, which we have heard they are already doing. Lastly, we build a new army with the men, women and refugees who are of fighting age. This is an all-in situation for Worchester, and this is where we show the world what we are made of. Messages must be sent to Ethan so that he can get a message to Emrick to tell him that he must be patient and protect every life if possible. A message must be sent to York that they must call in their farmers and put together as big a force as they can. They must be ready for either a field campaign or the defense of York. Leicester, Repton and Nottingham will have to do the same and if asked for they will need to join an army on our command. A last message must make London with the same instructions for East Anglia. They must stop what they are doing and meet at London ready to march.' John told us that this should take three weeks or more to arrange. We would then have the option to bring the full force of England on those gathered at Northampton. The biggest unknown was whether the army at Northampton could hold out.

Chapter 27

Extremes

We had only been waiting a week however I could see that the people in the palace were getting restless. Dorette was giving us constant updates as we usually shared one meal per day together. The pressure was building along the southern border with the Saxons as Otto continued to amass an invasion force. Apart from the men guarding the wall there had been no other deployment from the army. Dorette told me how this frustrated her and that her husband should have been back weeks ago. They left on the campaign five weeks earlier and besides Dorette the servants were all now beginning to worry. King Harold had most of his army north and since word came of victory nothing else had been heard from them.

I have been waiting for half a year for this moment and I felt like I would wait forever. I have Bran keeping me warm at night, but my heart is elsewhere. Bran and I do not discuss it which helps as I love Bran and need him but, in the end, we both know I will be Godric's when he is back. I have not even considered that he does not feel the same way. That look we shared just before he was captured at the Stonehaven dock. The look told me everything. It told me that he had forgiven me and that he still loved me. I have thought him lost on two occasions and each time he has managed to survive.

It is now early summer, and I have been spending many hours exploring Roskilde and the surrounding countryside. Bran is usually with me as being from Strath Clyde he also appreciates the open spaces and hates being crammed into a city. It is like being dogs trapped in a cage. You will end up accepting the cage as your spirit is squashed. There will be a sickness however you will not be able to pinpoint where the sickness comes from. This is the way we had started to feel in Bergen until the weather changed and we could spend more time outside the walls. Two days in this place and we were feeling the same. This is when Bran suggested we make the most of our time waiting by exploring the immediate region.

We have formed a close attachment to our servants as we have been kind to them which seems unusual. Most of the servants are Russian captives from up the Baltic Sea. They have accepted their position however many of the Danish seem to abuse their power over them. The servants live in dormitories like barracks and get one meal per day. They do everything from cleaning to preparing the food. The girls are expected to make themselves available to the males in the palace including the guards. Life for these many servants is harsh. Back in Carlisle we have servants however they are treated with dignity, and they have rights. They eat twice per day and apart from their tasks they have the rest of their time to themselves. Two of the servants which we have built an immediate relationship with are Arni and Kara. Both are inquisitive and both have come on adventures around Roskilde at some point. They speak Old Norse about as well as we do so between us, we get along. They are not meant to speak inside the palace unless they are asked a question. Once outside the palace they chatter endlessly. Both come from humble fishing villages which had historically been safe from raiding as ice sheets scared the raiding boats from attempting their inlet. With the climate changing the ice has been melting more every year and one day a fleet of raiding boats came right up to their town. They knew what it was and attempted to flee to the forests however the men stayed for days and hunted them down.

Kara had been a big help with looking after Ramsay. Kara has her own twelve-month-old baby in her dormitory and volunteered to look after baby Ramsay as often as she could. She did not know who the father of her baby was such was her position in the palace. Kara has been doing everything from putting baby Ramsay to bed and giving him his feeds when he screams for food.

We had begun taking extra food for the servants and particularly Arni and Kara. It seems that where they come from is like the country around Glasgow so like us, they thrived once given freedom outside of the palace. Arni had been a fisherman and Kara had been involved in home duties with her mother and aunts. They prepared meals and made clothing and blankets. On one such adventure along the coastline north of Roskilde we saw the flotilla of ships coming south across the Skagerrak straight. It could only be

King Harold and his men returning victoriously. Flags were flying from the masts on full display. Just then the clouds which had been building decided to open and we got drenched as we made our way back to the palace.

I longed to see Godric and to hold and be held by him however I was now feeling nervous. I had that sick feeling in my stomach, the one you get when there is a situation which you know you cannot avoid. Back at the palace I dried and went to find Tata. There was a commotion in the palace with the news that King Harold was returning. Arni, who was out with us took off as soon as we were back. I could see he was worried that he might be missed which will give him trouble. Tata and Stuart seem as excited as me as we climbed the steps of the palace to get a good vantage point over the docks. Despite the rain the docks were filling with people all trying to get a position to see their King or loved one's return. It was still raining those cold heavy drops and as I had just dried, I had no intention of going out into it again. From the spot we found we would get to see the men disembark from the boats and the procession through the town to the palace. The walkway where we were standing is four stories high giving us two stories above the highest buildings between us and the dock. We had the connecting road to the Eastern gate directly below us.

The men numbered in their thousands and not all the boats could dock at once. The first boat to disembark was the Kings as we watched the guard of honor form around what was obviously the largest and most spectacular boat. Although we could not be sure it looked like the king was the first to disembark. Then I saw Godric as he stepped from the boat to the docks. There was no mistaking his size, his flowing dark hair and beard. Godric has a presence wherever he is and even at this distance I knew it was him. His brother Tata was beside me and Godric is not that dissimilar to him. Tata is a couple of inches shorter but just as broad and of the same coloring. From our vantage point we could see that Godric was in close with the king and his men. Things must have gone well for them on this campaign. The people were cheering as the King and his entourage made their way from the docks and up the streets to the palace. Tata, Bran, and I stayed on the covered walkway and watched them all the way. They looked at ease and were smiling and laughing with the people who they passed. Even Godric, who seems to always be alert, seemed to be at ease. He would not know that I was here, and he would not have seen his brother for years. He was about to get one of the surprises of his life.

We stayed watching the procession beyond when the King and Godric entered the palace. Dozens of boats were now disembarking at the same time. This is a massive well-armed force which seems to have everything an army would want from armor to discipline. It was an emotional homecoming for most with loved ones in their thousands here to meet the men. Roskilde had been swelling with people over the last week in anticipation of the armies return. 'We have seen enough Tata, let's go and surprise your brother.' Tata smiled and put an arm around me agreeing that it was over time.

Guards met us as we went to walk into the throne room. I told them we were here to pay our respects to the King as guests of his Palace. The guards allowed us through and we were instantly surrounded by the excitement and a mass of people. King Harold is shaking hands and making his way to the throne. I saw Godric instantly as he stands out in any crowd. I was watching his eyes as he scanned the room. He now looked like the ever-alert Godric which I remembered. He takes in everything and is ready for any threat or surprise. As his eyes looked in my direction, I saw them linger on me for a microsecond longer as they moved on. He knew I was here and even though his eyes had moved on I could see a smile begin to fill his face.

At that moment he turned toward the throne as Amalie came running out and threw herself into his arms. Godric was meant to be getting the surprise however instead I was getting it. All at once I felt flush with emotions. I was furious, envious, and extremely Jealous. Stunned I did not move as I watched Amalie ply Godric with kisses. Worse was that he was giving them back, this really sickened me. I turned to leave when Tata grabbed my hand. I turned to him as he pulled me close. 'Hold your nerve Kenner. You are a princess and Godric has not seen you in a long time. Godric owes you nothing and you owe Godric nothing. Be calm and everything will work out as it should.' Wow Tata was more like his brother then I had thought. He knew how I felt about Godric and knew that I was going to flee. Tata was right as I needed to reconcile with Godric at some point and better in the open where I can control my emotions.

Tata pulled me with him as we made our way to the throne. At the same time King Harold was still making his way to the throne, and it looked like he would be sitting soon. Godric and Amalie turned as we came up to them. Godric faced us with his broad smile and open arms, I saw the threatening look Amalie gave me from behind his back. The look was one of hatred and it was laced with malice. It dawned on me that this was a dangerous situation for me as she is the Kings daughter. Tata and Godric embraced, ruffled each other's hair, and stood back and admired each other. 'My beloved brother, how I dreamed of this moment. You are every bit an Amity and our parents would be thrilled at how you have turned out.' Tata repaid the complements and Godric turned to me and pulled me into his arms. 'I am so sorry I pretended to hate you and for ignoring you as we crossed Pictland. I have thought of you almost every day since then and longed to be able to hold you and make amends.' Switching to Celtic Godric continued. I was amazed at his control and his ease with the situation. 'As you can see, I am currently sharing a bed with Amalie, this will not be for long as we must be home at the first opportunity. Be alert and be prepared to flee at a moment's notice, our time will come again.' He said the last looking directly into my eyes while holding both my hands. Godric also had his cheeky childish smile and I wished that moment could have lasted forever. He abruptly dropped my hands, put an arm over the shoulder of Tata and grabbed Amalie's hand with his free hand.

The king had taken a seat on the throne and those in the room had stepped back so that all in the room could see the king. At this point one of his men stepped forward and spoke to us. I later found out it was Gorm, the commander of the army. Gorm was an imposing man like Tata and Godric. He was probably Godric's height of around six foot two inches or in that range. Gorm held the rooms attention as he announced the return of the Victorious King Harold. He spoke of the expansion of the Danish empire which now included most of Norway. 'Norway now recognize King Harold as their king and have handed their lands and taxes to him. The victory was complete, and we now prepare for the Wends and the Saxons. We are powerful and the world should be put on notice that King Harold has your measure.' With that the room erupted in applause except for notably Godric, Tata and me. Gorm gave a real rallying cry to the nobles of Denmark.

The room eventually went quiet, and the King stood to address the room. 'We have been on campaign longer than we would have liked however we have had great success. King Leif Erikson was killed by the hand of Godric of the English. We swept into Kaupang and were able to secure it quickly and with limited bloodshed. The other southern strongholds of the Vikings took some securing however we were able to take control of Stavanger, Lindenies, Nordmarka and Horten. Norway is now Danish. We have left commanders and men over there to ensure the Vikings accept their new rulers. Although we do not have any real concerns as the people seem to have embraced us.' With this there was further applause and celebration. Food and drink were brought out and the celebrations really commenced.

I left the room as I did not feel like I was a part of it, and I could not stand to see Godric with Amalie. Amalie has a real dark side and I had to trust that Godric knew it and would be safe. He was right that I needed to keep my head down and keep myself out of the minds of the Danish. Baby Ramsay was my next thought as his life was in peril if we remained in Roskilde. I left to find Bran to tell him how the Kings arrival had gone. Once with Bran I felt a little better as he could understand our predicament. From the care Godric took when he spoke to me, I suspect that he is uncertain how he is going to get away and out of the clutches of the Danish and Amalie.

That evening I lay in bed listening to the festivities as they continued into the night. Tata had joined them along with Bran, Stuart, Elgar, and Ronnie. Baby Ramsay was sleeping however I had too much on my mind to sleep. I wondered where Godric was and if he was thinking about me. The way he held my hands and looked at me I know he still loves me. He apologized when he had nothing to apologize for. When I was the person who owed him an apology for my betrayal of him to my father. I had made the wrong choice and all the events since then are a result of that choice. Family is everything in this world however family could not always be trusted. There are times when we need to trust our gut instinct.

There was a gentle knock at the door which I only heard because I was awake. I quietly got out of bed and peaked around the door. Kara was there in her nighty holding a lamp. She said that she had been given a message to give me. She said that the Kings steward had given it to her and said it must be delivered immediately. I opened it at once and read it out loud. Not so loud as to wake baby Ramsay but loud enough so that Kara could here.

Meet me under the Dead Oak in the central garden. The dead oak is an ancient oak tree in the middle of the main Palace garden. It was reputedly struck by lightning some ten years back and progressively died over the following years. We will be away from prying eyes so I can really hold you and show you my love. I looked up at Kara and could see she had tears in her eyes. I held her hands and thanked her for the message. Godric is the man I have given my heart to even though Bran is my best friend in the world. Bran will understand. Kara was crying and smiling at me, and she offered to take Baby Ramsay back to her room while I went to see Godric. Thanking her I dressed and took a coat and kissed Ramsay on the way out. I was going to see my beloved where we could hold each other and hopefully make love in the garden where I have been spending so much time.

The rain had stopped which was a blessing. It was a mild night helped by the low cloud. There was light stretching out into the garden from all the openings to the adjacent walkway. I pushed on to the old oak where I was going to meet my beloved. He must still be with Amalie, or we would not have to be meeting in private. I guess it will be difficult for him to leave her without causing a stir. Amalie strikes me as being someone who is used to having her own way. We should all just leave tonight, forget everything, and make for Esbjerg and the boat. I know this is too soon however part of me thinks it would be the safest thing for us.

Finally, I reached the tree however there was no sign of Godric. I stood waiting for a few minutes as I was not sure if I was late or early. My instincts told me there was something wrong as I do not remember Godric being late or even vague when arranging something. I was about to leave back to the building when a voice behind me told me that she was glad that I had come. Amalie had crept up to me without making a sound. The wet ground had disguised here footsteps. 'Amalie, I was not expecting you.' She laughed at this and said that of course I was not as she knew I was pining for Godric. She had sent me the message so that they could have the chance to speak in private. I felt vulnerable out here and I didn't even carry a weapon.

Amalie started goading me about her love with Godric. 'Do you know that I carry Godric's child? Godric and I will marry and together our family will rule all of Denmark and beyond. With Godric we will conquer the Saxon's, the Wends and all the southern European nations. The Danish will be feared around the world, and I will bear the future generations of

Denmark royalty. You are nothing but a distraction as I saw the way he looked at you. There cannot be two of us in Godric's life, I hope you understand?' Amalie was laying it into me and the more she told me the more I knew my life was at risk. I told her that I saw love in his eyes for her and that I was now with Bran and would not have him back. I was doing my best to downplay my feelings for him while boosting what I thought he thought of Amalie.

Whatever I said did not seem to be making a difference as she had this vicious look in her eyes which was made worse as it was by the light of the candles, we both held. It was then that I realized that I had backed up to the old Oak tree. From either side men came from behind the tree with one of them shoving a rag into my mouth to stop me screaming. I struggled to free myself but could not break the grip. The men dragged me to the ground and began opening the buttons on my coat. Amalie knelt beside me and ripped open my blouse freeing my bosom to the mild night air. What was she doing to me, I thought? This was terrifying as I was totally helpless. I wanted to scream for help or at least to inflict some pain on my attackers but there was nothing I could do.

Amalie drew a dagger which looked to have been freshly sharpened. 'I can see that Godric is in your heart and that Godric loves you. You can say all you wish to distract me, and I commend you that you realized the threat that I am. I am striking quick before you have the chance to poison Godric against me. I am going to take your heart for myself and place it in a box to remind anyone who dares to give their heart to Godric.' Now I was really scared as I contemplated what she said. Time had slowed as I saw her lift the knife and bring the cold blade down to my chest. Pain shot through my body as the blade plunged through my ribs. I screamed into the rags from pain and terror. I now knew that I was going to die. Amalie was cutting out my heart. I stopped struggling and watched Amalie lift my beating heart out of my chest. She showed me my heart before putting it in a box she had nearby. I knew I was dead but still time slowed further. I thought of Godric and the wonderful times we had spent together, especially on our long horse rides to the secluded lakes around Carlisle. I thought about Baby Rick and Ramsay and how much love and happiness they had brought me and about what would become of them. Lastly, I thought of home and the wish to say goodbye to my family and friends.

Chapter 28

Rage

Coming up from the docks I could see Tata and Kenner looking down from the walkway above. I know they are not aware that I have seen them, but my sixth sense told me they were up there watching. The crowds are pressing us but they are mostly being held back by guards. This is a victorious homecoming and what the King has achieved deserves recognition as most of the Viking kingdoms have now been swallowed into the Danish empire. The king is under no illusion that the greatest battle is still to come. He offered me lordship over Norway although I declined as I said I needed to get back to England to see to the welfare of my people. I could see that he was not impressed however the mood was so great that he simply said, 'So be it.'

Since the offer I have considered the benefits of being lord over Norway. I am also surprised he offered me this as with the resources of Norway I could build a force to threaten Denmark. He either really trusts me or he already knew I would refuse.

The campaign was not all smooth sailing as the Viking states had risen against us. Particularly Horten in the north and Stavanger from the west coast. Both armies were large and threatening and fortunately for us they did not merge and attack as one. Horten, reached us first and not wanting to be trapped inside the city walls we met them on the fields north of the city. Our heavy horse and superior English/Danish longbows made short work to the initial attack. I had hoped that this would be enough to put them off the battle and convince them to submit. However they fought on until almost all their men were slaughtered. They all wanted Valhalla and thought dying in battle would get them there. I looked at their sacrifice as selfishness as they have families back home who would struggle and maybe perish for their deed. The last remaining sensible men surrendered and the threat from the north was removed.

Stavanger arrived a week later for which we had early warning. Stavanger had a larger army which was close to the number we still had in the Danish army. We decided to stay in the city as we had the river between us and them and we wanted to play it safe to preserve as many men as we could. Word had reached us that the Saxon's were amassing south of our wall in Denmark, and we knew that the battle against them was our biggest threat. From the security of the Kaupang wall we watched the Stavanger army relocate across the river outside of our northern wall. The aim of this battle was preservation of life. We had supplies in our stores and knew that the longer the army was in the field the more desperate they would become. We had many elevated locations where our archers could take down threats.

The siege lasted two weeks and, in the end, we lost patience and via our northeast gate we poured out of Kaupang and pinned the Stavanger against our wall and the river. There was blood spilt on both sides but by the time it was over it was a slaughter and many from Stavanger were needless killed. War seems like the best way of keeping population growth in check. With the men I have seen die in battles I am surprised there is still enough to form an army. One day this mindless destruction of life will end. One day I will be the person to end the waste of life in Britannia and maybe over here as there seems little chance anyone else is working toward that goal.

With the last of the resistance, we set up some control and Danish authority and once that was achieved, we made for Roskilde. I would say home however this place could never be home. Nobody seems to trust anybody, and I am tolerated because I am useful. I am under no illusions that the minute I stop being useful they will either slit my throat or throw me in a dungeon without a key. I have made many friends and for them I feel sorry. It is easy to see that people here are expandable. The value of life might be the one thing I have taught this King even if it is so he can get advantage over his foe.

Kenner is just as amazingly beautiful as I remember her to be. That she is here is sign enough of here feelings for me. That she continued our mission to rescue Tata and cross the seas is special beyond belief. I know I am married to Aethelswith, and I loved her dearly however it seems like a lifetime ago that I was in her arms and love. What is Aethelswith up to now and have we grown apart. She may even have remarried as she would have thought me dead. I do not know how things will work out when I finally get home however for now it was reassuring knowing that Kenner must still love me. I love my brother and it will be wonderful to hold him again. To arrive back home after the attack at Jarrow where I thought we were all dead. I have been blessed by God and I now have confidence that there is a higher purpose for my life.

Once inside the palace Harold told us he wanted to celebrate into the night, and we were all to gather in the throne room. I understood the need to celebrate as Vikings have always been a threat to Denmark much as they were to Britannia. The Viking raids will end now that he has conquered them., The land will also bring in additional taxes for the Danish. I was in the inner sanctum of his leadership group and since the victory the rhetoric about expansion including raiding the coastlines of Europe had me worried. The Vikings may be down, but they were not out, and it sounded as though the Danish were looking to follow in their footsteps or at least the vacuum they have left.

Before even reaching the throne room I had Amalie on me with all affection, jumping into my arms. I looked across at King Harold, when I could finally free my face, and I saw his smile of approval as it beamed back at me. I felt a little trapped as I had been a willing lover before the campaign however I did not know that Kenner would be waiting when I returned. I knew this was a sticky situation however I would resolve it by fleeing back to England with Kenner. I did not feel brave enough to face Amalie as I knew she had a nasty side which I did not wish to test. It was not that I feared Amalie however I knew that her father could make life very difficult for me. Consequently, I grabbed her hand and whispered into her ear that I had missed her. This was not a lie as I had genuinely missed her firm athletic body on the drunken nights in Kaupang. Amalie was always enthusiastic no matter what the opportunity or adventure. She was depressed to have missed out on the campaign to take Norway and I would not be surprised if she still held a grudge against her father. It looked like all was forgotten as we walked into the throne room hand in hand for the entire court to see. I felt like Amalie was putting me on display and I had a suspicion that this was because of Kenner. There was naught to be done until I had a chance to speak with Kenner.

Scanning the room, I saw her and even though I could see her discomfort with the situation she looked stunning in the dress which she wore. The dress was nothing fancy, long, and grey however it hugged her shapely figure. I had to be careful not to draw attention to her as now that Amalie had made a public display that we were lovers Kenner was in extreme danger. The court would see Kenner as a foreigner with the potential to unsettle the balance of power. I know that King Harold will not willingly let me go and the behavior of Amalie only confirms my suspicion.

At last, my brother and I come face to face. I can't do anything other than hug him as tears come to my eyes. 'From the battle of Jarrow to Denmark, who could have written about it? I have longed for this moment and the one where we both return home.' I was speaking in English as I did not need prying ears listening to my sentiments. 'You look so strong and well, the quarry seems to have done you no harm physically. I thank you and Kenner for coming to my aid. We will talk more tomorrow when we get some time together.' With that I turned to the Women I have loved since we first met a decade ago. I was young and a captive of her fathers. I had favorable conditions as I was a blacksmith, and this is a useful trade. Kenner and I both love horses and this commonality brought us together. Those carefree days are some of my fondest memories apart from the ones where I was at home with my family.' I took Kenner's hands and apologized for sulking and not speaking to her. In Celtic I told her about my situation with Amalie and to be prepared to leave on a moment's notice. This was all I could do at that moment as the room was full of nobles and commanders but more importantly Amalie was standing behind me.

I endured the Kings speech with a hint of boredom but also of alarm. The king was talking about bringing war to the peoples of Europe once they defeated their old enemy the Saxon's. I was starting to hope that the Saxon's could blunt their army and ego. Finally, the speeches were over, and the food and drink arrived. I had not eaten since we left this morning, and I had a pain which needed filling.

'Tell me that you love me,' Amalie whispered in my ear. 'Let's go somewhere private so that we can catch up where we left off. I long to have you in me, to have you be my man again. I also have some important news which I can only tell you in private.' Amalie was at me to leave with her and as appealing as this was my mind had now switched entirely to Kenner. I was also hungry which is what I told her. The truth was I had not eaten since sunrise and wanted, almost needed to make the most of this food. Looking into her eyes I kissed her passionately and hoped that this would be enough to put her on hold.

Gorm came over with mugs of mead carrying one for me. Gorm put his hand around Amalie and told her to leave me alone. 'He is just home from war women, give him some space,' as he handed me a mug. I welcomed the intervention and used it to fall into conversation with them both. I could sense that Amalie was getting bored and sure enough she let go of my hand and disappeared into the crowd. While in the conversation I casually looked around the room but could no longer see Kenner. I could however see Tata who were conversing with another man and some women. It was reassuring knowing that Tata was here as I know his character and strengths and by my side, we would be difficult to take down. It had been so long, but the sight of my brother filled me with joy. I chugged down my drink and demanded another. This brought a slap on the back from Gorm as he commented that they would make a Dane out of me yet.

Through the course of the night, I was able to share a drink with Tata. He introduced me to Elgar whom he is currently bedding. Elgar is wiry but muscular evidenced by her exposed arms and neck. She would be around Tata's age and like me Tata has done what he has had to do to survive. Tata has a wife back in Worchester in Seren however she may have remarried thinking Tata was dead. My brother and I were more alike than we knew, and we were alike in many ways. From our point of view our relationships made sense. We were men who had needs and high on the list of needs was to be loved. If our wives have remained faithful to us and they find out that we have taken other women, they may be deeply offended. Our wives may have thought us dead and would thus have an excuse to remarry however we know we are not dead so for us there is no excuse. This was a humbling thought as I thought of my vows during the wedding ceremony and went on to think about God's protection, I had always received even though I had lied to him when getting married. The marriage vows cannot be as important as the other purposes he has for me. I said as much to Tata when we were alone, and he just laughed at me.

Tata told me he had given up on there being any God years ago when he passed a hundred back breaking days in that northern quarry. 'My body no longer ached, and I no longer felt the icy conditions. I had prayed every day for a hundred days that there would be some opportunity for escape. I prayed that someone would come to my rescue, and I prayed for you. By the time a hundred days came around I gave up. I spent the best part of two years in that quarry. Seven-hundred days breaking and hauling rocks, chained to my fellow human beings. Chained while defecating and pissing, chained while eating. The blessing was I could sleep chain free although the lice had their way with me once the chains were removed. The bed lice lay in wait for my exhausted body to hit the mattress. I gave up on god and instead I believed in myself. I used the punishment to build my mind and body and with the work crew my mission became helping them mentally and physically if needed. Eventually I was rescued, and I guess this could have been God coming through.' Tata took a big swig of his drink and became somber with his thoughts. I could understand where he was coming from however could it not have been God who had given him the strength to endure what would have broken most men. Finding me here in Denmark was like finding a stick in a haystack. The chances are so small so surely this also could have been God's work.

Stuart and Ronnie came over to share a drink. I did not know either but was soon introduced. Stuart had been in the quarry with Tata and Ronnie was Viking from Bergen. They told me a little about their time there but of most interest to me was how they learnt that I was in Denmark. Hearing that Sigvald was alive broke me out of my deep reflections and gave me reason to eat and drink some more. Sigvald, or Stern as I had called him had been my captor turn friend. Sigvald and I had travelled with Bjorn down the spine of Norway to present to King Leif Erikson. The king had taken me captive and slit Bjorn's throat. I suspected a similar fate for Sigvald so was joyed to hear he was well and at home.

The night had dragged on and there was no sign of Amalie. Tata and the others said that they were going to bed and looking around I thought I had best do the same. I felt drunk and I knew I needed sleep after the day I had had. We all went our own ways, and I was again faced with a dilemma, to find Kenner's room or make for Amalie's bed. In my condition I could have made the wrong decision as I was surely tempted to follow my heart. My head won by the smallest of margins, and I made for Amalie's room.

Amalie was not in her room which surprised me. She proclaimed love for me, but she may have another lover in the palace which would not be unusual for a princess. I was too tied to dwell on it and thought it a blessing as rather than make love I could crash, exhausted.

The following morning, I was awoken by a naked Amalie astride my body. Immediately all my senses were awakened and without thought I knew what to do. It was only when midway through making love that the thought of Kenner came into my mind. There was nothing to do but continue and enjoy my situation, and I have to say, six weeks away with smelly men was nothing compared to the sweet perfumes and soft skin of Amalie.

We lay down, side by side with Amalie's head on my shoulder and her free hand stroking my chest. Amalie told me that she was pregnant and from the way that she said it she was sure that I was the father. I knew not to question a woman when they say this as it would throw their commitment and virtue into doubt. I kissed her and told her how wonderful this news was. I had children all over the world so what difference was another one. This child would not know their father as I knew I had to leave as soon as I could. Although I had been given the perfect waking gift my head still ached from the alcohol the night before. There was light coming through the window shutters so I knew it was later than I would have liked.

Breaking the spell of our intimate time in bed I rolled out of bed and got dressed. Amalie asked where I was going and with a kiss, I told her I was going for morning practice. She knew me to be fanatical with my routines and practice so did not question me.

Outside the room I started searching for Kenner, Tata, and the others. I came across a servant and asked if they knew where lady Kenner's room was. He told me that they were in the dormitories on the ground floor around the central court. I headed that way and when I reached the dormitories, I found an open door with a servant girl in it. She was startled when she saw me and then she broke down. I entered the room and comforted her. The girl was almost inconsolable. Eventually she began to speak, and she told me the story. She told me that her name was Kara and that she had been friends with Kenner. Kara said that she had delivered a message to her just before midnight. 'The message said to meet her at the old dead oak tree in the main palace garden. She was to meet Godric at midnight, so the message said. I know this as Kenner read me the message. Kenner dressed and gave me the baby. She looked so happy, and I felt joy that she was going to at last be with her love.' Kara burst into tears again and it took some time to calm her.

I was alarmed instantly as I knew I did not send the message. I told Kara that I was Godric and I had not sent the message. 'Do you know who could have sent the message,' I asked her? She said that this is Kenner's room and she did not return. Kara told me that she could not think who could have done it. Kara told me that Kenner's body has just been found in the Palace garden. She broke down again with sobs and a held her in my arms for comfort. I looked around at Kenner's bedside table through the tears which were now filling my eyes. Here was the letter, the poison which led Kenner to her death. I picked up the letter and ran my eyes over it. I knew instantly who had killed Kenner, the letter even smelt of Amalie. At that moment Tata arrived at the door and was confused by the situation.

'Can you show me the body,' I asked Kara. Tata enquired about which body, and I knew I was coming around as I calmly answered Kenner's body. 'Kenner was killed in an act of treachery during the night.' My sore head had also disappeared, and all sensors were now alert to threats. I could see the shock on Tata's face followed by anger and alarm. Tata said that we are all in danger and must leave at once. I countered that I needed to deal with Amalie for her crimes. 'She will not get away with this, I will ring her neck for what she has done to Kenner.'

Tata put one hand on each of my shoulders and told me that I was too valuable to throw my life away here. He said that Kenner and the rest of them had risked everything to bring me home. I was listening but not hearing. 'It would be Kenner's wish for you to make it home. You must honor her and make it back home. You have a baby to raise and children at home who need their father. If you stay, they will kill you.' I was hearing but I was not listening. I asked Kara to take me to the body and told Tata he needed to be ready to leave. At this point Bran appeared in the doorway. His first question was about where Kenner was. Tata told him that Kenner had been murdered and Bran simply collapsed in a heap and broke down. My anger boiled as I saw the instant grief which had taken over the warrior in front of me. Tata told Bran to prepare to leave and to meet us outside of the inn which they had first tried to book into when they arrived in Roskilde. Bran was coming back from despair and shook his head. Kara added, don't forget baby Ramsay. I had heard that Kenner had a baby earlier and had taken note. The thought had been pushed to the back of my mind. The baby must be mine and it would be cherished as my memory of Kenner.

Kara was on her feet, so I also stood and said to her to take me to Kenner. Tata said that he was coming with me which made me hesitate. I nodded and agreed as I wanted to have my brother with me when I took Amalie's head. He could bear witness that justice had been served. We waited for Tata to grab his weapons and pack and then we were off following Kara. I was already armed as I had told Amalie I was heading to weapons practice.

There were many guards in the garden as Kara pointed to where the body was. Kara was reluctant to go any closer and I do not blame her given her rank and station. Tata thanked Kara and said that she and her family were welcome to come with us. We will be going back to England where he said he would do everything in his power to give her safety and a good life. She said that she has a baby son of similar age to Ramsay and no other family. 'Do you know where we are to meet, Tata asked her?' She nodded and said that Kenner had told her where they had first tried booking into. 'We will meet you there but do not delay.'

I made my way over to the old dead oak tree and pushed through the guards. The guards moved out of the way as they all knew who I was. I was a commander in the Kings army and ranked well above them. A blanket had been put over the body. I knelt and rolled the blanket back. I could see it was Kenner and looking down I saw the hole where her heart used to be. There was blood everywhere which was now congealed and sticky. I had not noticed that I was kneeling in it. Tata put a hand on my shoulder which helped calm me. I could feel my berserker mood rising in every muscle in my body. I wanted revenge and God help anyone who gets in my way. 'Is there any sign of the heart,' I asked the guards? They said that they had looked but the heart was gone. Giving Kenner a kiss on her bloodied lips I rose to my feet with death in my every being.

Walking back toward the palace Tata pulled me to a halt and said we are going to the inn. We are leaving now, or we will never get away. I went to push past Tata, but he was strong and with both hands he held me firm. You are the first King of England. Your people and family need you as England is being squeezed from the north and the south. Your people are dying by the thousands and that lady has crossed the world to bring you home. Do not fail her and the legacy she has given you. Be Kenner's warrior and bring security and safety to England. You are its first king, and your number one duty is to your people, not revenge.' Tata was firm and was looking directly into my eyes as he laid down the law. He was right and the conviction which Tata had used was enough to snap me out of my desire for revenge. With dried tears all over my face, beard and my clothes covered in congealed blood, I asked Tata to lead the way.

Chapter 29

The Rolling Hills of England

The others were at the Inn as planned and the moment Tata and I arrived we took off toward the western gate. Bran was carrying a baby which I took to be Ramsay, my son. As we walked Bran handed me Ramsay and confirmed that this was Kenner's and my child. Bran's face was covered in dried tears and at that moment I could not have loved someone more. I gave him the biggest of hugs and told him that he would always be like family. 'Your love and support of Kenner on her quest to rescue me will not be forgotten lightly. I know you share the same grief as me and only a life well lived will repay Kenner for the love, she showed both of us.' These were still raw moments after such extreme grief. I was coming around, but I could see that Bran was more sensitive than me.

We walked out the gates without question which was reasonable as we were not entering Roskilde and people were coming and going. Elgar knew the way, so we all followed her. We needed horses so at the nearest farm I paid gold for eight horses. Kara had shown up at the inn and had brought along a friend who I had met earlier, Arni. We made good time with the horses and before long we were well away from Roskilde. The further we got the better I felt. It felt good to be free and I realized it was the first time I had felt this way since being captured at Jarrow some three years earlier.

There was no stopping except to rest the horses for five minutes every hour or so. The plan was to reach Esbjerg and the west coast before nightfall. There will be accommodation and a chance to rest. We will meet up with the rest of the crew and with all going well we will be on the boat and off to England tomorrow. Elgar did mention that the weather would need to be favorable as there was no point heading out into a storm. I nodded agreement but thought that I would have even headed out into the greatest of storms. Delaying out departure could place us in a situation much akin to a manmade storm.

I did not know any of the men or women who we met at Esbjerg. They were all still at the Fair-Weather Inn. Although I did not know them, they all knew of me and that I was Tata's brother and Kenner's lover. The news of Kenner's death was a downer for all of them as it seems Kenner had made a big impact on them and their lives. Thinking about it, this made sense as Kenner had been a part of the group to rescue them from the quarry and a part of the group which helped the Vikings from Bergen to rebuild through the winter. Tata had told me the story of how they had come on Bergen after it had been sacked. Winter was on them, and the women, children, and old people were going to perish. Kenner had been a part of the team which had taken leadership and led the rebuild of Bergen. Sigvald was there now continuing with the work. All I remember of Bergen was from a cage in the chieftain's tent and that night of the attack when I was almost burnt alive. Fortunately, Sigvald came to my rescue, and we fled into the mountains. We toasted Kenner that night and ate well as we had not eaten all day. The inn keeper was pleased to have so much custom as the crew had been accommodated there.

The Vikings had been conversing and they said that they believed the weather conditions would be favorable the coming days. They said that it should not take more than three days to cross the sea. We spoke to the publican in the inn and told him we would be leaving the following day. We requested food and water for all of us for three days. We needed dried and salted meat which could last the journey and keep our energies up. He said that this would be difficult, but he would see what he could do. I flashed him some gold and flicked him a coin for starters. He bit down on a corner and smiled. 'I will see what I can do for you all.' Thanking him I went back to the drink and conversation.

A lot can change in twenty-four hours and my last twenty-four hours is testament to that. Yesterday I was a returning war hero and now I was fleeing for my life. My lover has been murdered by my mistress and I have found out I am a father again to a healthy baby boy. If I had time, I might like to write a book about my adventures.

I was not up for a late night, so I headed for my room. Kara was looking after baby Ramsay and had already taken him to bed. Kara was already feeding her own baby and it was a blessing that she could feed Ramsay also. Neither Kara nor Arni have family which is a sad reality for many of the servants in Roskilde. Many were captured when only children and taken from their loved ones and towns. Their loved ones were killed in many instances leaving them with no other option then a life of servitude. One day I would like to end the suffering of servants which are more like slaves. They are not treated well, and they have no rights.

The knock on the door came before first light. I cursed the sound as I knew it meant we were leaving. I could have slept for days and the bed I had was the most comfortable bed since I was back in Glasgow with Kenner. Even Amalie's bed was uncomfortable as it was filled with dozens of cuddly toys and blankets. Her room was always heavy with perfume which tended to make me feel a little sick. I was up and packed and along with the others we headed down to the docks. I had a box of provisions, and I could see half a dozen other boxes being carried down to the boat. I had seen a few longboats and this one was as good as any I had seen before. Tata told me that they had built it to cross the north sea to Bergen. He said that they had built two, but one had been sunk in a storm during the crossing. He also said that he had been on the other boat as they had smashed together in the storm. It was only luck which had saved him as he swam toward the direction of the smash to where he thought the other boat was. A wave had thrown him into the side of the other boat and the crew had pulled him aboard. All the others bar one, had drowned. A Viking called Sven was the only other survivor. I was told by the Vikings that this is the nature of the sea. Every now and then it rises to claim sacrifices for the times it grants safe passage. I told them this was not reassuring however they said that this was the perfect season for crossing the sea so luck would be on our side.

By mid-morning we were out of sight of land and clear of the Danes. I still thought that one day I would get revenge for the death of Kenner. I was realizing that time never stops and if I stuck around long enough events and situations come to pass which we least expect. Tata was sitting with me and told me to look back on all the wonderful times I had shared with Kenner. 'Look at the positives my brother. Think of all the time you spent together which you might not have. There is all the joy you gave Kenner. She was alive on this adventure, filled with the one-track mind of rescuing you. She was very similar to you my brother and she was successful. Kenner rescued me and you with her persistence. God will reward her for completing her mission. He will reward her love. I know I said I did not believe in any Gods but maybe I was wrong. I am starting to think that only with the help of God could you and I still be alive and heading home.' I hugged him and wept. Tata was right in every sense. Kenner had been successful and due to her persistence both Tata and I were alive.

True to their word we saw land three days after leaving Esbjerg. This was my home, and our amazing journey was coming to an end or so I hoped. Closer to land Elgar was able to tell us we were coming in close to Colchester. It seems that Elgar is well travelled due to her family connections back in Bergen as she has even been down along this coast.

The emotion overcame me again as we pulled in at the dock at Colchester. This was England and I was home. As we pulled into the dock it seemed like the whole town including the guard were waiting for us. By the time that we tied up the guard had realized we were no threat. I hugged Elgar and thanked her and the crew for getting us home. I felt overwhelmed that I was at last back in England and free. Along with the others we alighted from the boat. The captain of the guard enquired about our purpose and who we were.

Reaching down and placing both hands on the ground I took a moment to compose myself. I knew I still had tears in my eyes. The emotions were so strong. Standing back up, I must have looked menacing as all the guard and towns folk around me took a step back. The guard placed their hands on their weapons. I told them that I was Godric, son of Osgar Amity and the first King of England. 'Who is Queen, where were you supposedly killed and who leads the Worchester guard?' The leader's questions were shot back at me. I easily answered the questions and with that everyone dropped to a knee and bowed. The captain bowed, stepped forward and offered me a hand of welcome. 'I am Rohan, captain of the Colchester guard. Welcome to Colchester my King. We thought you dead and it is great tidings that you arrive on our docks. Please let us know how we can be of service.' It is a testament to the faith and hope of the people that they were so quick to embrace my return and believe that I am the King of England.

I thanked Rohan and told the people they could stand. 'We have come a long way and only because of the friendships we have with the Picts and Vikings. The world is a large place with many different peoples but from what I have seen the people all want the same thing. The people want peace and prosperity but too often our leaders send us into conflict and heartache. We would welcome the re-provisioning of our boat so that our friends can return home. A warm meal and a bed for the night would also be welcome. Then tomorrow after our friends have returned for home, we would welcome a guard of twenty men to escort us through to London.'

We walked from the docks surrounded by the excited crowds. Rohan told us he had much to tell us as I said that it was three years since Jarrow, and I needed to know what had been going on. A few of the Vikings stayed with the boat to help with loading provisions while the others all headed into town. Colchester is a good-sized settlement which was Viking owned for decades. I could see Viking characteristics in the people and buildings as I looked around. The excitement with the people was obvious for all of us and the purpose of everything we were about came back to me. These are the people we fight for, and these are the people we sacrifice everything for. It is our responsibility as leaders to give these people security and prosperity. We must give them a safe environment to raise their children, one with opportunities for a long and happy life. The death of my mother and father was the trigger which set this entire plan in motion. We needed to get back to Worchester and deal with our enemies. We needed to reignited hope in the people. That night we drank to being home and I quietly drank and thanked Kenner for her sacrifice. I was at long last back in England.